THE GIRL AND THE TWISTED END

A.J. RIVERS

PROLOGUE

Then

It wasn't supposed to be this way.

Quick. Simple. Clean.

She knew what to do, and how to do it. When to tighten. When to breathe. When to walk away.

How did she get here? How did it come to this?

It was never supposed to be this way.

MARIE CLAWED AT THE GROUND AT HER SIDES, THE ROUGH SUR-face scraping away the skin of her fingertips and pressing back her nails as she searched for something, anything, to grab onto. She didn't know if there was anything there. She didn't know why she was searching.

She wouldn't be able to pry away the ground and find something to save her. No one was beneath her waiting to take hold and pull her back from the edge.

Her eyes closed tightly, and she could feel the aching burn of tears swirling over their surface. It stung like they were etching the membranes, melting the veins to bring out the blood.

The rush of adrenaline through her body tried to combat the gray coming to the edges of her thoughts and the heavy panic coming to depleted muscles and malfunctioning lungs.

It wasn't supposed to be this way. It had never been this way.

I hope you know what you're getting yourself into.

The words echoed through her mind. She knew who said them, but she didn't. She wished she could make sense of the fragments of voices that hung loosely together in her thoughts to make up the warning. She had only just heard them. Or maybe it was days, months, years before. Someone said them to her. To warn her, to chastise her, to mold her into something she should be, or make her spring back to what she had been before.

She wanted to hear something else as the ache spread behind her eyes and down the base of her skull to her throat. She wanted other words to come to her as the gray settled in.

Her fingers dug harder at the ground and then in the air and then on skin. On hair, on clothes, on blood, on nothing. Maybe she could tatter them all, peel them all away and find something else to hold onto. Something that would remind her heart to beat and her lungs to fill and her brain to fire and pulse and stay awake.

But those were the only words. The same ones she'd heard, coming to her in thin, fragile layers of voices. At least her mind was giving her that. If she couldn't have strength, she could have comfort.

But it was a taunting kind of comfort.

She was glad for the voices, even if she couldn't make them form any other words. She was beginning to understand there would be nothing after this, and she didn't want the last things she heard to be the other sounds around her. She wanted those voices to surround her, to fill her ears and her head, to protect her at least from that part of her suffering. No matter how hard she clawed and reached, she would find nothing to save her life.

But the memory of the voices could save her final seconds. They could shield at least a part of her. Even if they were also tormenting her.

Marie thought she didn't need to hear that warning, to give it any weight.

She believed she *had* known what she was getting into. She always had before. It would be just like all the other times. The meeting place didn't matter that much. It wasn't familiar, but they rarely were. What mattered was what was waiting there. Like she always did, she would go, get what she needed, and leave. It would carry her through long enough until she needed more, then the pattern would happen again.

She knew the realities. She accepted the risks.

But it wasn't supposed to be like this.

It wasn't supposed to end like this.

Something went wrong. She didn't know until it was far too late to go back, to change her mind, to stop. By the time she realized it, there was nothing she could do.

As her body shut down, she wished she could speak and have the words stay crystallized in the air around her so that they'd be there when someone found her. There were so many things she'd want to say. She wondered what she'd choose. Then there was nothing left to wonder.

Mere steps away, a pair of eyes dry and painful, marked with scattered lines of reflected blood, watched for Marie's chest to rise again.

The light of a phone intruded on the funeral shroud of night over her.

Then a voice, outside of her mind, beyond the protections of silenced memories, calm and steady.

"It's me. I have a situation that needs to be cleaned up."

CHAPTER ONE

Now

"The whole thing started in 1972 when Marshall Applewhite and Bonnie Nettles met and started on what they called a 'spiritual journey.'"

"A lot of young people did that around that time," Dean says, reaching forward to turn the computer slightly to see the screen better. "I've talked to a bunch of the old PIs from those days. Teenagers, even people in their early twenties, would get it in their minds that they needed to 'find themselves' and disappeared into the ether."

"Do people generally misplace themselves?" Xavier asks. "I always just assumed other people were the ones who had lost me. But maybe that only applies to when I know where I am."

"I don't think that's what he means," I say. "They were trying to figure out who they were. Usually because they didn't like what their parents thought they should be. And I'm going to go out on a limb here and say that's similar to what was going on with these two when they met. The difference being these two weren't nearly as young as you would want them to be.

"It's easy to understand a teenager wanting to venture forth on their own, away from their parents' influence. They think there's got to be more to life than what they've known. So they go out and figure something out on their own—and maybe make some pretty terrible decisions in the process. But most people get themselves together by the time they are really grown. But these two were already in their forties by the time they met and started up what they thought of as their own religion."

"Which actually means a cult," Dean intuits.

I nod. "That's pretty much how these things go, right? They went through a couple of different names. They started out as The UFO Two. Then when they got some people behind them, they became Human Individual Metamorphosis."

"I've done that," Xavier says. "I don't recommend it."

"And Total Overcomers Anonymous. The one they are actually known by in this day and age, they didn't even start using until the last couple of years before the end. That was Heaven's Gate."

"I like Total Overcomers Anonymous better," Xavier says. "It sounds more supportive."

"And that's what we all need in our cults—emotional support," Dean adds sarcastically.

I stare at him for a few seconds. "Actually, I think that's exactly why people join cults."

He thinks about it for a moment, opens his mouth like he's going to respond, then snaps it closed again and gives a single nod.

"Valid. Anyway, Heaven's Gate."

"Yes," I continue. "Heaven's Gate. They believed human bodies were just vehicles for the actual soul and that after what they called the 'classroom' period of being on Earth was over, a ship would come and take them to the planet of Heaven. And Applewhite believed his body had the same alien spirit presence that used to live in Jesus, and it was his duty to bring the group forth to a new evolutionary level of spiritual ascendance. Or something like that. It's all a little complicated. Anyway, along the way, things went a little sideways when Nettles died."

"She was murdered?" Dean asks. "The apple guy got her?"

"No. Applewhite didn't kill her. She died of cancer."

"People tend to do that," Xavier says. "Even in cult circumstances."

"Yes," I say, pointing to him. "But they didn't think so. Remember, they thought they were going to walk up onto a spaceship and it was going to whisk them away to the next plane of existence. They didn't think they could actually die. Then one of their leaders up and died. So, that ruined that whole belief system. So, Applegate decided that it meant she had gone off to prepare the ship and everything for them, and that when they were ready, they wouldn't be able to bring their Earth vehicles with them.

"But in the more than two decades of learning and preparing on Earth that they'd gone through, none of them had figured out how to just climb up out of their vessels when the time came. Which brings us to the big plan… mass suicide. They'd all die like their leader did and then hop on her ship."

"Which was coming on the Hale-Bopp comet," Dean says.

"Right," I nod.

"Yeah, I retained that part. There's just too much crazy in that detail not to hang onto it. Besides, I can appreciate wanting a comet to be more than just a flaming ball of potential devastation and demise for the planet."

"I mean, yes, that is somewhat more hopeful. The thirty-nine people still left in the cult didn't so much avoid their demise, but I can see where you're coming from," I say.

"They wanted to give meaning to the death of their leader," Xavier offers. "It went against all they had believed in. It shattered their entire reality. All they could do was gather up the little bits and hope they could make something new out of them. They didn't believe they would die, but then she did. They had to make it mean something. They couldn't just experience her death and accept that they'd been completely wrong. It would be too painful.

"They'd put all of themselves into following that belief, into preparing themselves for something. They'd already gone from their families, gotten rid of worldly possessions, and completely devoted themselves to this cause. It was the only way they could comprehend it."

"Sunk cost fallacy," Dean mutters.

Xavier shakes his head. "More than that. This wasn't some cynical calculation of costs or benefits, or an attempt to save face from the humiliation, uncertainty, and grief of trying to find normalcy again. These were true believers. They had no choice but to believe. Because it was the meaning they'd been seeking from the beginning. Going back wasn't even an option. It was like a revelation being granted to them. And they knew—not just believed, but *knew*—that Nettles's death was part of the process, and when they heard the comet was coming, it was the sign they'd been waiting for. They'd chosen to live like their leaders, and now they were going to transcend like them, too."

"That's exactly what they decided to do," I added. "So when the comet approached, and the thought of all of them getting sick spontaneously was a bit far-fetched even for this crowd, they settled on spiking their pudding with phenobarbital. Applesauce for the ones who didn't like pudding. While wearing bags over their heads."

"Well, that's not an elegant solution," Dean says.

"Not particularly. They were all wearing the same outfit, including some very nice Nikes that were henceforth vilified, which adds a nice uniformity to it all, but that's not really the point," I say.

"Emma?" Xavier calls from the kitchen. When exactly he made his way in there, I'm not sure.

"Top shelf of the pantry. There's a little silver metal container. I think there's chocolate and butterscotch. Maybe vanilla, but I'm not positive," I call back.

"Thank you."

"I think you've lost me," Dean says. "Were there survivors of this thing that had something to do with Salvador Marini? And Sam's cousin, too?"

I shake my head. "No. I mean, yes, there were survivors. Not of the suicide, but of the group. But that's not the point I was going for. It's how the whole thing went down that got me thinking about them. I was reading an article about Dr. Villareal and how she spoke about her role in everything that happened at Baxter College, and when I heard about how Heaven's Gate handled the suicides, it started to click."

"Losing me more," Dean says.

"I can help find you," Xavier chimes in brightly, coming into the room with three glass bowls of pudding precariously balanced together in his fingers in front of him. "It shouldn't be all that hard."

He walks carefully over to me and holds the bowls out to me.

"Thank you, Xavier," I say, taking the closest bowl and hoping moving it doesn't disturb the structural integrity of the entire thing. He hands another of the bowls to Dean and sits back down with his. I eat a spoonful of the pudding and look down at the bowl. "What flavor is this?"

"Chocolate-butterscotch-vanilla."

"Ah."

"Heaven's Gate," Dean says, encouraging me to move along with the conversation. "Suicide in matching shoes."

"Right," I nod, putting the bowl down so I can pull up an image of one of the victims of the cult's ritualistic suicide. "Again, the suicide itself wasn't my point. It's how the rest of the group handled the deaths after they happened. They did it in waves rather than all at once. It took three days. For each wave, the people would get in their uniforms, eat the poison, then put the bag over their heads. And then they would lay down in their bed and wait to die."

"Jesus," Dean mutters.

"Once they were dead, people came in to take the bag off and clean them up, arrange the body, and cover each of their faces with a purple cloth. Then that group went, and it continued on until the very last group ate their pudding. They were the only ones found without the cloth. The group had gone to a tremendous amount of trouble not just planning the deaths, but also dealing with the aftermath. They wanted to show dignity and respect, and make sure that the scene was crafted to give a very specific message to the people who found them."

"That message being?" Dean asks.

"That it was intentional. That this wasn't something to be mourned over or seen as a tragedy. It was a ritual, a religious expression they wanted to be celebrated. In fact, there were videos of the cult members saying goodbye to the people they loved and several of them point out they don't want to die. They aren't suicidal. That's not the point.

"In those moments they weren't thinking about what they were about to do as killing themselves. They were just releasing themselves into the next level, something they deeply wanted. The way the waves of people handled the deaths was an extension of that very methodical thinking. They were creating a narrative through death."

"Like the Cleaners," Dean says, the realization settling in.

"Exactly. Different reasons, but same concept. Death is a construct. It's not just the death itself that matters. It's the entire experience surrounding the death."

A glance at Xavier just shows he's fully invested in his pudding concoction. I wait. This feels like a moment he would usually have something to say about. But he remains silent.

"Xavier?"

He glances up at me, slightly wide-eyed in the way he does when he's not sure if he missed something and is somewhat unsure of how much time has passed since he was connected to what is happening around him. Still nothing.

"Alright." I look back at Dean. "This. This whole thing is making me rethink what I thought about the Cleaners."

"What do you mean?" Dean asks.

"All I knew about the Cleaners is they had something to do with Salvador Marini and Marie's deaths. It was the only thing that made sense after what Jonah said. 'Find the Cleaners, find the truth.' As I thought about it, the only thing I could think was that this meant they were killed by this group. That someone put a hit out on them," I say. "Now that I've dealt with Dr. Villareal and read about this…" I glance at the screen again and let out a breath. "I don't think it's that simple. Maybe it wasn't the death itself they were called in to handle. Maybe it was just the aftermath," I say.

"And Jonah knows that," Dean says. "But you said it yourself that he was mad about Marini dying. He wanted him to go to jail. If he already knew what happened to him, that these people dealt with him, why was he angry about it?"

"He didn't know when it happened," I say, but even as the words come out of my mouth, I start to question them. My voice trails off and I feel my eyebrows tighten in as the thoughts start filling up the edges of my mind like dark storm clouds rolling in.

Dean notices, leaning toward me slightly. "What is it?"

The slight shake of my head might not have even been perceptible by the others, but it feels like there's too much energy surging through the tangle of thoughts in my brain to devote any more to actually moving parts of my body.

"Commas have value, Emma," Xavier says.

There it is.

CHAPTER TWO

SEARCH THROUGH THE PAPERS ON MY DESK, TRYING TO FIND THE folded note that had been concealed in the Christmas ornament we found in our front yard months ago. It had accompanied pictures of both Marini and Marie, drawing a link between the two cases we still didn't understand.

Of course, it's never been far from my mind that this all could have been yet another of Jonah's mind games and manipulations. But this time it feels different.

I find the note and bring it over to show Dean and Xavier.

"Jonah called me after Marie went missing to say how sorry he was about it. Of course, we know Jonah. We know he wasn't really calling to give his condolences. At least, that's not all he was doing. But it really got to Sam. When we found the ornament in the yard and got it open, it was full of all those pictures of Marini after he died. That was how I figured out that his fitness tracker is missing. It took a while before I realized the top of it opened too, and that's where we found the picture of Marie and this note."

I know I'm telling them things they already know, but I feel like everything has been torn down to the base foundation and I have to build it up again. I have to go through it all, explain it to myself all over again, to make sure I haven't missed any of the tiny breadcrumbs that might tell me where to go.

"Find the Cleaners, find the truth," Dean says.

"Right. But just like Xavier said, the comma. It's important."

"Commas were the bane of my existence when I was in school, and I'm pretty sure they still are now," Dean remarks.

"One little interrupting plop of ink can cause all kinds of turmoil," Xavier says. "Especially in the cutthroat world of style deviations." He shakes his head sadly. "So much division among the devoted."

"And you?" I ask.

He holds up a solidarity fist at shoulder level. "Oxford comma for life."

"Good to know." I point to the paper. "Look at this. The first 'find' has a capital. Then there's the comma, then the second 'find,' which is lowercase. That's why I've always thought of it as a cause-and-effect statement. Find the Cleaners and you will find the truth. That's what I told Sam when we were talking about it. He thought Jonah had something to do with Marie's disappearance and death, but we couldn't figure out what it would be, and it didn't make sense to me. He didn't know Marie and he really had no reason to do anything to her. Besides, if he did, he wouldn't go to the effort of covering it up only to tell us to figure it out. He's played sick little games like that before, but they always had some kind of goal.

"He pointed out that Jonah uses riddles a lot. He likes to twist words and make you figure out what he's saying. This is a man who tied his entire identity to a complex bastardization of religious and cultural mythologies that set him up as both a god and a martyr, tasked with the protection of humanity through chaos and its ultimate destruction." I sigh. "He enjoys screwing with people's heads."

"But in being straightforward and declarative in his statements, he creates confusion regarding whether he is truly being as simple as it seems, or if there is something much deeper and more complicated going on," Xavier points out. "Thereby causing you to think even further into what's happening, coming to increasingly complex and convoluted conclusions that distance you from the actual intention of the statement, making you tangle yourself up by overthinking it. He knows you'll overthink it, so he says something simple. It's the ultimate head screw." He takes another mouthful of pudding. "And mean."

"Right. And that's the thing. I tried to think of it in the simplest way possible. He is so determined for me to sort out the whole situation with Miley and Serena, and he knows I've reached the end of my tolerance for him," I reply. "He told me he wasn't playing games anymore and wasn't going to try to make things more confusing for me. Just that there were things he wasn't able to tell me. It's like when he first asked me to clear his name in Serena's murder. He couldn't give me any of the details."

"Because then there would be nothing you could bring to the police," Dean says. "It would all be hearsay, or they would want to know how you had come to the conclusions and it wouldn't be enough solid evidence to actually lead to arrests, much less convictions."

"Exactly. I had to investigate and work it out on my own, using only the barest details he could give me. But it worked. And that's what he wanted for Miley, too. So I wanted to think the note was just as clear-cut as it seemed right from the beginning. He was dropping the hint about the Cleaners, but it was up to me to find out who they are and what they did. And if I did that, I would know the truth. Right?"

"Right," Dean nods.

"But what if it's not?" I ask. "At least, I don't think that's the whole point of the message. There's a comma and there's a lowercase letter. Then after the word 'truth,' there's this."

I point to what had initially looked like just a continuation of the end of the letter 'h,' but now I'm looking at it differently.

"A smear?" Dean asks.

"Another comma," Xavier offers. "Note the swoop."

I'm not sure there's an entire swoop to be seen, but at least he can see where I'm going with this.

"I think there's more to the message. It's not just this part. There's something else. Which means it's not as easy as it seemed. It's not just a cause and effect."

"Alright. So what's the rest of the message? If it's not cause and effect, what is it?" Dean asks.

I get up and head for the back of the house and the steps leading into the attic. It's a space of the house that always seems to be in flux. Sometimes I'm happy with it just being stuffed to the gills with boxes containing holiday decorations, seasonal clothes, and things Sam and I don't use but I can't bear to part with. Other times, I get it in my head that I want to make something more out of the space, something that would go with the small room in the back I reclaimed and redecorated after excavating it from a sealed-over wall years ago.

Right now, we're in one of those phases. All the boxes and set-aside furniture are off to one side and the rest of the room is empty except for one rocking chair on a rag rug in the center of the floor. Dean comes to a sharp stop when he sees it.

"What the hell is going on there?" he asks.

I look at the chair. "Oh. I was considering a craft space up here."

He gives me a look that I can only interpret as befuddled. "Do you craft?"

"I could," I say. "I draw. And Xavier taught me to crochet."

"She is a whiz with the half-double," Xavier interjects.

"Thank you, Xavier. And I've gotten interested in clay sculpting."

"And by that do you mean you went to the homemade Play-doh class at the community center in between the seminars you taught and now you're disappointed you didn't have the little star extruder set when you were little?" Dean asks.

"It was the barber set," I say. "And I think I might make scented ornaments for Christmas this year."

"So you need a creepy ghost chair sitting in the middle of your attic all summer and fall?"

I glare at him. Sometimes I think Dean is trying to make up for all the years we didn't have together when we were kids and should have been poking at each other like this. It's in those moments I wonder what it would have been like to grow up with him. If we would have been like siblings going through everything together. But just as soon as those happy thoughts and the memories I pretend exist come along, reality hits.

I have to remind myself that that kind of life never could have actually happened.

That would mean Jonah was never ousted from the family, that my grandparents never had to make the heart-rending decision to cut one of their children out of their lives because of the horrors he'd already put them through. It would mean my father would never have witnessed his identical twin brother fall in love with his wife and torment him in an effort to win her, and that Jonah never would have tried to take me believing I was his daughter conceived on a night he stole with my mother.

And because of that, Dean never would have been born.

My cousin only exists because of all that. Jonah's madness and his descent into the depths of delusion led to my grandparents and parents excising even the acknowledgment that he had ever lived from their thoughts and my awareness. I never really knew him. I'm sure I saw him a handful of times when I was very young, but I never would have processed I wasn't looking at my father. By the time everything he ever owned and every shred of tangible evidence that he had ever been was locked away in that room in the attic and sealed over, the family believed he was dead.

There wasn't any superstition behind my grandmother taking all those things and hiding them away in the wall. It's not that they thought it would act as some kind of protective talisman. They already thought he'd been killed in a fiery car accident.

She did it so I would never have to know.

As a mother, she couldn't bring herself to completely rid herself of all reminders of her son. He was still her child, and she had memories of him from before everything went wrong. My father does, too. He's just now getting to the point where he'll talk about them sometimes. He'll tell stories about when he was young and occasionally, I'll hear him say "my brother." Never his name. Never anything more than that. But the acknowledgment is there. It means something. Not for Jonah. For my father. He's letting himself move on.

But all of that means Dean is here. Jonah's obsession with my mother and her rejection of his advances is what led him to a vulnerable, frightened woman who had just been brought out of a horrible situation by the rescue organization my mother devoted her life to. No one knew that he'd slithered his way into her trust and then her affections. Or that when he tossed her away because just looking and sounding like my mother wasn't enough to satisfy him, she was already carrying a son.

Dean and I could never have grown up together. He could never have been the extended family I'd longed for. Because his very existence depends on the destruction of that family.

But even despite all of that, I'm glad that he's here.

CHAPTER THREE

W ITH THE ROCKING CHAIR PUSHED INTO THE CORNER AND THE rug sitting at the top of the steps to be brought downstairs, I go back to the original reason I came up to the attic. A plastic tote on the far side of the room sits by itself rather than being stacked among the red and green boxes of Christmas decorations or the orange and black ones stuffed with everything related to Halloween. I drop down to my knees on the floor and drag it toward me, taking off the lid and tossing it aside.

"What's that?" Dean asks.

"Remnants," I tell him as I start digging through the seemingly random contents of the box. "They're pieces of cases and investigations I've hung onto because…" my voice drifts off and I realize I'm not entirely sure how to finish that sentence in a way that would make sense to anyone else, "because I needed to. They were particularly significant or had an impact on me. Some of them I felt like meant more than I'd figured out, and I didn't want to give up on them. Some I just felt like I couldn't get rid of them. So they went into the box. Like a scrapbook. Only with considerably fewer stickers and die-cuts."

"I should start a scrapbook," Xavier says. "I have precious memories I'd like to entomb for the foreseeable future of humanity. Or as long as the tape holds out."

"That's not exactly *entombing* memories, X," Dean says in the way he does when he's trying to gently bring Xavier back somewhere in the vicinity of other people's reality.

"What if I made sure to use acid-free tape?"

Dean and I share a quick look and he breaks out into a grin. "Sure. That could probably work."

Dean is a vital element of Xavier's life and there have been moments between the two of them that have broken my heart and moved me to tears. And then there are moments like that one. They might be my favorite. It makes me think of a bird trying to land on the reflection of a branch in a window. It might look like the same thing, but it's still bouncing off a piece of glass.

"One of the things I put in here is the ornament from Jonah," I say, bringing everyone back to the reason we're up here in the first place. "I sure as hell wasn't going to put it away with the rest of my Christmas decorations and let it snuggle up with the yarn popcorn garland and the walnut mice. But I also didn't want to throw it away." I continue to dig through until I finally find the large, multi-sided decoration. "Maybe there's something in it I missed."

Since Dean's eyes are still flickering over toward the rocking chair like he's sure any second it's going to start moving on its own, I carry the ornament downstairs before examining it. At first, it looks exactly like it has since I discovered the note and the picture of Marie in the hidden top compartment. I open that section again and run my fingers inside to try to detect any inconsistencies in the surface that might indicate another hideaway section. When there's nothing, I start looking at all of the pictures of Salvador Marini again.

These are the pictures that told me there was something more to his death than just a heart attack brought on by the stress he had to be going through, knowing he was about to walk into a police station and turn himself in for a list of brutal crimes against Serena. He knew that was the end of the life he'd known. He'd be giving up unimaginable luxury and power for a tiny cell in a crowded facility where he was far more likely to be prey than predator.

But I knew those crimes weren't the only ones he'd committed. He would never be brought to justice for the string of dead women scattered across several states, or the men he left used up and broken in situations made to look like accidents. He'd never be held accountable for the lives he'd destroyed. He'd never be forced to tell about the ones who were simply never seen or heard from again. Like Miley Stanford, who conveniently disappeared not long after entering his orbit and who I still haven't found any trace of.

It would make sense for the stress and anxiety of facing that kind of future to give him a heart attack. And the medical examiner confirmed it. But there are inconsistencies. Troubling signs in the autopsy and in the events after his death that only further prove the truth has yet to come to light.

The pictures inside the ornament aren't from the police record but show Marini after his death. They showed me that someone else had been there and had tampered with the scene. But maybe they told me something else and I didn't listen.

I touch one of the pictures, feeling for how it might have been attached to the inside of the ornament. It's firmly in place, probably glued. I feel the rest of them. They all feel just as stuck in place—until the last. It slides just slightly. Using the edge of my fingernail, I lift up the picture and ease it away from the ornament.

Part of me is expecting another little piece of paper to fall out from behind the picture, but it doesn't. Instead, I notice something written on the back of the picture.

"What does it say?" Dean asks.

"Find the solution."

"Emma, look," Xavier says. "The corner of the picture."

I look more closely and notice the paper at the corner seems doubled, like the backing of a sticker. I brush against it with the pad of my thumb until it comes the rest of the way loose and I can peel it away. Beneath it are two more words. I lift my eyes to Dean.

"End it."

Dean takes the picture from my hand and glares at the writing. "He just can't help himself, can he?"

"No. He can't. But this is exactly what I was saying. It isn't cause and effect. It's instructions. Step by step of exactly what I'm supposed to do to handle both of these situations."

"According to Jonah," Dean says.

"What do you mean?" I ask.

"This is just more of his agenda, Emma," Dean says. "More of him exerting his control over you. You said you didn't think he was playing any games with you, but then you find out he's been hiding more obnoxious little notes in places you would have no reason to be able to find."

"But I found them," I say.

"Yes. You happened to find them," he says. "You happened to look in just the right place."

The anger is making the edges of his eyes look red and the tension in his jaw so taut it looks like the bones are going to come through his skin. Dean swore once that he was never going to think of Jonah again, but I knew all along the truth: he did, and still does. He believed fully within himself that he could encapsulate the father he never knew and always hated, scrape every bit of him out of his mind and heart and being, and expel it. He thought he'd overcome everything and didn't have to let the bitter truth of how he came into this world weigh him down anymore.

It wasn't true. I wanted that for him, too. I wanted him to be able to walk out of that jailhouse visitation room and never have to think about Jonah again. I would love it if he never had to see his face behind his eyelids or hear his voice in his dreams. It would be nothing short of a miracle if my cousin could go the rest of his life without ever being burdened by him and what he has done again. Unfortunately, I've been through enough and seen enough to know that doesn't happen.

My one hope is that when I bring him down—and I *will* bring Jonah down—it will release Dean enough that he can let the memories fade and live with a scar rather than a wound.

"No, Dean. I found them because I looked for them. I know how to play his games. He's fucked up, but if there's one thing I've learned in the years since I found out about him, it's that there's absolutely nothing any of us can do about that. We're not going to change him. We're not going to scare him or ignore him or manipulate him or grind him down into being anything but what he is. And even if we could... What would you want him to be? Is there anything he could be now that would change what he has been?"

Dean stares at me angrily, his blue eyes flashing. Finally, he shakes his head. "No."

I nod. "Okay. Then we stop waiting for him to be like anyone else we deal with, and we meet him where he is. I don't like it any more than you do, but what I like even less is thinking about what might have happened to Marie, Miley, and countless other people. They deserve to have their stories told, and we're the ones who can do that. If that means amusing Jonah for a little while, as much as it makes my skin crawl, it's something I'm willing to do."

Dean still looks stiff and resistant. He doesn't want to bend. Relenting even the slightest bit would mean giving in to Jonah. To Dean, that would mean he won.

"Refusal isn't going to do any good, Dean," Xavier tells him. "You can hate him with everything in you, but the people who were hurt shouldn't have to pay for that hatred. You feel like pushing back against everything he does will keep you in control and take from him what he wants, but it won't. You're giving him power. Over you and over everyone he has ever hurt and who he might hurt. He hasn't stopped for you, and he won't stop because of you."

Dean draws in a breath and sets a less virulent look on me. "Alright."

It's one word, growled low under his breath, but it's enough. I'll take it.

"Neither death is what it was made to look like. Which means we need to go back to the beginning. We have to find out what really happened to both of them."

"But why would Marie have anything to do with the Emperor? What possible connection could they have?" Dean asks.

"That's what we have to find out. And why someone would want them to be Cleaned."

CHAPTER FOUR

THE SHEER NUMBER OF SALVADOR MARINI'S VICTIMS, CATALOGED in pictures spread out across the dining room table, is daunting. I've seen all of them so many times they aren't individually shocking anymore. They've been reduced down to the details so when I look at them, what I see is the trail of clues, the signature of the man who exerted the brutality and constructed the scenes of his sick fantasies.

But when they are all together, it's something different. Seeing all these images spread across the table, piled up in places because there are too many of them and not enough space, forces me to face the sheer magnitude of what he did.

The individual murders are bad enough by themselves. Any of these victims would be a grisly, horrifying case for any detective or investigator. Any of these images on their own would be enough to haunt their dreams and change the way they looked at the people around them when they walked down the street every day.

But Salvador Marini didn't just stop at one. He killed again and again.

But it isn't just the fact that he kept going. It isn't the body count he racked up or even the way he left his victims scattered across several states, some of them so broken and reduced to nothingness they still don't have names. I'm sickened when I look at these pictures because of why he killed and how he managed it.

He killed for the sake of entertainment and out of a pure sense of entitlement. He believed fully that he had the right to use people however he wanted, whether it was as his fantasy sex slaves or as gladiators in brutal fights to the death. But it wasn't just him. He manipulated people into a sense of loyalty and service that resulted in them finding and delivering his victims to him.

Because of his grotesque crimes and the lives he left in tatters, I want this to be simple so it can be over. It isn't.

Looking at these pictures seems to both answer questions and create more of them.

"The Cleaners aren't assassins," I say.

"At least, that isn't all they are," Dean offers. "I would venture a guess they killed Marini. A heart attack is all too convenient an excuse, considering what he was going through, but it doesn't make sense that he would be Cleaned after dying of natural causes, especially considering someone would have to know it had happened, and it was already established he was supposed to be alone in the house but we've found out he wasn't."

"Exactly," I say. "He clearly didn't have a natural heart attack. It wouldn't make any sense for things to be going according to plan, then for him to spontaneously die, and somehow it gets handled that quickly. The time between his death and when the police responded wasn't long enough for someone else to realize he'd died, and have people come in to... do what?"

"What do you mean?" Dean asks.

"It would mean they made a heart attack look like a heart attack," Xavier says.

I point at him, nodding. "The medical examiner hasn't changed the cause of death, so it is still officially a heart attack. But the scene wasn't staged to make it look like anything else. It wasn't like they came in and shot him or broke his neck or something to make it look like he was violently murdered after the fact."

"That would be fairly pointless," Xavier counters. "If they arrived any later than the moment of death, the victim wouldn't bleed. That would be a dead giveaway that the gunshot wasn't actually the cause of death."

I lift an eyebrow at Dean. "Did Xavier just make a pun?"

"No," he answers without hesitation.

"Alright, well, that is a good point. Marini seems to have legitimately died of a heart attack. But there were notes on the medical examiner's report, and I noticed some things myself, that seemed inconsistent or at least noteworthy. Marks on the body. Some discoloration. Things that wouldn't immediately seem to correspond with a heart attack. Which means that might be how he died, but it wasn't necessarily brought on naturally. Think about it. People go to fairly extreme lengths to make murders look like accidents or suicides or even natural deaths. But no one is going to go try to make a natural death look like a murder."

"Unless there's a life insurance policy in place that has a clause agreeing to pay out double the policy amount in the event of a murder," Xavier says.

I stare at him for a second. "Well, that's something I'm going to tuck away in my back pocket and potentially consult on later. For this particular situation, though, I don't think that's what's going on. I absolutely believe he was murdered. His fitness tracker was taken. His dry cleaning was brought up and put away. Not to mention the pictures of his body that were taken before the police arrived. Someone was there when he died and immediately after. And considering everything, we're going to assume that was the Cleaners.

"It's easy to look at the situation and say it's obvious why someone would want to make sure he was dead. As businessman Salvador Marini, he was no peach, and as the Emperor, he is confirmed to have killed more than a dozen people, and I guarantee you that number is actually far higher. And he also tortured and discarded many, many more. If we're just looking at people related to his victims, that could be hundreds, maybe thousands of people who wanted revenge."

"That'll do it," Dean says.

"Right. But is it really that easy? There's still the question of why someone would want to kill him and make it look like a heart attack. I'd think anyone wanting to kill someone like him would either want to make sure it was as bloody and agonizing as possible to put him through some of what he had done, and also send a message to the world—or they wouldn't care what anyone thought. The murder would be for them. Constructing the whole idea of a heart attack seems too careful and almost dignified for a vengeance killing.

"Besides, even putting aside the why, who would do it? The details of his crimes weren't made fully public. Even the families of the victims don't know who he is, what he did, or how to find him. There would have had to be a massive leak and then the people would have had to track him down and figure out how to get into his home without anyone noticing. There just wasn't enough time for any of that. And his victims are either dead or incapacitated," I say.

"I'm not," Dean points out. "I think I count as one of his victims, right? And so does Eric. We might have both been battered around, but neither of us is dead or irreparably damaged. The situation is a little different with Eric since he was a plant. A self-done plant, but a plant nonetheless. He put himself in the path of the Emperor's assistant for the sole purpose of getting kidnapped and trying to figure out what was happening. He survived because you rescued him and Mark Webber before they could kill each other. Without you there to raid the arena, he very likely wouldn't have made it. Neither of them would have.

"But that's not what happened with me. I got out. I just don't know how. What I do know is there was someone else in there with me and no bodies have been found in the area, so there's a chance whatever happened that led to me escaping and ending up by the side of that road might also have involved another intact survivor. And there could be others we just don't know about. We have no idea how many people he captured or even for how long he's been doing this. Someone who made it out alive could have wanted to make sure he paid for what he did."

"But he was on his way to prison," I say. "Anyone who was in any proximity to a TV or the internet during that time would have heard his name and seen his face, and known what was happening."

"Maybe it wasn't enough. He wasn't going to prison because of what he did to them. Or to any of us. It was because of Serena. And with the way money and power work, it was entirely possible he'd be able to get the case overturned and get out. I mean, none of the other details of his crimes were made public. Maybe one of his victims who *did* know what he'd done didn't want to risk that. Someone might have not wanted to face the possibility he would get out of prison," Dean says.

"And if that was the case, it wouldn't necessarily be violent," I say, his point settling in. "Because the goal wouldn't just be to kill him for revenge. It would be the death itself, purely the act of removing him from existence. Making it look like a heart attack would not only help the killer escape suspicion but prevent Marini's name from being amplified any more than it already was. It would keep him from being a victim in the eyes of the public, make sure he could never inflict such pain on anyone else ever again, and make him suffer. Three birds with one stone."

Dean nods.

"But even if that is what happened, there's still so much missing. Starting with the most basic. Who?"

CHAPTER FIVE

"**A**LL OF THIS KEEPS COMING BACK TO THIS NEPHEW," I STATE. "No one seems to know who he is, even Louisa and Angelo. She heard him introduced. That's it. I've talked to people who knew him, people in his circle, and only one mentioned ever having met someone he referred to that way. Marini never even gave his name. It was just an introduction in passing, but Angelo remembered being surprised because he didn't think Marini had any family. No one else had heard of him. Add to that the simple genealogical hiccup of him only having a sister who does not have a son, and we're at a standstill.

"They aren't making him up. The lawyer, Nathan Klein, responded to my email about him without any indication he didn't know what I was talking about. But even if that wasn't the case, it wouldn't make any sense. The only reason the staff would have to make someone up is if they had something to do with his death. We know that's not the case. Not only do both of them have alibis with their new employers, but the only benefit they would get from his death would be knowing he wasn't around anymore.

"While that has been proven to be enough of a motivation for plenty of other murders, I don't see them doing that. Just talking about him shook Louisa up. The threats he made stayed with her. I don't think she would go through with that kind of meticulous plan. Not that it isn't a relief to her that he's dead, but I think if she was going to kill him, it wouldn't be this carefully thought out. It would be a gunshot or poisoning. Something she could do quickly and at a distance.

"Besides, it's far too easy to prove Marini didn't have a nephew. They wouldn't go to so much effort to cover up a murder by making it look like a heart attack only to make such a colossal mistake when it was uncovered that the death wasn't as clear-cut as it might have originally seemed."

"And we've exhausted all the options for trying to find out who this guy is," Dean says.

I nod. "Everything I've been able to think of. I'm going to go through all the contacts again to make sure. If you could take another look at all of the social media and news posts about Marini and his company that have pictures and see if you can see someone we might not have noticed before. Other than that, we just have to wait for Nathan Klein and what he's going to tell us." I gather up the pictures and put them aside so I can empty another folder onto the table. I pick up one of the new pictures and let out a breath. "And until then, we think about Marie."

Sam's cousin smiles up at me from the picture. Bright sunlight glistens on her hair and a close look at the lenses of her sunglasses reveals a reflection of ocean waves breaking on the beach a few yards in front of her. The picture doesn't show it, but I know just beneath the frame she's wearing a blue polka dot bathing suit and reclining in one of those beach chairs that sits almost against the sand. To the side of her, a pink towel spread across the sand has a collection of books and drinks along with several seashells she dipped in the water and laid out to dry.

I know the picture because I took it from her long-dormant social media early in the investigation of her death. She used to be far more active, posting and keeping people updated on her life. But then her posts dwindled until she was only posting every few months. The platforms went silent a year before her death, but her mother Rose told us she didn't think it was something to be concerned about. Apparently, she was losing interest in social media as she got older and had decided to simplify her life so she could actually live it rather than existing in the virtual world for so much of her time. She felt like it was a waste to constantly be posting updates and reading posts from other people, especially ones she barely even knew.

Her New Year's Resolution the year before her death was to focus on the real relationships in her life and put her energy into things that enriched her existence. According to her, if she couldn't pick up the phone and call or text someone, that person didn't need her time or energy.

But she hadn't pulled down the profiles. They just sat there, now a memorial. Rose told us how grateful she was to still be able to go on them and look at the little flickers of her only daughter's life. She liked to read her thoughts and see the pictures she shared. This one was a favorite of hers, which is why I chose it. Marie posted it after a spontaneous trip to the beach at the very end of the season, when the stretch of sand was nearly empty and the waves were more gray than blue. It was still hot enough for her bathing suit and to dig her toes in the wet sand reflected in her glasses.

Marie was happy. The smile on her face was genuine. I can see only the faintest outline of her eyes through the dark lenses, but I know if I could see them, they would be sparkling with the same kind of playful spark I see in Sam's when he's happy. They don't look alike. Not in the way that people looking at them would automatically know they were related if they were in the same room together. But there are some pictures where you can see a resemblance that ties the family together. Their smiles look similar. Their eyes sparkle in the same way. I've seen pictures of the whole family celebrating Christmas together and the two of them had fallen asleep next to each other on the couch, both of them curled in the exact same position. Sam still nods off like that. I'm sure Marie did, too.

The resemblance makes me smile, but it also makes it harder to look at the pictures knowing she'll never grin like that again. I hate that I'll never get a chance to get to know her better or see her and Sam spend more time together. They were so close when they were younger, and though they'd drifted somewhat, as tends to happen when growing up, I know he would have loved for us all to be together more.

All I can do now is find out what happened to her. What took that smile out of the world. Because I know it wasn't her. I glance over at another picture of her, this one of the way we found her body, given to despair and ruin. She didn't do that to herself. The official ruling is that she overdosed in the abandoned building and lay there, falling victim to her decaying surroundings, until we found her.

I don't believe it. I *won't* believe it. And now I have no reason to. I know Marie didn't overdose alone in that dirty mound of debris. Something else happened to her, and someone wanted to make sure no one found out.

"Understanding why someone would want Salvador Marini to be Cleaned is pretty easy," Dean says. "But nothing you've told me about Marie has made it seem like she'd be someone's target."

I shake my head. "I'm not going to sit here and pretend she was an example of the perfect human or anything. She went through things just like everybody else. But Sam is very honest about her, and he doesn't know anything about her or her life that would make me think she might have put herself in a dangerous situation."

"What do you think about the drugs?" Dean asks. "I know you said her mother is convinced she never did drugs, but that's what most parents would say, isn't it? They wouldn't want to believe their child had a double life, especially not one like that. But do you think it's possible she actually was involved in drugs?"

"I didn't know her well. I can't tell you with absolute confidence one way or another. It's obviously possible she was involved in things her family didn't know about. Looking at it as an investigator, the evidence is there. Obviously. It was enough to make the local police say she was clearly wrapped up in drugs and probably just wandered off and overdosed. Possibly whatever she was doing was laced. But," I shake my head again, turning my attention to one of the pictures of her apartment, "the very fact that so much evidence was found so easily..."

"Makes you question it," Dean says.

"It doesn't feel right. We've established the Cleaners are used to literally set a scene. To create a particular image of someone's death. That might mean actually committing the murder. It might mean simply coming in afterward and arranging things to make it look a certain way. And yeah, for a serial killer with so many connections like Marini, I can definitely see something like this happen. But I can't imagine what could justify that for Marie. It isn't like they tried to make her out to be a kingpin or even a mule. All the evidence that was found pointed to her just being a buyer and a user. No different from any other."

"Who ended up dying," Dean adds.

"It's not an uncommon ending to that storyline," I point out. "It's an unfortunate reality that people who get sucked into the drug world usually don't get out alive. They spiral further and deeper until it takes them, and overdose is one of the primary causes of death. And if that was really what happened to Marie, what exactly did the Cleaners do? It took us a while to find her, but not years. It isn't like she was hidden well. She was just there. All we had to do was follow the clues. Clues that were laid out right there for us to find."

"Making a heart attack look like a heart attack and an overdose look like an overdose does lack imagination," Xavier chimes in.

"It does," I acknowledge. "Which makes me think that's not what the Cleaners did in Marie's situation. Think about all the evidence that was found in her apartment. It was right out there. Tucked into a drawer, hidden under some stuff on the table. It was made to look like it was just pieces of her everyday life. Like she had put them there on a regular day, then walked away from them. But if somebody was supposed to handle her death because it related to her drug use, why wouldn't they remove those things?

"And remember, someone was seen going into her apartment after her disappearance. Through a window. It was the only reason anyone went inside after the police denied the request for a welfare check. They were never able to identify who it was. The neighbors who saw him didn't give a good enough description to narrow it down past it being a man who didn't live in the building. And there isn't any security camera footage to give a better look. I think that was one of the Cleaners. He didn't go inside to take things. He went inside to leave them."

"So people would find them," Dean nods, taking the thread from there. "To plant the narrative that Marie had something to do with that drug dealer."

"Gerard 'Rocky' Collins," I say. "I think that's exactly what they did. The fact that there was no welfare check performed is a huge red flag. It's still sticking with me. And it makes me wonder if that compromised the Cleaners' plan, or if it was part of it."

"Dirty cops," Dean murmurs.

"I know Sam had words with the locals about there not being a welfare check, but it still really bothers me. That isn't how situations like this are handled. Checking in on somebody who has been missing is standard practice. Even if there's no reason to believe something is wrong, there's no excuse for the way they seemed to completely blow off Rose's request."

"Not responding is reason enough to believe something is wrong," Xavier says.

Those of us familiar with Xavier know that better than most.

"It should have been. That's the point. The fact that Marie hadn't answered any of her mother's phone calls or texts for days was enough to get them to the apartment, but they knocked on the door and she didn't answer, so they left. They should have gone in there to see if everything was alright. But instead, they said she was an adult and could leave whenever she wanted. She didn't have to report to her mother. And she didn't have to respond to any calls or texts if she didn't want to. Which is all true, obviously. But frankly, to me, that nearly crosses the line from negligence to outright malpractice.

"But was the responding officer negligent because he was bad at his job, because he thought he was doing the right thing, or because he was intentionally not doing what he knew he was supposed to do? Did he make a mistake or a choice?"

"Watch the Director's Cut," Xavier says.

"The Director's Cut?" I ask. "Of what?"

"Of this situation," he clarifies. "Feel free to cast me as you please."

"I'm going to need more to go on than that."

He looks at me in that way that always makes me wonder how what I say sounds to him when filtering through his brain.

"The movie that ends up in a theater or shown on TV isn't made up of all the footage that was filmed for the project. Usually there are hours and hours of other footage that ends up being cut out."

"I know," I say.

"Well, the director doesn't always get the final say. They usually have a lot more that they want in it, or different scenes than were finally chosen, or they shoot a few different endings and the one they wanted isn't chosen. So sometimes they release a Director's Cut of what they really wanted the movie to be like, or even just a version with the option of adding on different endings."

"Xavier, are you still in this conversation, or are you somewhere else right now?" Dean asks. "Are you still angry about the ending of *Pretty in Pink*? I told you I will show you *Some Kind of Wonderful* and it will make you feel better."

"No," Xavier says. He thinks for a second. "Yes. But not right now. This is about Emma. You said there could be different explanations for why the officers didn't do the welfare check at Marie's apartment. The guy who responded to the call didn't know how to do his job well enough—or maybe he decided he wasn't going to do it because he thought it was the right thing to do—or he was purposely trying to keep anyone out of her apartment because he knew there was something going on. Right?"

"Right."

"So, you get to direct it. Come up with all the alternative endings and play them all out. What happens in them? How would each of those reasons change how the rest of the story goes?"

Now I feel like I understand where he's going.

CHAPTER SIX

W E DON'T HAVE A CLAPBOARD HANDY, BUT XAVIER MAKES DO BY holding up his hands in front of his head and slamming them together.

"Action!" he calls out.

The words come flowing out of me so fast that I'm almost convinced they're bypassing my mouth and going straight from my brain to everyone's ears.

"Alright. There are two branching paths, two divisions here: either it was a mistake, or it was intentional. Either way, that specific failure in the investigation delayed us from finding Marie. I don't believe it has anything to do with her death, though. She was already dead by the time Rose realized she hadn't heard from her in too long. So it isn't that a welfare check could have saved her life. It's whether the lack of one changed how the Cleaners did their job.

"Without saying it explicitly, we've been assuming that the lack of a welfare check was a part of the puzzle. That if there was a conspiracy behind Marie's disappearance and death, the police who refused to go into her apartment were in on it. Which would mean they were trying to keep anyone from realizing that Marie wasn't there, or that there was incriminating evidence inside. Dean, you're up."

Dean takes center stage like it's his turn to start monologuing in a movie. Xavier keeps his hands up like he's filming the whole process.

"But that doesn't make sense. Obviously, people knew she was missing. Her family wasn't just going to stop wondering where she was because they didn't go into her apartment. If the police were actually thinking the situation through, they would realize not getting answers would only make her mother and other people who care about her more worried and eager to find out what was going on. And if they weren't letting anyone inside because they knew there was evidence in there that would link Marie to the drug dealer, which could possibly incriminate him, why did they just leave those things there?"

He furrows his brow and starts pacing some more. "In all that time between the initial welfare check being denied, and their hands being forced because of the neighbors reporting the person sneaking into the apartment, there had to be opportunities to go inside and remove that evidence. If the police were working with Rocky for some reason, blocking the welfare check to prevent people from finding out he, or one of his associates, was responsible for Marie's disappearance, they would have made sure that evidence disappeared. But why? Why cover for a relatively low-level drug dealer who was already in prison?"

He looks at me as though to pass the baton back. Xavier follows along with his fake camera and zooms right in on me.

"Which brings me back to my thought that the evidence was planted," I say. "It's too convenient to have those things right out in the open, especially in the home of someone who was supposedly keeping their secret life of drug use away from their family. If she was putting so much effort into keeping up the appearance of living out a normal life, not trying to cause any alarm with Rose or Sam or anyone else, why would she be so careless about leaving drugs readily visible? Why go to the trouble of getting a second phone just for her drug deals, only to have the dealer in her contacts and have the phone easy to find?

"And then there's the fact that Sam interviewed the dealer himself. He made it very clear he didn't know Marie and had never had any contact with her. He'd never sold to her and since he was in custody, it would mean someone else would have to be running his business under his name, which he did not allow. Of course, that doesn't mean it wasn't happening. One of his associates could have seen his incarceration as the ideal opportunity to get a jump on his own business ventures. But it does mean Collins didn't have anything to do with it.

"And that leads us to his untimely demise. The day after Sam's interview with him, Rocky was found dead in his cell. It's obvious he was murdered, but it hasn't been solved. Sounds like a very neat way to tie up those loose ends. He's dead so he can't ask around, find out who is behind his name being wrapped up into all this shit, and start naming names. Marie is already painted as a junkie, the trail leads to her body, it's declared an overdose, and it's all over."

"Little did they know that Emma Griffin was going to be on the case. Which means it was most certainly not over."

I look up and see Sam leaning against the wall at the entrance to the room. He looks tired, but there's a softly amused smile on his lips.

"Hey, babe," I smile. "When did you get here? I didn't hear you come in."

"Yeah," he says, pushing away from the wall and coming toward me. "I noticed. I've been listening for a little bit. Fat lot of good that alarm on the doors is doing."

My husband has a habit of periodically augmenting the security features of our house. His most recent addition is thankfully much simpler than the high-tech cameras and sensors he installed and I promptly disconnected but have since selectively started again. The simple alarm connects to every door and window leading to the outside of the house and lets out a chirp every time one of them is open.

Every. Time.

On his specific request, I've left it in place, but my brain has apparently decided to occasionally receive the tone as only white noise.

He leans down for a kiss, and I notice his eyes flicker across the pictures of Marie as he straightens back up.

"That evidence was definitely planted. There's no question about that. And I think it happened after the officer knocked and left without going into the apartment," he says.

I nod. "So, in that version of the alternate ending, the Cleaners staged the scene where her body was found, expecting that someone would eventually check on her and realize she wasn't there..." my voice trails off as I realize the thought process I'm following feels strained. "And then what? Just wait for her body to be discovered in that abandoned warehouse eventually?"

Dean steps up and Xavier follows him with his camera motion. "Stay on your mark, Dean," he murmurs.

Sam gives me a bemused look.

"We're filming the Director's Cut of what really happened," I explain in a stage whisper.

His face scrunches up in confusion, but he nods, clearly going along with it anyway.

Dean returns to his spot and clears his throat. "Anyway. If the Cleaners weren't responsible for her death, if they were just there to fix things afterward, maybe it didn't matter when she was found. All that mattered was that people knew she wasn't in her apartment and that there wasn't any sign of a struggle there," he suggests. "They knew she would be found at some point. Places like that attract people. Other junkies might just ignore her body because they don't want to get involved, but people who think of themselves as urban explorers would have stumbled on her at some point."

"Not other," Sam says, his voice lower. The tone means he's trying to control emotions building up.

"What?" Dean asks.

"You said 'other junkies.' Junkies might just ignore her. Not 'other junkies.' Marie was not a user. She wasn't an addict," Sam tells him. "She didn't go out to that junk heap and shoot herself up. She didn't sit there and die by herself. She is *not* one of them."

Dean's jaw tightens. These two men haven't had the smoothest, easiest time adapting to each other. They get along far better now than they did when Dean first became a part of our lives, but there's still tension. I wait for Dean to react, but he restrains himself. He can tell this isn't the moment to try to jockey for position.

"Next ending, Emma," Xavier mutters out of the side of his mouth, still arduously filming the proceedings on his fake hand camera. "Go to the next ending."

"Alternate ending," I announce, pushing the conversation forward past the thickness of the air around us. "The person who hired the Cleaners isn't satisfied with just waiting around. They don't want questions. They want to make sure her body is found, and her death is quickly explained.

"Which means they had reason to believe what actually happened could be traced if too much time passed. So they send the Cleaners in again. They access her apartment for two reasons: first to plant the evidence that supports the story they want to tell, and second to make sure they are *seen*, so the police are notified and are more likely to go into the apartment."

I look at Sam. "The person who gave the information that led the search to the factory. Were the detectives ever able to conclusively make a connection between him and Collins?"

"He said he was one of his associates," Sam says.

"I know. But could they prove the connection? Did they even try to?"

"Why would someone lie about being connected to a drug dealer?" Dean asks. "Especially one whose name has appeared in a missing persons' case?"

"After Rocky was murdered, this guy showed up to talk to the detectives. He was able to convince them he knew Rocky well enough to be able to say with certainty he didn't know Marie and hadn't had any contact with her. But he did mention several people in their circle who did know her and some of the locations where she frequented," I tell him. "That was the tip that eventually led us to that broken-down warehouse. Think about it: there was nothing in her apartment to indicate where she could be found. All that *was* there just furthered the narrative that she used drugs. It wasn't until they talked to this supposed associate that Sam got the information that sent him searching. This is someone who the police have heard about but have never had direct contact with. Rocky would never give him up."

"But he just suddenly decides to walk in and talk to detectives," Dean says sarcastically.

"Even if he was angry about his fallen leader, I don't see that being the approach he would take. I don't think him going in there had anything to do with finding out how Rocky was killed, because I think he already knew. It was arranged as part of the coverup. The Cleaners, or possibly whoever hired them, might have assumed the police would take the information that Marie was using drugs and go to locations known for users frequenting them. When they didn't search the right places, they had to find another way to ensure she was found."

"What does Rocky Collins have to do with any of this? He was already in prison. He didn't even know Marie. Why was he targeted?" Dean asks.

"Maybe the Cleaners were cleaning up two messes."

CHAPTER SEVEN

G ETTING UP IN THE MIDDLE OF THE NIGHT ISN'T UNUSUAL FOR ME. In fact, that moment of opening my eyes and realizing it's still dark tells me that at least I was able to fall asleep, and there have been many times in my life when there were fewer of those than not.

What is unusual is waking up and not feeling Sam right beside me. I find comfort in the warmth of him, the depression of his weight in the mattress. In the feeling of sturdiness and peace that comes from snuggling back against him and waiting either for sleep or for dawn cresting through the window.

But tonight when my eyes open to only darkness, I reach across the other side of the bed and don't feel him. I listen, thinking maybe he has gone off to the bathroom and will come back any second. I don't hear his footsteps and when I glance over, there's no glow coming from under the bathroom door. I fumble around under my pillow looking for my phone so I can check the time.

It's that time of year when even if I get up early, the sun is already creeping its way up the horizon, if not already all the way up, so waking up to a cloudy or rainy day that obliterates that light can make it seem like it's still night. But it's not morning yet. At least, not the kind of morning that means I should be getting up out of bed. And certainly not Sam.

Worry starts to trickle in. I get up and throw a lightweight robe on over my pajamas. As I walk for the bedroom door, instinct ingrained in me from my years in the FBI has me take my gun from the nightstand drawer and slip it into my pocket. I know I'm just walking through my own house, but there have been plenty of situations when that meant nothing.

Walking out into the hallway, I pause to listen to my surroundings. Except for the low drone of fans in the bedrooms, the house is quiet. I continue downstairs to find Sam sitting in the living room, his elbows propped on his thighs as he leans forward with his head hanging down and a cup dangling precariously in the tips of his fingers.

"Babe?" I ask, coming into the room.

He looks up at me and I can see the hurt in his eyes.

"Hey. I'm sorry, did I wake you up?" he asks.

I shake my head, taking my gun from my pocket and setting it on the side table as I curl up beside him and rest my hand on his back.

"No. I just woke up and realized you weren't in bed with me. What's going on? Are you all right?"

Sam sits up and leans back against the couch. He lets out a long breath. It's not really a sigh. More just an exhale to make room for the energy to talk about what he's thinking and feeling.

"I just can't stop thinking about Marie," he murmurs. "When I came home and you were talking to Dean and Xavier about it..."

"I didn't mean to be talking about it behind your back. It's not like I was trying to hide it from you. I just..."

"I know," he says, cutting off my hurried voice. "Ever since you read that article about Dr. Villarreal and made the connection with the cults, your brain has been churning. I can see it. And it makes sense that you would talk to them about it. Dean has his experience with private investigating and could have different insights about it. Xavier can do whatever it is that Xavier does. I'm not upset that you were talking about it. I'm glad you care as much as you do."

"Of course, I do," I say.

Sam's face tenses. He looks down again. "I just can't stop thinking about all the pieces that don't fit together. None of it makes sense and yet everybody wants me to just accept the explanation they're feeding me. The people supposedly investigating her disappearance were so eager to first say there was nothing to be worried about and that she had just wandered off on her own because she's an adult and was clearly trying to get away. And then when we found her body, they still wouldn't admit there could be anything going on.

"They wanted to write her off as fast as possible. Just say it's an overdose and push her aside, like she's disposable. They refuse to acknowledge the inconsistencies, the problems that seem to be showing up at every step. I know I'm probably idealistic because I'm Sheriff and I watched my father in the job and his father before him. It's all I've ever wanted to be. I grew up believing in justice. Really believing that anyone who puts on a uniform and a badge does it because they are truly dedicated to protecting people and finding the truth when a crime happens."

"But you and I both know that that isn't the case," I finish the thought for him. "It's unfortunate, but we've dealt with plenty of bad cops or agents in our career. As much as we'd like to believe that people who choose this line of work are still committed to it because they want the old cliché, to make the world a better place, safer and kinder and gentler for the next generation... that simply doesn't always bear out. People get corrupt, or greedy, or complacent. They turn the other way and lose focus on what real justice means. Maybe they lost it somewhere along the way, or maybe they never had it. Maybe they only ever signed up to be a cop for the thrill of it. But it makes the work the rest of us do that much harder. And that's why you and I have dedicated our whole lives to the pursuit of justice."

Sam considers that for a moment and nods. "And you know the worst part? It's not just necessarily whether or not they were corrupt, or bad cops. Maybe it isn't that they lost their sense of justice. For all we know, they might really be great officers. But they were so selective about it. They thought she was a junkie, and thus, she didn't matter. Like she wasn't worth their time. Trying to find Marie and then figure out what happened to her wasn't a priority because of how they saw her. I don't care how they saw her. I don't care what they think of her. That shouldn't matter. Even if they believe completely that she was just an addict who had gotten herself in too deep, they should still care about her because she's a person. She's *human*." He hesitates. "She was. I know there's a lot more to her death than those investigators want to admit. And now that I've heard your thoughts about the Cleaners, it's eating at me."

"I don't know for sure what they did. I was just throwing ideas around. There's still so much to figure out," I say.

We had all ended the conversation a couple of hours after Sam got home without any real conclusions. All those alternate endings are still hanging in the air, unresolved. The truth is, I know just as well as Sam does that Marie's death isn't what it looked like. Even if I had never heard of the Cleaners, I would still have the twisting feeling in my gut that says something isn't right. I just don't have the answers.

"I know there is. And I need to be the one to figure it out," he says.

"Then do," I say. "Be her voice. Keep standing up for her the way you have been since the very beginning. You know I'm here to help you in any way I can. And Dean and Xavier. Eric. All of us. We'll do whatever we can to help you."

His head rocks back and forth, not really a shake, just a swing like his body is rejecting what I'm saying before his voice can even catch up.

"I have my department to think about, Emma. No matter what's going on, I am still Sheriff of Sherwood. The people here depend on me. I have to take care of them. I can't sit here and say how frustrated I am about the investigators not taking her case seriously, or just tossing her aside, only to do the exact same thing to the people here. Maybe we don't see as much crime as in other places, but the people here are still just as deserving of protection and leadership."

"They are. And they adore you. Every person out there who has elected you to this position time after time does it because you are amazing at what you do. Because, like you said, you were raised for it. And you've never faltered in your dedication. But that doesn't mean that you have to sacrifice yourself and your family," I tell him. "They can get on without you for a little while. You've trained the other people in the department and they can step in for you if they need to. You need to do what's right for you."

"The rest of the department, the city council, and the people of Sherwood might not be so understanding. I could be recalled for taking more time away from work. And I could essentially hand the election to whoever comes up against me."

"Then that's the way it is," I shrug. He looks over at me and I move closer so my arm stretches all the way across his back and can hold him against me. "I know you love being Sheriff. I know you love the department and the town. But if it comes down to making a decision between staying here so you don't upset anybody and following what's in your heart to do for your cousin, there shouldn't even be a second of hesitation. You need to do what I know everything inside of you is telling you that you have to do. Even if that means leaving the department."

"Are you sure?" he asks.

"Absolutely. I'm your wife, Sam, before anything else. I will be supportive of whatever you need. Talk to the department. Meet with City Council and the County Supervisors. Talk to the Governor if you have to. Explain the situation and request a leave of absence. If they give it to you, that's great. But if they won't, you can just walk away. Marie and Rose need you. And you need to do this for yourself."

He looks touched as he nods and leans in to rest his forehead against mine.

"I love you," he whispers.

"I love you," I say.

"I'll talk to them tomorrow." He stands up. "But for now, I'm going to try to get some sleep. Are you coming?"

I nod. "I'll be there in just a minute."

"Okay."

I wait until he's upstairs to stand up from the couch and walk over to the window. The night beyond the glass is still and peaceful. It looks like the world has simply been turned off. Just looking at it as it seems, everything is just as it should be. But as my eyes move to Janet and Paul's house, and the tiny light glowing in the back where I know Paul is sitting in his office, and the house across the street where I can close my eyes and still see blood on the door and feel car fumes filling my lungs, I know there's always something beneath the surface.

CHAPTER EIGHT

I GRAB A COUPLE OF HOURS OF SLEEP BEFORE GETTING UP TO MAKE breakfast for Sam and send him off to work. He doesn't need lunch today. He's planning on bringing his deputies to Pearl's Diner for lunch so he can broach the subject of his leave of absence.

This is somewhat of a strange situation. Because he's an elected official, Sam doesn't have a boss he can go to in circumstances like this to ask for the time off he needs. There's no supervisor or HR department to which he can submit a request and the plan put into action. Instead, he has to navigate this in real time and figure out an ad hoc solution.

It's one of the benefits of Sherwood being such a small place. Little towns like this with deep roots and close ties can sometimes get steeped in too much tradition so nothing changes. But at the same time, it can also make things much more flexible. If Sam was in a big area like Richmond or DC, this would take mountains of bureaucracy and paperwork. But in Sherwood, we have enough leeway to make an exception to take care of our own. And if there is anybody in this town who could be considered one of Sherwood's own, it is Sheriff Samuel Johnson.

I'm doing my best not to show how worried I am about him. He hates to see me upset and the last thing he needs right now is something else to make him feel like the world is on his shoulders. He's my rock. I know he'd never push me away or tell me he didn't want to listen to me if I needed to talk through how I was feeling. He is always there to comfort and reassure me, or just be the wall that absorbs my rants and anger at the world, knowing it's not really directed at him, but that I just need to be heard. It's like the tree falling in the forest. If there's no one around to hear my rage, have I really let it out?

Sam is always there for me without question, without hesitation, and sometimes without restraint. Like a multitude of locks and alarms on the house. Like all the times he has tried to talk me out of an investigation or change my mind about rushing headlong into something reckless, he sometimes tries to take care of me to a fault. The least I can do is try to do the same for him in return.

There's no question he is the more logical and calmer of the two of us. If I was in his shoes, I probably wouldn't even go to the effort of asking. I would just tell them I was going to investigate my cousin's murder and would be back when I could be back. I'd deal with the consequences later.

But that's the kind of approach that has gotten me in quite a lot of trouble, and is at least partially responsible for the network of scars on my body. I've gotten better at controlling my compulsions and thinking through things more before I do them, but Sam is always going to be the one that keeps both of us firmly planted on the ground.

I can only hope enough of my impulsiveness has worn off on him that he'll be able to do what needs to be done. I know it would hurt him to have to walk away from the department and not be Sheriff anymore, but it would torture him for the rest of his life if he wasn't able to solve this for Marie.

Dean comes into the kitchen as I'm dumping another pan full of scrambled eggs onto a platter. I hand it to him and gesture at the table so he can put it next to a stack of buttered English muffins and a jar of Janet's homemade apple butter I broke out of the pantry.

"I love coming here," he grins, grabbing a link of sausage from another plate and biting it in half.

Breakfast is my favorite meal to make, so he's used to at least having something in the mornings when he's here, but the spread on the table is definitely more elaborate than usual.

"Yeah, well, you can thank Sam for getting extra spoiled this morning. Where's Xavier?"

"He said he was going to the backyard. What's going on with Sam?"

I move the curtain on the kitchen window aside and look out into the yard. Sure enough, there's Xavier, sitting on a blanket under a tree, his jars of sourdough starter arranged around him like his children.

"He's having a playdate with his starters," I say.

"Sam?" Dean frowns, sounding confused.

"No, Xavier."

"Oh. Yeah, he says they like the sun in the morning. It helps them get extra bubbly. I think he's planning on a lot of baking today, just be ready for that," Dean says. "He should be back in pretty soon. He usually doesn't stay out there very long. I think he's worried they'll get sunburned."

"Well, then I guess we'll be having biscuits with dinner. That will be good."

I let out a heavy sigh as I drop down into the chair across from him, holding a cup of coffee in both hands and feeling like I forgot something.

"Sam," Dean says. "What's going on with him that inspired the hotel breakfast experience?"

I explain what happened last night and his plans for the day.

"I'm trying really hard not to be pushy. This isn't my decision to make. I know that. I told him he needs to do what's right for him, and that's exactly what I meant."

"Only, you know what's right for him and you want him to do that," Dean says.

"This is going to stay with him. The rest of his life. He will never not think about her and what happened to her. The only way he's ever going to even come close to recovering from it is if he's able to find out exactly what happened. And maybe I'm being selfish. I want to know, too. I want to know who the Cleaners are and why they got involved with someone as unassuming and non-threatening as Marie.

"I know I can't do this for him. I can help. I can offer whatever type of support and assistance I can. But this is something he needs to do, and the only way he's going to be able to do it is if he goes to Michigan and investigates."

"He will."

The alarm on the back door chirps as it opens and Xavier comes inside, the blanket draped over his shoulder and his arms full of jars. I get up and take some of them, helping him transfer them to the counter. I take him coming in as a chance to break away from worrying about

Sam. He has to make this choice and do what he's going to do without me interfering. I just have to wait and see what I can do to help.

I refresh the coffee in my mug before sitting back down at the table. Xavier joins us and starts filling his plate.

"Did they enjoy their morning outing?" I ask.

"They seemed to," he nods. "Dough and Behold is seeming a little sluggish. I'm thinking about adding a bit of rye flour to the feeding later."

I lean back slightly and look over my shoulder toward the jars. "Get well soon, D and B."

"What are your plans for the day?" Dean asks.

I take a sip of the hot coffee, enjoying the sting of the heat and the bitter taste.

"So far I've settled on taking a shower. Xavier?"

I look over at him and watch him methodically fill each divot in his muffin with tiny globs of apple butter. He shakes his head.

"I've already taken a shower, but thank you."

Dean and I look at each other and my cousin fights not to laugh. I shake my head at him.

"Any other plans?"

"I have a couple of theories I'm working through. I'm almost certain I'm right, and I hate to be the kind of person who would rely on preconceived notions and prejudices to form opinions, but it's hard to have total faith in the word of a man with spiderwebs tattooed on his eyelids and his tongue split so it looks like a snake."

He still hasn't looked up from his English muffin. I wait for more information, but don't get it.

"Xavier?"

His head lifts long enough for him to stick his tongue out and flick it a couple of times before sucking it back in and going back to his muffin.

"No, Xa—never mind. Dean. What about you?" I ask. "Are you working on something specific today?"

"I was just planning on doing some research on my computer. Why? Is there something you wanted to do?"

"If you had time, I was thinking we could go down to the Community Center. One of the programs I helped develop is happening today. I'm not speaking at it because I'm pretty sure everyone who lives in Sherwood has come to one of my talks, but I'd still like to stop in and see how it's going."

"That sounds good," he says. "What time?"

"Late this afternoon. We could probably pick up something for dinner after and get back here right before Sam gets home."

"Sure." His eyes move cautiously over to Xavier. "Xavier?"

One finger comes up to ask Dean to wait and he fills the last of the crannies. He picks up the muffin and displays it proudly.

"Good distribution." I finish the last swig of my coffee as I stand. "I'm going to throw some laundry in the cold wash and get in the shower. Be out in a bit."

CHAPTER NINE

'VE ALWAYS BEEN ABLE TO DO SOME OF MY BEST THINKING IN THE
shower or bath. When I can't untangle something, or when I feel like
my emotions are going to get the best of me, I get in the water and my
mind seems to clear. I'm hoping for some of that clarity to come to me
today, and I have my back to the water, trying to find that moment of
peace, when my phone alerts on the counter.

Leaning out of the shower, I dry my hands on a nearby towel and
reach for my phone. The alert was an email from Marini's lawyer, Nathan
Klein. I'm surprised to hear from him, but I'm even more shocked by
the content of the message.

He got in touch with Marini's sister. She wants to talk to me.

Dropping my phone back down onto the counter, I get back in the
shower long enough to finish up, then jump out and get dressed before
answering his email. Drying my hair with a towel, I head out of the bathroom, already calling out loud to Dean and Xavier.

"You won't believe what I just got in my email. That lawyer just messaged me to tell me that Marini's sister not only tracked him down, but she wants to talk to me. She wanted him to get us in touch with each other, but he has a policy against sharing personal contact information. Which, I guess is a good policy, considering the nature of his work and the types of clients he's known to associate with. He was emailing to ask permission to give her my information so she can get in touch. Of course, I told him to give it to her. I really want to know what she has to say. He said her name is Gwendolyn Russo."

I walk into the living room expecting Dean to be on the couch with his computer, but he's not there. "And I'm talking to myself." His computer is sitting on the couch and there's a cup of coffee on the side table. "Where the hell are you?"

I check out the window to see if he has gone to get the mail or get something from his car, but I don't see either one of them. The kitchen is also empty, and I don't see them in the backyard, either.

"Dean?" I call out. "Xavier?" I walk down the hallway toward the small home gym and call their names again.

My office door pops open, and Dean steps out, holding his phone to his ear. He gestures at it.

"What do you need?" he mouths.

I glance around him into the office to see if Xavier is in there with him, but he's not. I make the shape of an "X" with my arms and then hold my hands out in a questioning gesture. A look of concern immediately crosses Dean's face, and he walks around me so he can go down the hallway. I follow and we walk through the bottom floor of the house, checking in each of the rooms, but he isn't there. He ends the call, promising whomever is on the other line he'll call back soon, and shoves the phone away into his pocket.

"Where is he?" I ask.

"I thought he was in the living room," Dean says. "That's where he was when I got my phone call and went in your office so we didn't distract each other."

"Come on. Let's check his room," I say.

The room Xavier chose as his was the one I slept in when I visited my grandparents in this house as a little girl. The yellow paint is the same and it doesn't have my grandmother's angel collection that scares the hell out of him. Those are in Dean's room.

The door is standing partially open when we get to the top of the steps, and I already know he isn't in there. Xavier doesn't like the ambiguity of a door that is somewhere between open and closed. He says it contributes to personal crises of optimism versus pessimism in the people who see it and the world doesn't need more conflict, internal or otherwise. He also just really doesn't like not knowing the protocol of whether to knock or not. I've seen him accidentally push a door closed by knocking on it when it was standing part of the way open and end up locking the person inside. That person being me.

"Damn it," Dean mutters. "Where is he?"

"Between doing the laundry and taking my shower, it couldn't have been more than an hour. How long were you on the phone?" I ask.

"I got the call just after you went into the bathroom."

"Alright, so maybe forty minutes," I say. "Where could he have gone in forty minutes?"

I try to call Xavier, but he doesn't answer.

"This is Xavier, Emma. For all we know he could have rigged Sam's riding mower and be on the fucking moon by now." Dean rubs his hands down his face. "Alright. What's around here that he would go to? There isn't an amusement park anywhere. He just ate, so he didn't go to Pearl's."

"You try to call him. He always responds to you."

Dean calls, but there's still no answer. I can see the worry building up inside him. I distinctly remember the last time we lost track of Xavier for any considerable length of time. It didn't end well for him. But this time is different. The Dragon is gone. We don't have a serial killer hunting us. Xavier must have decided he wanted to go somewhere and didn't want to wait for Dean to get off his phone or me to get out of the shower.

"He said we were both going to be researching today. He likes when we're both working on something," Dean postulates.

"By the description of his source of information, I'm going to take a wild guess and say he's looking into something he found out while he was in prison. He must still be trying to show how Jonah escaped."

Dean nods. "He says he knows how it was done, but knowing it and being able to prove it are two different things. He has to be able to prove it before he talks about it. He wants to hammer out the details and get empirical proof. Honestly, I think he might just be creating a *MythBusters*-style show in his head."

I try to call again, but it still just rings as Dean looks around the room. He stops in front of the desk, and I end the call.

"Did you find something?" I ask.

"Maybe." He picks up a piece of paper. "This is Xavier's handwriting. But all it says is 'two-point-three miles.' No address. Just the distance."

"Come on."

I stop in the bedroom for my gun before running downstairs and snatching my keys off the hook by the door as I push through it. We drive out of the neighborhood without knowing which direction we should be going.

"What's around here at that distance?" he asks. "Which way do we drive?"

"There are only three roads leading through Sherwood. One direction is the main area of town. The green, the shops, other neighborhoods. The other way is industrial, some woods, the schools. The other way is more woods."

"I don't think he would have any need to wander around in the woods by himself," Dean notes. "And if he did, he would have stuff with him. A backpack. Water. He'd prepare. He was heading somewhere."

"He's probably on foot, since there aren't any rideshares in Sherwood and I don't see him using one anyway, but he's speedy when he wants to be. He could have gotten a pretty good distance in this time."

"Alright," I nod. "Shopping? Did he need anything?"

Dean shakes his head. "I can't think of anything. And unless it was really urgent or there's a self-checkout, he wouldn't go alone."

"Two-point-three miles," I mutter, trying to wrack my brain for anything that is that distance from my house and that might appeal to Xavier. "What was he researching? You said he was doing that show in his head. What was he trying to figure out?" Almost the instant the words are out of my mouth, it hits me. "Shit."

I pull the wheel hard to catch a turn that brings us toward the other side of Sherwood.

"What?" Dean asks. "What is it?"

"A junkyard. Scrap metal, discarded appliances. Old cars. Remember all the questions he's been asking about Jonah being able to cling to the bottom of a car and how long he could hang on if the car was moving?"

Our eyes meet and a sudden shock of panic bursts in my chest. I pull off to the side of the road and Dean flings himself out of the car before it's all the way stopped. He drops down to the ground and sticks his head underneath to look up, and by the time I've gotten out, he's climbing back to his feet, shaking his head.

Relief relaxes my shoulders, and we get back in.

"So, that was probably a long shot," he says.

"And yet..."

He nods knowingly as we continue to the junkyard. Even though it's less than a mile away at this point, it feels like the drive is stretching on endlessly. Dean has tried to call Xavier several more times from both of our phones, but he still hasn't answered.

"Explain to me again why he's able to track all of us, but none of us have hung a beacon around his neck or something," I gripe as we pull through the chain-link fence into the cramped junkyard parking lot.

"Because in theory, he's almost always with one of us," Dean says. "And if he's at home alone for a few hours, he's fine. Usually, he gets misplaced in a relatively small area and we're able to locate him. I didn't think it would be an issue considering we're in a town with no access to public transportation, a ride share, or even his unicycle to get him anywhere."

He pulls this one on me as I'm getting out of the car, and I glare across the roof at him.

"You got Xavier a unicycle?" I ask incredulously.

"He got it for himself," Dean says like he's defending himself. "And I might have been supposed to not tell you that."

"Damn it, Dean," I say, slamming the car door. "He's easy enough to lose when he has all his faculties about him. The world didn't need him more mobile and with the need to concentrate on staying upright on a single wheel."

We take off jogging toward the entrance to the junkyard, calling for Xavier as we go. Dean calls him again and I think I hear a faint ringing in the distance. I stop, reaching out to grab Dean.

"Did you hear that? I think that was his phone. Call him again."

He calls and I hear the ring again. This time, Dean's eyes widen. He nods and we run toward the sound. It carries us around a corner made up of several beaten-up cars piled up on top of each other at tenuous angles. I skid to a stop, my panic bells fully ringing in my head now.

Standing in the middle of the grass walkway that winds and weaves through the piles of cast-off metal in the yard is a large man in heavy boots and a t-shirt emblazoned with the name of the junkyard. He's focused on an old school bus in front of him, but I see a phone in his outstretched hand.

"Xavier?" I call, my hand instinctively moving to my gun.

"Emma?"

The man turns enough for me to see more of the bus and there's Xavier. Clinging to the underside like a monkey.

"X, what in the blue hell are you doing?" Dean asks.

"Bruce?" Xavier calls out.

The man looks at the phone in his hand again. "Thirty more seconds."

"Be with you in thirty seconds," Xavier tells us.

We stand and wait until Bruce gives Xavier a signal. He clings for a few moments longer, then drops away from the bottom of the bus and rolls toward us.

"Did you walk all the way out here to try to hang onto the bottom of a school bus?" I ask.

"I didn't try," he clarifies. "I did hang onto the bottom of a school bus. And I didn't walk all the way here. I was towed."

"You were towed?" Dean frowns. "You don't have a car."

"I wasn't in one. I was doing my research and trying to figure out if my assumption of what happened was accurate. I found out about this lovely junkyard and decided maybe the proprietors would be able to help me. So, I called and got a hold of Bruce here. I asked him if he might have a decommissioned van or truck readily available that he could bring to me so I could cling to it for a while. He said he couldn't do that, but he did have a school bus and I was more than welcome to come see it. When I explained that I didn't have a motor vehicle I could drive to the location, but I could walk there, he said he could come tow me. So, he did. And he agreed to time me."

He reaches for his phone from Bruce. "Thank you, kind sir."

"I thought he meant his car was broken down. I have a mechanic shop next door and was going to see if I could fix the car up for him. I never have towed just a person," Bruce says.

I don't tell him he still hasn't. What he did was give Xavier a ride. Still ill-advised, but not nearly as dangerous as I would have originally thought hearing that story. Him clinging to the bottom of the school bus, on the other hand, is still causing me concern.

"And why are you clinging to the bottom of the school bus?"

"I told you, research. And, it worked out," Xavier says.

"Great. Can we go home now?" I ask.

"Sure," Xavier says, nodding. He looks at Bruce. "Have a lovely afternoon. I may come and browse again sometime."

We start away from the bus, but Bruce stops us.

"Hey." We turn around and he points at the bus. "My turn."

CHAPTER TEN

" TOLD HIM IT WAS HARDER THAN IT LOOKED. BUT HE REFUSED TO believe me. I hope he's going to be okay."

"Xavier, why did you go to the junkyard by yourself? I was right there in Emma's office on the phone. You could have waited for me," Dean tells him.

"And I was just taking a shower. If you needed something, you could have just knocked on the door and let me know. I would have gotten out and brought you," I add.

"I know you would have. But I did it myself because I could. I think sometimes people forget that," he says. "Things are harder for me. And there are a lot of things I need help with all the time. But I can do things myself sometimes. And even if I find out I can't, every now and then I still like to try. I don't want to be a burden to any of you. Ever."

"You aren't," Dean says.

"None of us think that," I say. "We want to help you."

"I know. But sometimes it feels good to be able to do something on my own. I spent a long time being told what I could and couldn't do. And then I went to prison, and everyone is told what they can and can't do there, so I thought maybe it would be easier. But it wasn't. It was just worse there. And then when I got out, it was the same thing. I still had other people deciding everything for me. Sometimes I just want to be able to do things like everybody else does," he says.

"X..."

"I know," Xavier says again, looking at Dean with an emotion in his eyes I've never seen exist in anyone else. "I know I'm not like everyone else, Dean. I'm reminded of that every single day. Do you remember when Ava asked you what it was like not to remember?"

Dean stiffens and a muscle in his jaw twitches. He gives a single nod.

"I do."

"Don't you ever just stop and think about something to make sure you remember it? Go over what you did during the day, or everything you bought at the grocery store, or what you talked about on the phone?"

"Yes," Dean nods.

"That's what I do. Just for a second, I see what I can do."

"Alright," Dean says. "But can we just agree that you let me know where you're going? Or at least answer your phone?"

"I couldn't answer my phone while I was hanging from the bus," Xavier points out.

"Right. But in other situations."

"Not when you're riding your unicycle," I say quickly. "And can we also just establish right now that the unicycle is not a long-distance mode of transportation?"

"I thought we weren't going to tell her about that," Xavier mutters, looking through narrowed eyes at Dean.

"It slipped out," he admits. "I was worried about you."

"I appreciate your worry. There have been plenty of times in my life when there wasn't anybody around to worry about me. Actually, there were people who said they were worried about me, but I don't think it was the same sort of sentiment. Anyway, I know if I do try to do something and it goes wrong, you'll be there for me."

"Of course, I will," Dean says.

"And if you ever can't remember, I can be there for you, too. Look."

He takes out his phone and scrolls through a few screens. I glance over from behind the wheel to try to see what he's looking for, but I can't. After a few seconds, he holds the phone between the seats so Dean can see it.

"What am I looking at?"

"Scrapbooking supplies. I ordered them yesterday. It's enough to outfit my whole scrapbooking room."

"Xavier, we don't have a scrapbooking room," he frowns.

I glance into the rearview mirror at my cousin to watch the moment when he realizes that somewhere in his house, there's either a room he doesn't know about, or one that has been repurposed without his knowledge.

On the way home from the junkyard, I take a detour through the main village to get a milkshake. It feels like that kind of day. With each of us putting a valiant effort into sucking down the ultra-thick handmade shakes from a tiny little shop that opens each summer by the green, we make our way back to the house.

We haven't talked any further about why Xavier felt the need to cling to the bottom of a school bus or what that has to do with Jonah, but sitting on the wicker furniture on the front porch seems like the right atmosphere to go ahead and descend into that nightmare again.

"Why a school bus, Xavier?" I ask.

"Because it was the only kind of bus available," he shrugs. "And the basic structure is the same."

I'm about to move right past that when the realization strikes me.

"Prison transport buses. They're the same as a school bus. Did you go through all of this because Jonah latched himself to the bottom of a prison transport bus and that's how he escaped?" I ask. "You wanted to test that?"

"Yes," he says calmly. "I mean, that's how he got out the first time."

My eyebrows raised and my mouth falls open.

"The first time? There were subsequent times?"

"At least one. When he didn't go back. I'm not sure if there were times in between those, but it wouldn't surprise me if there were."

"You're telling me Jonah attached himself to the bottom of a bus and rode it out of prison, then turned around and rode it back in?" I ask incredulously.

"I don't know if I would say he attached himself. I suppose there could have been some sort of rudimentary seat belt operation in place. Maybe a sling. But that would all require far more time and preparation than I think he was willing to devote to that plan."

"That is not the part of this I want you to be focusing on," I say. "Get back to him escaping and then putting himself back in prison."

"Oh. Yes. I am almost positive he did that on at least one occasion. But, again, I'm somewhat shaky on the credibility of my source. Webster was involved in some shady dealings in his life on the outside."

"Webster?" I ask.

Xavier closes his eyes and splays his fingers out over his eyelids like he's creating spiderwebs.

"Webster."

Dean leans slightly closer to me so he can whisper out of the corner of his mouth. "The man's name is Webster?"

"Why did he tell you he thought that was what Jonah did?"

"He watched him do it. He was on that transport and saw him get under the bus. Everything I've tested and other people I've spoken to have validated everything he said. Maybe his reputation isn't completely warranted."

"But if he got out, why would he go back in? Why would he go to the effort of escaping, apparently unnoticed by anybody but old web-eyes...?"

"Webster."

"Only to risk being caught, not to mention his life, by doing it again in the other direction?"

"He wasn't ready to fully escape yet," Xavier says. "Remember we talked about him having several different plans in place. He didn't want to get out and instantly become the target of a manhunt that would get him captured or killed within a few hours or a couple of days. He wasn't escaping just for the sake of not wanting to be in prison anymore. This wasn't a reckless, impulsive decision. He escaped because he had, in his mind, unfinished business. It's very difficult to finish business when you've been shot down running across the field."

"That's true. So is that why you had me arrange that transport? The guy needing to go to the hospital with the specific guard?" I ask.

"No," Xavier says. "That's for a different test. Did you arrange it?"

"Yes. It's happening in a few days. But I don't understand. What does that have to do with Jonah's escape if it isn't because he was hanging onto the bus when it went to the hospital?"

"He was on it," Xavier says. "Inside the transport bus."

I shake my head. "No. I went through all the records of every one of his movements myself. He wasn't listed as being transported to the hospital at all during his time at Breyer. And he never got on one of the buses."

"He did," Xavier says. "But it wasn't reported. According to the guard and the official paperwork, he was only transferring one patient that day. And when the bus got back to the prison later that afternoon, that's how many got off. But it started with two."

I listen as Xavier describes Jonah's escape to me, my heart thumping in my chest and my stomach twitching and clenching angrily as the story unfolds. When he's done, I'm disgusted by what he's told me. I put my milkshake down on the table in front of me and take out my phone.

"What are you doing?" Dean asks.

"We're going to take full advantage of this situation," I say.

"What do you mean?" Xavier asks.

"That guard made himself a pawn for Jonah. Now he's going to be bait."

CHAPTER ELEVEN

Twenty minutes later, I have everything in place.

"I'm going up there the day of the planned hospital transfer. And I'm going to have a little meeting with Deandre Wright. We're going to talk about the time he brought Benson Mandeville to the hospital for treatment and showed back up at the prison almost two hours late."

As I go to put my phone back down on the table in front of me, I notice the email icon at the top and remember the message from this morning. "I can't believe I forgot to tell you about the email from this morning."

"Is that what you were talking about while you were walking through the house?" Dean asks. "Before we lost Xavier?"

"I knew where I was," Xavier says in his own defense.

It might not sound like much, but my experience with him says that's a valid statement for him to be making.

"Yes. While I was in the shower, I got an email from Marini's attorney. I honestly didn't think I was going to hear back from him voluntarily. I thought I was going to have to hound him until he talked to me again. But he messaged to tell me about Marini's sister."

I tell them about the email.

"That's huge," Dean says.

"I know. This could be key to really finding out what happened to Miley Stanford. And maybe even getting the answers to everything Marini did. She is his only living immediate family member. Unless a will spontaneously shows up and can be verified as authentic that leaves his estate to anyone else, she will likely inherit everything. She'll have to go through probate and make sure there are no other claims to it, but otherwise, it's hers. Which means she'd be able to provide us access to vaults and safes, bank records, any of that."

"Do you think she will?" Dean asks.

I'm surprised by the question. "Why wouldn't she? Don't you think she would want to help an investigation like this?"

"An investigation of her brother," Dean points out.

"Her brother who is a known murderer and who she has apparently little to no relationship with. That doesn't sound to me like anything she would be too protective of," I say.

"Just be careful," he says.

"I know," I acknowledge. "I'm trying not to get too wrapped up in it and not think it all the way through. This is what I've needed to happen in this investigation from the beginning, but that's why I need to be cautious. We know someone was helping Marini at the time of his death, and I can't imagine this is a situation where his death suddenly broke the spell on his accomplice.

"They're still out there somewhere. I can't imagine they want me getting any closer to finding out more of what he did. He might be dead, but if they are still loyal to him, they might not want his name sullied any further. This could be a trick. But at this point, I haven't even heard from her yet. When I do, I'll be careful."

I didn't realize how late it's gotten, and I hurry to change clothes and put myself together a bit more before we head to the Community Center. I get a rush of pride and satisfaction when I step through the doors to the bright, bustling center. I still remember when this wasn't here at all. This used to be the grounds of the old high school, and after it sat abandoned for many years, it was the site of a horrific murder, and where I apprehended the killer.

That was the conclusion of the case that brought me back here to Sherwood and it left a scar on everyone who lived in and loved the little town. Up until that point, the tiny town had a sense of complete safety and peace. Of course, there was the occasional fight or domestic violence. Maybe a robbery. But for the most part, people felt secure here. It was the quintessential sleepy little town where people said that those kinds of things happened in other places. People didn't destroy lives or kidnap people's babies in Sherwood.

But they did. And after that, some of the innocence of the town was lost. The run-down, dilapidated high school was like a wound that wouldn't heal. Even though it was set back from the rest of the town and not immediately visible when traveling through. We all knew it was there. It was a place where before the kidnappings and murders people still went to run laps on the track or get a bit of an adrenaline thrill by sneaking inside and walking along the long-unused corridors. After, it was a burned, bloodied reminder.

Creating the Community Center was a way to try to heal some of that pain. It took what was so horrific and turned it into a place where the people of Sherwood could come together again. I played a small part in getting it off the ground and have done several programs and events for them, but I take absolutely no credit for how amazing it has become. That all goes to Bianca Hernandez.

She is nothing short of a force of nature; a former girlfriend of Sam's who he stayed close with even after they broke up, and the mother of a child who was kidnapped during the crime spree. And now she has revitalized this humble building into a bustling, thriving place for the town. I am always amazed by what she's able to come up with and how she manages to get things done.

I help out on committees whenever I can, but coming here is more than that. A good portion of the money Greg left me came to the Community Center as an anonymous donation. I never want anyone in the town to know I'm the one who gave it, but I like to come here and see the impact it has had. Greg was a good man and gave his time, energy, and talents diligently to help other people—and me, even when I didn't return his feelings. It was that dedication that ended up costing him his life.

It's still horrifying to think of what he went through in his last months and the fact that he was finally saved, finally out of captivity, only to be brutally murdered within days. One thing that comforts me is knowing that the money he left behind has been put to amazing use. Equipment and supplies, programs, and even a scholarship fund startup all exist because of his memory. He would be proud of that. He'd be happy to know his life continues to have so much value and purpose.

We stay at the Center for a couple of hours, watching the children and talking to some of the adults from around town before we take a moment of quiet to duck out.

"Do you get asked to host murder mystery weekends often?" Dean asks as we cross the parking lot to the car.

"Just about every time I go in there," I tell him. "As soon as I told them I was going to take a little break from doing the seminars and crime classes they started approaching me with this idea for a fundraiser. All I have to do is plan out an elaborate murder plot with several suspects and red herrings, make sure it ties up into a neat bow and that non-law enforcement professionals could easily pick up on the clues to solve it, and then teach performers how to present it so that it could be drawn out over the course of a weekend."

"So easy," Dean remarks with a smile. "I don't know why you don't just jump on that. I think it's something you could do every weekend."

"Clearly," I say. We get in the car. "And you know what? It's not even that the idea of a murder mystery weekend is objectionable. It could be fun. Like living in a game of Clue for a little while."

"Aren't you terrible at Clue?" he asks.

"Yes," Xavier chimes in.

"Uncalled for. But anyway. I get caught up in the whole idea of having to plan the thing and be the one to make it fun for other people. Murder and fun don't work together in my head that way," I shrug.

"Maybe that's why you're terrible at Clue," Xavier suggests.

I choose not to respond.

Dean calls an order in to our favorite pizza place, and we get it back to the house just a few minutes before Sam gets home. He walks in and takes a deep breath of the delicious garlic and cheese-scented air.

"Honey, I'm home," he sing-songs dramatically. "Is dinner ready?"

I lift the box up from the dining room table and tilt it to display the pizza to him.

"I made it myself," I grin.

He comes around to hug me close and kiss me. "And you even went to the trouble of putting it in a box for me. You're the best."

"And don't you forget it, buster," I say as I pepper a kiss on his lips.

"Like I could ever forget you," he replies.

Dean's phone rings in his pocket and he walks out of the room to take the call as I distribute slices of pizza onto the plates around the table. Xavier comes in carrying cups and a jug of sweet tea.

"Hi, Sam," he says. He looks at me. "How did his meeting go?"

"I didn't have a chance to ask him yet," I say under my breath. He makes an encouraging sound and gestures like he's nudging me until I look at Sam. "How did your meeting go?"

I'm hoping the question won't break the good mood he seems to be in. I'm relieved when his eyes don't darken.

"Everybody was really receptive. Most of them already knew what was going on, at least to some degree. I caught them up and told them I feel it's my place to be in Michigan with my aunt right now, making sure my cousin's case is not forgotten. Everybody in the department agreed and said they were willing to work around my time off or anything I needed. The County Supervisor I met with didn't have a lot to say about it, but agreed to take the matter to others this afternoon and I'm meeting up with the board and the city council again in the morning."

"That's good," I smile. "I told you everybody was on your side."

"On your side for what?" Dean asks, coming back into the room and sitting down.

Sam tells him about the meetings and Dean gives a nod of acknowledgment. It's at least something.

"Well, I have a couple of meetings coming up myself later in the week," I say, filling him on Gwendolyn Russo and Deandre Wright.

As I'm explaining Jonah's escape, Dean's phone rings again. He rolls his eyes and stands up, still swallowing a bite of pizza. Xavier finishes his pieces and wipes his mouth on a napkin before getting up and running upstairs.

"Was that planned?" Sam asks with a raised eyebrow. "Is this an intervention of some kind?"

"Don't interventions generally involve people ambushing someone in a room, not abandoning them in it?" I ask.

"The world is changing, Emma," he says solemnly, making me laugh.

I lean in for a kiss that's broken a second later by Xavier appearing back in the room carrying a box of Twister.

"You said we could play," he implores us.

I look at Sam and shrug. "I did. I told him we would play."

He sighs and stands up. "Alright. But if right hand red is what takes me out, I am haunting you forever."

CHAPTER TWELVE

S AM GOT THROUGH RED HAND RED JUST FINE, BUT IT TURNS OUT left foot yellow has it out for him.

Xavier insists the specified body part has to move to the correct color on every turn with the exception of when all of the colored spots are full, which means Sam has now moved his left foot to three different yellow spots in a row. I am positioned particularly precariously under him, but over Xavier, so things might get very uncomfortable rather soon.

Dean comes back into the room just as I'm trying to navigate moving my hand to a spot my spine might not allow me to reach. He sounds like he's in the middle of saying something, but the words fizzle out in his mouth when he sees us. My head is upside down, but I can still see his face change.

"I leave the room for ten minutes, and this is what happens," he says.

"It's Twister," I tell him.

"I'm aware of what it is," he replies, muffling a laugh.

It's enough to make us all collapse and I have to disentangle myself to get back to my feet.

"You sure are popular today," I say as I pull my ankle out from underneath the crook of Sam's knee and step off the mat. "What's with all the calls?"

"It's a case I'm working on," he sighs. "Thomas Auden. His wife was kidnapped by an escaped prisoner and held for ransom a few years back. He got her back, but the prisoner escaped. She became a small-time celebrity in her area for a while going on the morning shows and everything."

"The name doesn't sound familiar," I say.

"It probably didn't register too much to you at the time. If I'm right about the timing, you were in the middle of two really intense investigations then. You probably weren't spending a lot of time taking in the news," he says. "Anyway, his business partner hired me a few days ago. Both Auden and his wife are now missing."

"They were abducted?" I ask.

"He doesn't know. They don't have any other family except for a couple of really far-flung relatives, apparently, so he's really the closest thing to a next of kin they have, and he hasn't reported them missing to police."

"If he is concerned enough about their safety that he hired a private investigator to find out what happened to them, why isn't he notifying police?" I ask.

"I don't know if 'concerned about their safety' is the right terminology to use here," he clarifies.

"What do you mean?"

"He wants me to find them because he believes they embezzled a massive amount of money from their company and have gone into hiding with it," Dean explains.

"Oh. So, he doesn't think they're in danger, he just wants his money back," I note.

"That's what I'm getting from him. Definitely not my most sympathetic client ever, but it's not really up to me to judge why someone wants to find someone else. It's just my job to find them."

"That's kind of a slippery slope," Xavier says.

Dean looks at him and Xavier makes a point with the fingers of one hand and shoots it through the air like it's sliding down said slope.

"First, I agree with Xavier on that one. Which is new," Sam starts. "Second, it still doesn't make sense that this guy isn't calling the police if he thinks these people stole a ton of money from him. Wouldn't they be a better option for tracking people down and actually doing something about it than relying on a private investigator?"

"I find the people I'm looking for," Dean replies in a low, even tone.

My body tenses as Sam's face changes. He draws in a slow, deep breath and lifts his chin. The muscles along the bottom of his jaw tense and twitch. I put a protective hand on his back and meet my cousin's eyes.

"Dean," I say.

"It's fine," Sam says, standing sharply. "It's late. I'm getting a shower and going to bed."

It's hours earlier than he usually goes to sleep, but I don't question him. He needs to not be in the room with Dean right now. I don't blame him. Sam kisses me goodnight and walks out of the room. I wait until I hear the sound of our bedroom door closing before I turn back to Dean.

"What is wrong with you?" I hiss.

"What?" he asks.

"Don't do that," I say. "Don't act like you don't know exactly what you just did. You know how much this situation with Marie has hurt him, how hard he's been fighting just to have anyone recognize that she's more than the statistic they want her to be. And you also know how hard it was for him, for both of us, when she was missing and we didn't know what we were going to do to find her. That was completely out of line, Dean."

"I didn't say anything about that. He asked me why Auden's business partner hired me to search for them rather than calling the police," Dean protests.

"It's a valid question, Dean," I fire back. "This is someone who already witnessed his business partner go through the abduction of his wife, and now he thinks that the two of them stole a considerable amount of money from him, but neither of those situations seems to warrant actually getting law enforcement involved? That is a strange situation. And you chose to make it personal."

"And I'm handling it," he huffs. "Again, why people hire me is their business. It's not up to me to decide who should and shouldn't be found."

"And again, slippery slope," Xavier says, repeating the gesture when Dean looks over at him.

I shake my head and follow Sam upstairs without another word. He gets out of the shower and comes into the room a few minutes later. I'm already in my pajamas, tucked into bed with a book. I've been holding it since I got under the lightweight white blanket that appears over the sheets as soon as the weather starts to get warm, but I haven't retained any of the words I've read.

Sam is silent as he moves around the room getting ready for bed. It's the same routine he follows every night. At this point, I could probably use some of those white footprints instructors used to use for ballroom technique to create a pattern on the bedroom floor and he would never miss a step. It's comforting in its familiarity, but tonight it's unsettling in its force and intensity. His anger is evident in the heavy fall of his footsteps across to the dresser, in how hard he pulls out the drawer, and even in the way he yanks his pajama pants on and throws his towel into the hamper against the side.

There's tension in that silence. Threatening like the horizon before a thunderstorm. That feeling you get when stepping out into air already carrying raindrops and your body can feel the roll of thunder that hasn't happened yet.

Finally, the heaviness breaks.

"He really does think he's something, doesn't he?" Sam says sarcastically.

"He didn't mean anything by it," I say.

"Yes, he did," he replies with a scoff. "He absolutely meant it. And you just sat there."

My mouth falls open. I can't believe he's pulling me into this.

"I just sat there?" I sputter. "What is it that you expected me to do? Was I supposed to fling my body between the two of you and demand he apologize? Possibly challenge him to a duel at sunrise?"

"You're being ridiculous," he says.

"*You* are being ridiculous. Did you hear yourself just now? Look, babe, I'm sorry he said that. It was a pretty nasty little crack. But don't get mad at me for not jumping in and turning it into a fight. As soon as you left, I defended you," I say. "And just so you know, he feels like you were the one being an ass to him, so the two of you are even."

"Now you're on his side?"

"I'm not on anyone's side," I say with exasperation. "This is not a game of dodgeball on the school playground. What is it with the two of you? Why can't you get along with him?"

"I don't know," he says, his voice dropping close to a growl.

"You do know," I press. "What is it that makes you like this?"

"I don't know," he repeats with a hint more insistence.

"It seemed like things were getting better between you, and that you might even be starting to get close. And then all this starts up again. I just don't understand why my cousin and my husband…"

"Because he acts like he's entitled to your life," Sam snaps. "As soon as he showed up you were completely wrapped up in him."

"He's my cousin," I say.

"You seem to forget he was also your stalker," he presses.

"He didn't stalk me."

"He had no idea who you were and he followed every facet of your career, he tracked Jonah's movements around you. He knew you were going to be on that train to Feathered Nest. He sat behind you. He followed you around it trying to get information about and out of you. He showed up in Feathered Nest and continued to hang around you all the time, even before you figured out that you're related. If it was anyone but someone you happened to find out was the son nobody knew about from the uncle you didn't know about, you would think of it as stalking and cut it down in a second," Sam points out.

"That was literal years ago, Sam. Listen to me. I was never wrapped up in him. He helped me solve the case on the train. So did you. But you were on a different train. You couldn't help me with the bodies. You couldn't figure everything out with me in real time and distract the conductors and watch my back. You were doing what you needed to do. Then he was instrumental in Feathered Nest, going to the hospital and finding the medical records that proved Jake Logan's mother was my mother's nurse when I was born.

"Figuring out that he's Jonah's son wasn't a happy thing for him because he learned he came from a monster, or for me either. I had to watch that devastation and know the man who had been tormenting me had someone else in his sights, too. But at the same time, it did make me happy. It made me extremely happy. I didn't have a big family growing up like you did, Sam. I never met my grandparents on my mother's side. My mother died when I was a little girl. I had my grandparents and my father. That was it. No other relatives as far as I knew.

"There was nothing about finding out about Jonah that was good. But making the link that Dean is his son, my cousin, was huge. He's my family. He's the cousin I never got to have when I was little. And even more than that, he was robbed of the life that he should have had as a member of this family."

"So, he feels like you owe it to him now," Sam says.

"I don't *owe* him anything. But I do believe he deserves to know things about his grandparents, and this house, and holidays. The things he missed out on. We missed out on everything about each other growing up."

"I missed out on you, too," Sam says, the emotion stronger in his voice.

My heart twinges and my breath catches in my chest. I lean slightly toward him.

"Sam," I say, "I've told you how sorry I am about how things ended between us when we were teenagers. I've told you I never wanted to hurt you and I hate that I did."

"It isn't just those years," Sam continues. "It was horrible being without you for those, but it wasn't the first time you were just gone, and I didn't know what to do. It happened over and over when we were kids. Ever since that day when your ball rolled in front of my bike, you were a part of me. And I learned quickly to try to suck in as much as I possibly could, because I didn't know when you were going to just disappear again.

"You'd be right there with me at school or playing in the park or going to movies, anything, together one day, then the next you'd just be gone. No one ever talked about where you went. Not the school, not any of the other students at the school, no one. Either they didn't think I deserved the information, or they didn't care that they didn't know. They were never able to say where you went or why. But worse, they could never say when you were going to come back. It might be weeks, it might be months, it might be years. I never once said it, but there got to be some points when I thought you might not come at all.

"That's what I missed, Emma. I missed you. I never stopped missing you. I never stopped loving you. Dean barely knew you and you'd already devoted yourself to him. I've been here. The whole time. It feels like you're trying so hard to construct a life for him that never existed. I knew your father. I knew your grandparents. I knew you. But he comes in and suddenly there's something the two of you have that I can't ever share."

"And we have something that no one can," I say. "You don't need to compete with him. You are the boy I always came back to. No matter what. I can't give you back those years I spent away from you, but I can tell you that you were always with me. I don't need to try to construct a life with you because we already had it. We always had it."

"We didn't for seven years. You told me you were never coming back. You looked me right in the eyes and said you were leaving and I wasn't ever going to see you again," Sam presses.

"But you did," I point out. "I was wrong. I've told you that. Leaving you wasn't because I didn't love you or didn't want to be with you. It was because I loved you so much and wanted to be with you more than anything. I didn't think I would be able to focus enough on my career and do what I needed to do for the world if I stayed."

"Because I held you back."

This isn't how this conversation was supposed to be going. I came in here because I wanted to comfort him, to show him my support, and instead, I feel like I'm in a corner. The worst part about it is I can't really blame him for anything he's saying. I hate hearing it. I wish I could put it completely behind me and not ever have to think about it again. But I can't.

"You didn't hold me back," I tell him. "I was out of my mind then. I wasn't thinking clearly about anything. Walking away from you was one of the worst decisions of my life, Sam. Maybe the worst. And I missed you every day. I thought about you. I wondered how you were and what kind of life you were living. I wanted to know someone was making you happy, and I really didn't want to think they were at the same time."

"You didn't want to come back here when I called you to ask for help," he says. "I could hear it in your voice the second you answered. I was the last person you wanted to hear from."

"You were the last person I thought I was going to hear from," I correct him. I'm fighting against his pain so hard I know I'm not being fully honest, so I make myself stop. "And you're probably right. I didn't want to hear from you. I'd just come through something horrible and was supposed to be taking some time. Hearing from you complicated everything that was already so complicated. It meant coming back here, which I never thought I was going to do. Having to be confronted by all the memories of my father, my grandparents, my mother. Everything. And I didn't know if I could cope with seeing you.

"I didn't know if I was going to come back here and find you married to some perfect woman with a stairstep collection of perfect children and a perfect dog, and I was just going to have to deal with that. I was going to have to be here acting like there wasn't a part of me that was still the girl who wanted to run right into your arms and let you make everything feel better the way you always had."

"Do you know how hard it was for me to call you? Do you have any idea how much I went back and forth with myself about even considering asking for your help?" he asks. "I thought you were going to laugh at me or tell me to leave you alone, that you didn't want anything to do with me. But I knew if there was anyone in this world who was going to be able to help me with a case like that, it was you. Getting your help was the only hope I had."

"I'm glad you called me. It had been seven years of avoiding being here. I had a life here, Sam. I was pretending I didn't. I stopped talking about this town and everyone and everything in it because I hoped that if I just didn't talk about it and I pretended it didn't matter to me anymore, eventually I could convince myself it was true. Because as much as I was convinced when I left Sherwood that I was doing the right thing, even if it hurt like hell, the further away that moment got, the harder it got. But I was too afraid and too proud to come back.

"I didn't want to come to a town that had forgotten me, or that didn't want me around. I didn't want to show my face in a place full of people who knew me differently than anyone else in the world, and who might be standing there ready to hold up a mirror to show me what my life had become. I don't regret my career. I'm proud of what I've done and the people I've helped, but I don't know if I would have been able to keep feeling that way if I'd come back here and been forced to see the other option.

"It took me a long time to come to terms with this life, Sam. I needed to figure out for myself that I could have both halves of me. I didn't have to choose. I didn't have to try to stop loving you and try to avoid you so that I could focus on my work. I didn't have to be afraid of what it would do to you if something happened to me. Or far worse, be afraid that something was going to happen to you because of me. Which it has. And I'm still afraid of that. All the time. But I love you and the life we have together far too much to not have that fear anymore," I say. "I'm sorry it took so long for me to get to that point."

"But it was so easy for you to accept Dean. He just got folded right in," he says.

"It wasn't easy for me," I admit. "But I had to accept that he is my family. Nothing is going to change that. And it's not his fault how he came into the world or what he's been through because of it. He's been extremely helpful and made a massive difference in a lot of cases, not to mention what he's done for Xavier. It isn't just about me."

I get out of bed and shove my feet into the slippers under the edge of the bed before throwing on my robe. "You know, Sam, you're lashing out right now because I was able to form a relationship with a part of my family, and for some reason, you're threatened by that and by the work he does."

"I'm not threatened," he protests.

"Yes, you are. And it's ridiculous. It's like you're jealous of him. But I married *you*, Sam, because I l love you. Because you complete me. I don't understand why the two of you can't just figure it out. Or at the very least, realize this isn't something that's going to change and learn to deal with it without making things miserable for the people around you."

I start toward the door but stop to look at him again. "I know you're upset. I know this whole situation has been so stressful. And what Dean said is out of line. I'll be having words with him about that, too. But please don't take it out on me, Sam. It's not like you. I love you very much, but this conversation isn't productive."

I head for the door and Sam takes a step closer.

"Emma, stop. Don't just walk out of here because you're mad. You always do that."

And he's right. I do. But this isn't that.

"I'm not mad," I tell him. "I just need to not be in here right now."

CHAPTER THIRTEEN

DEAN AND XAVIER ARE STILL PLAYING TWISTER WHEN I GET BACK into the living room. When Dean notices me standing there, he drops out of his position, very nearly crushing Xavier's head in the process.

"Hey," he says. "I'm sorry. You're right, I was out of line."

I hold up a hand to stop him, closing my eyes and shaking my head. "I don't want to talk about it anymore. Sam's exhausted so he's going to sleep, but it's too early for me to go to bed. I'm going to get a snack and watch TV and just relax for a bit."

Dean nods. "That sounds good."

Xavier looks at me from under his arm. "Are we done playing?"

"I think so," I tell him.

"Okay," he says, dropping down onto the mat. "Rematch tomorrow."

While they put the game away, I go into the kitchen to pop some popcorn. A few minutes later, we each have a big bowl in our lap and a documentary about a defunct water park on TV. I'm not letting myself think about Sam or the argument we just had. Not right now.

"I'd try it," Dean comments during a segment about a death-defying water slide designed by the park owner. "It looks like fun."

"Did you miss the part about the escape hatch at the top and all the teeth embedded in the plastic?" I ask.

"Life isn't any fun without risk," he says. "Imagine the adrenaline rush."

"And the communicable diseases," Xavier adds. "That water does not look properly chlorinated."

"I think the level of risk I already have in my life is sufficient to preclude me from needing an adrenaline rush brought on by surviving a poorly planned water slide, dirty water, and lifeguards who don't actually guard anything," I comment. "But I could use a spin around a lazy river right about now."

"Not unless I don't have to use a tube," Xavier says.

I nod and pat his shoulder. "I know."

The last time we went to a water park, Xavier got overly enthusiastic with his inflatable tube usage and ended up floating around with his hips submerged in the water through the hole in one tube, each foot dangling in a separate one in front of him, and his arms draped over one to either side. It seemed like a great idea at the beginning of the journey around the circular pool, right up until the path of the water diverged. One stream went off to the right at the same leisurely pace as the rest of the way had been, but jets strategically placed along the walls of the pool made the stream to the left fast and choppy.

Unfortunately for Xavier, the left half of his floats got caught up in the jets while the right half tried to keep going along the slower path. He couldn't figure out how to get himself out of the tubes, which resulted in a lot of flailing and the general peacefulness of the afternoon being ruined by a woman screaming and almost falling into the water when she saw just Xavier's foot sticking up out of one of the tubes as it floated by. We obviously managed to get him untangled, but I'm pretty sure he's sworn off inflatable tubes for a good while.

Dean's phone rings again and he sighs as he puts his bowl of popcorn on the coffee table and walks out of the room while taking the phone from his pocket.

"You know," I say, nodding toward the TV and the teenagers talking about working the questionable attractions at the park, "that reminds me of when you and my father kept building things and running around in the backyard. Some game you were working on. Whatever happened with that?"

"Infallible design thwarted by the iron curtain of nostalgic game show confidentiality."

"I hate it when that happens," I say.

"Always trying to keep us down," he nods, tossing a handful of popcorn into his mouth.

We watch the show for a few more minutes before Dean comes back into the room. I look over at him as he sits.

"This guy is seriously concerned about finding his money, isn't he?" I ask.

Dean shakes his head. "Actually, that wasn't him. That was the friend I was telling you about. The police officer who told me about the lair they believe belonged to Marini."

"The one on the contested property that hadn't been developed in years even though it was bought by a private owner who wanted to turn it into something," I reply.

"A neighborhood and shopping district," Dean says. "Right. Well, remember how they couldn't get permission to actually go into the lair because the land is privately held? There was nothing they could present to a judge that justified a warrant to give them access. Because there was no proof anything criminal happened there, they couldn't just go inside without permission."

"And they couldn't get proof of anything criminal happening there without going inside," I say.

"Exactly. But they were able to get in touch with the owner. Jason Hoyt. He's been out of the country on business, but he's going to be back in a couple of days. He's more than willing to cooperate with the investigation, on the condition he is present when anyone goes inside," Dean tells me.

"I guess that makes sense. I'm fairly certain if he was actually responsible for building it, he would have told the police that and made them get off the property. Since he didn't do that, we can assume he wasn't aware the underground structure was even there. I'm sure he's curious about what's in there and wants to see it, but probably also wants to make sure he's in control of it."

"What do you mean?" he asks.

"He's going to want to make sure he's fully informed of everything that was found, how, and by whom. That way if there is anything criminal in there, he'll be prepared and not held responsible. A situation as unusual as this, especially with all the power Marini held, you can't argue that there might be some rotten cops that could be tempted to plant evidence or skew what they find to come to a faster solution."

"Unless there's treasure," Xavier offers. "It was a well-known practice for settlers with a strong distrust of banks to put their savings and valuables in bags or trunks and bury them on their property to be dug up later if they needed it. They would often draw maps to those locations and send them to their loved ones back home so if anything ever happened to them like sudden injury or cholera, their families could go get those savings."

"I see we're back to cholera," I mutter to Dean from the corner of my mouth.

A little while back, I was tapping into Xavier's extensive and wildly assorted knowledge base to help me figure out a series of complex and confusing murders when I inadvertently sparked a fascination for cholera and the bubonic plague. He hasn't tried to diagnose anyone with one of those diseases in a while, but apparently, they're still kicking around in his mind. I have to admit, though, this time it seems applicable.

"People like to think about buried treasure as being a fantasy of the romanticized pirate lore, but it really did exist in a smaller, less bullion-based form with situations like that," Xavier continues, ignoring us. "So maybe Mr. Hoyt thinks there could be something valuable in that area and wants to make sure he stakes his claim on it rather than any of the responding officers trying to take it. Or a museum." He shakes his head. "Greedy curators always trying to say the museum has rightful ownership of things other people found just because they're old weapons or pottery or skeletons."

"Well, preservation of history is a sacrifice we all make," I say. He sighs and nods. I shake my head and turn back to Dean. "I definitely want to talk to him. I know he told police he bought it because he wanted to develop it into something, but it hasn't turned into anything. I want to know how he found out about the property. That isn't something that would just be posted on real estate sites. I also want to ask him why he hasn't developed it into anything. He must have noticed some sort of potential in it, or he wouldn't have bought it in the first place. So, why did he never do anything with it?"

"As soon as he's available, we'll set up a meeting," Dean nods. "My friend already knows you want to be there when they go through the lair. He'll let me know when they're going to go in."

"Perfect."

I'd been waiting to hear from the owner of the property and to get permission to go through the underground structure that had been identified there. Ever since Dean got the tip from his friend on the police force in the area, questions about that property have been swirling around in my head. The curiosity is almost too much to bear. I can't help but think this might be a critical step in understanding the full extent of what the Emperor did and how many lives he really stole.

He's dead, but I'm not going to stop without answers to the questions that keep piling up. I won't be done until we know when he started and where, find every one of his lairs, and can give peace to every single family who lost someone at his hands.

I didn't lose Dean or Eric to him, but I could have. It isn't lost on me how close Dean was to dying in the dirt of that underground arena, or that I might never have found him if he did. He just would have been gone and we never would have known what happened to him. Just as disturbing, though, is how he survived. We don't really know the details of how he managed to get out of the gladiator fight alive. He doesn't remember.

The blackouts he has experienced since he was a teenager seem to have obliterated everything from that day. He doesn't remember a thing: not who took him from his house, how he got to the underground lair, or what happened between then and when he was found by the side of the road. The one thing he does remember is the sound of a gunshot. But he doesn't know if he shot it or if it was shot at him.

What I do know, even though he can't tell me for sure, is that there were other people there with him and we don't know who they are. There was another fighter in the arena with him. Maybe someone Dean killed. And there was also someone who got him there. Another of the Emperor's accomplices. It's very possible that same person allowed Dean to survive. He could have escaped. He could have somehow managed to figure out how to get away from the arena, then ran and ended up by the side of the road.

That seems unlikely, though. Marini wasn't new to this. He'd gone to incredible lengths to painstakingly create the underground arenas for his gladiator fights, complete with cells where the fighters were kept, and opulent side rooms to use with the women stolen and groomed to be his sex slaves. That kind of attention to detail didn't just falter. He made mistakes, enough for his secret to be revealed, but I'm not convinced he would have such a failure in one of his arenas that it would allow a fighter to get out alive.

But now that Dean has been a part of my life for a few years, I've learned very distinctly to not put anything past that man. It seems like one of those things that runs in the family, but he is stubborn, headstrong, and driven to do everything he puts his mind to. Whether or not those things are ill-advised, potentially dangerous, and quite possibly illegal. Sometimes very likely illegal. This means I can't fully discount the possibility he figured out the system while he was in the arena and got out.

Even if he did, though, the question lingers of why whomever was helping Marini just let him go. They'd done the work of tracking Dean down and bringing him to the arena. It's hard to believe they would just let him slip through their fingers alive and capable of telling what happened to him to whomever would listen. Which leaves me with one possibility: the shot he heard did come from him. And it killed Marini's twisted loyal servant.

Dean turns to me and gives me a reproachful look.

"Hey, Emma?"

"Yeah?"

"I really am sorry about earlier. I shouldn't have said that to Sam. It was completely uncalled for."

"It was," I nod. "Honestly, I'm kind of shocked you even went there. You really wounded him, and you wounded me, too. I don't know what's going on between you and Sam, but the two of you need to work it out. He's my husband and you're my cousin; you're both here to stay. But I'm not living out the rest of my life with the two of you at odds like this. So you better fix it, and don't drag me in the middle of it."

He nods thoughtfully. "Okay."

CHAPTER FOURTEEN

I F I MOVE THE BIG, OVERSTUFFED RECLINER IN THE LIVING ROOM over to right in front of the window, I can sit in it and watch the house across the street. That little bit of knowledge came about soon after Sam picked out the chair and had it delivered.

Both of us assumed it would come in a big box and we'd have to put it together. We didn't realize until after the fact that he actually ordered a floor model, so Mike, the owner of the furniture store up in the village, just put it in the back of his truck and plopped it on the front porch. I found it when I was walking out the door to go to a meeting, so I didn't have time to rearrange the rest of the living room furniture and actually fit it into place. I just shoved it inside and headed out.

That night, I sat down in it just where it was and realized I had the perfect view of the front window across the street. It's quiet and unassuming now, but only a few years ago, that window started a spiral that nearly cost me my career, my sanity, and my life.

Right now, the moon is hitting it just right to make the edges of the panes glow. There are some early mornings when I do my jog and pause a little in front of the house. In those misty first moments of light when most of the neighborhood is still asleep, or at the very least trying to wake themselves up and get their blood pumping with a shower, the house looks different. Somehow it is both more and less foreboding when it's just it and me in the pale, still hours.

"Emma?"

I hear Xavier behind me and I glance back to see him. He's standing just inside the living room, clutching a drink like Cindy Lou Who in green and black plaid cotton pajamas.

"Come on in."

He glances around. "I am in. Should I leave and come back?"

He backs out of the room.

"Xavier, come in."

He walks over and stands beside the chair, looking out the window with me for a few silent seconds.

"Is it bothering you for me to be here?" he asks.

"No. All the important meetings happen around here when people are supposed to be asleep." I look at him curiously. "What are you doing awake?"

Xavier holds up his drink. "My throat was dry. Either I needed some water or I recently developed an allergy to the color yellow. I figured I'd try this approach first."

"Probably a good plan. How is it working out for you?"

"I was thirsty."

I nod. "Good conclusion."

Xavier tugs an ottoman over and sits down beside me. It puts him several inches lower than me, and he stretches his neck to continue looking out the window with me.

"Who are you having a meeting with?" he asks.

"Myself, I guess," I say. I look out the window again. Clouds slide over the moon, obscuring some of the light and casting shadows across the front of the house across the street. "I can't let go of that house. I don't know why."

He follows my gaze and seems to examine the dark, blank front of the house for a few moments.

"Did you put in an offer on it that was rejected?" he asks.

I let out a soft puff of laughter and shake my head. "No. I don't want to buy it. I don't ever want to go inside it again."

Xavier's mouth opens and then closes. "So, you just really like looking at it?"

"Not particularly. It still gives me chills."

"It could use some sprucing up. The flower beds would be nice with some actual flowers. I'd prefer a lightbulb or two somewhere in there. But if it bothers you so much, you really shouldn't look at it. If it has required you to change the interior design of your living room, it seems like more stress than it's worth," he points out.

I don't ask what level of stress would be worth what he thinks is an ongoing obsession with the ugliness of a house. He has that answer inside him. There's a good chance it will come out of him at some point. No point in rushing things.

"It's not what it looks like," I say. "It gives me chills because I witnessed a murder there. At least, I thought I did. It turned out what I saw wasn't as simple to explain as I thought."

"The people were dancing?"

"No."

"Rehearsing for a play?"

"No."

"Practicing Greco-Roman wrestling?"

"No."

"I've run out of ideas," he admits, throwing his hands up in the air.

I coyly smile at him. "She didn't exist."

Unfortunately, because Xavier is Xavier, the reaction I'd hoped for doesn't appear. He just blinks and takes it in. "So no one was murdered?"

"I didn't say that."

Without another word, Xavier stands up and walks out of the room. I think he might have just decided he'd had enough and was going back to bed, but he comes back a few seconds later with a plate of chocolate chip cookies and two glasses of milk. He sits back down on the ottoman, dips one of the cookies in milk, and gestures at me to continue.

"Go on."

I tell him about Ruby Baker, the woman who briefly took up space in the house across the street and showed up on my sidewalk one morning to introduce herself. He listens, absently eating his way through milk-logged cookies, as I describe my interactions with her, my horror at witnessing her death, and the frantic, horrifying spiral that one moment, on a night not too unlike tonight, sent me down.

"Everyone thought I was losing my grip on reality. They thought the cases I'd been working on had made me crack. And maybe there was a little while there when I thought they were right."

"But you didn't stop," Xavier says.

"Of course, I didn't. I couldn't. Maybe I thought briefly that I'd lost my mind, but that wasn't enough to make me not want to help her," I tell him. "It almost got me killed. So, that wasn't great. But I figured it out. I ended it."

"Then why are you sitting here in the dark staring at the house?" he asks.

"I don't know," I admit. I look over at him. "Do you have any words of wisdom on that front for me?"

"Not yet, but I'll let you know if any pop up."

I nod. "I appreciate it." Looking back at the house, I let out the breath that feels like I've been holding it even as I've been speaking. "I do this. Not a lot. But enough that I sometimes wonder if it's a problem. I end up here more when a case I'm working on really starts to bother me. When I can't figure something out and I feel like it's sitting right there in front of me. Right now, I have three of them. Four, if you count the Emperor's crimes and Salvador Marini and his death as two different issues."

"I think that's appropriate."

"Then four. Four cases that are sitting there, waiting for me to find the pieces that are going to put them together. And I can't do it," I say.

"It isn't that you can't do it, Emma. It's just that you haven't yet. You'll get there."

"What if I don't? What if this is the time that I can't find the answer? If these are the cases I don't solve?"

"Well, you can't really say these are the cases you didn't solve until you die and are officially out of the crime investigation industry. And I figure you have a few good, solid decades ahead of you until you turn your badge over to Jesus, so there's still plenty of time for you to work things out," Xavier says.

His expression is compassionate as he nods slightly at me.

"Thank you, Xavier," I say. "That's very comforting."

"I'm always here for you, Emma," he replies.

"I know," I say, patting his hand and accepting the cookie he holds out to me.

"Which case is bothering you the most?" he asks.

"I don't know. They all seem so tangled together, it's getting harder to pull them apart."

"Have you talked to Jonah about any of it?"

"Not in the last few weeks. I snapped after the incident in Myrtle Beach and told him I don't want to hear from him again, that I'm done.

I didn't actually expect him to pay attention to that considering all the other times I've told him I'm done, but it seems like he might have actually listened to me this time," I say.

"How do you feel about that?" he asks.

"How do I feel about Jonah not reaching out to me all the time? To not having to wonder if it's going to be his voice on the other end of the line every time a number I don't recognize pops up on my phone? I'm elated," I say.

"Are you?" Xavier asks.

"What's that supposed to mean?"

"You want him out of your life, but you also know he is inextricable from the rest of what you're trying to find out. Whether he has the information and just isn't giving it to you, or you think he would be able to confirm things as you find them out, he is a part of all of this. He's the reason you got wrapped up in the Emperor case, in Miley's disappearance, in Serena's death. He told you about the Cleaners," he points out.

"Obviously I want to know anything he does and be able to use it to solve these things. And it pisses me off to no end that he dragged me into these things and is trailing me along. I honestly hate that I care so much."

"No, you don't." Xavier says it in a firm, unyielding tone that doesn't hold a shred of the gentleness he had a few seconds ago. "You don't hate it. Caring is the only reason you keep going. What you hate is that you can't stop yourself from wanting to do this even though it helps you. What you want is indifference. You want to not care that he exists or if he is a part of your life, whether he contacts you or not, whether he is out in the world or in prison or dead. You want to not care.

"But you do. Your hatred of him shows that you care. If there was nothing, you wouldn't be able to hate him. You wouldn't have the fire that burns in you when you think about him and everything that he's done. You can't be indifferent to Jonah, Emma. That doesn't mean you're never going to escape him and the hold he has on you. You're going to get away from him. You're going to put him behind you and never have to deal with him again. But before you can do that, you have to find a resolution. You can't ignore his connection to Miley, Serena, or Marini. And you can't forget those cases.

"You hate who he is and what he's done. You hate how many people he has affected. But I think even more than that, you hate his humanity."

"His humanity?" I raise an eyebrow.

"He isn't a caricature. He isn't an abstract concept or just a story. He's complex and contradictory. He has a clear-cut set of rules and morals that guide his life and how he sees other people. Consider his relationship with Marini and how he holds himself up against the actions of the Emperor. His morality allows him to hold himself in higher regard than Marini. He believes what he has done is justified, and what Marini did was reprehensible. He can revile the same things and people you do. He can feel sympathy, pain, guilt, and sadness. Even if his form of humanness isn't the same as everyone else's, you see it. And that's what you hate."

"He's delusional," I say.

"Yes," Xavier nods.

We sit in silence for a few moments, watching the moonlight come out from behind the clouds and illuminate the house again.

"What do you think about the lair found out on that land?" I finally ask.

"You knew there were going to be others," he replies. "Marini hid them well. They weren't just thrown together. They were carefully planned and exceptionally built. It would be interesting to find who made them and know what they thought was being done in an underground structure like that."

I nod. "I've thought about that, too. Maybe they didn't think anything of it. I've seen those shows about the enormous treehouses and the elaborate backyard grottoes and things. Maybe they just thought it was something like that. They wouldn't know the true purpose of it."

"What do you hope to find when you go see it?" he asks.

"Anything. Anything that's going to tell me something about Marini and what he's done." I let out a breath. "When I told Dean about the Shepherd, before I knew everything behind it, he described her introduction as an origin story. Some thought she was a hero, some thought she was a villain. It's hard for me to wrap my head around the idea that anyone would actually think of Salvador Marini as a hero, but he definitely caught the attention and loyalty of several people. I want to know why. I want to know that origin story and see where this all came from. And I want to put an end to it. A real end. Not just his death."

"What kind of end would that be?" Xavier asks.

"I want to say the names of everyone he has hurt. I want to give families back the people they lost and let them finally be able to grieve them fully. He took them because he believed he was entitled to them. He believed he was important and powerful enough to own these people. He can't own them anymore. That's the end I want. When I'm able to take every single one of those people back from him so even his memory doesn't have possession of them anymore."

Silence settles around us again and I sit with the feeling of Xavier next to me. He's not a big man, but he takes up so much space. He drowns out the silence with the intensity of his own.

"What are you afraid of, Emma?" he asks when the quiet has started to throb in my head.

The question takes me aback. It's definitely not what I expected him to ask.

"In life?" I ask.

"In this," he clarifies.

"I'm not afraid," I say, tempted to scoff like the sound will act as punctuation for the assertion.

"You are," Xavier replies without hesitation. "You feel like ice."

I've gotten used to Xavier seeming to have a sense the rest of us don't have, one beyond the general five to something that transcends just normal engagement with the world. I know he's not literal when he relies on those perceptions, but they are the only way he knows how to express them. It's up to us to try to sift through them and figure out what he means.

"Cold and hard?" I ask.

This wouldn't be the first time someone described me as being like ice. Every variation of "Ice Queen" that has ever been crafted in the minds of people even vaguely creative has been slung at me. I've stopped reacting when I hear it. It feels like they're too accurate to fight.

"Fragile," he says, taking the slight hint of a bemused smile from my lips. "Smooth and calm to a quick glance, but seconds away from shattering into the dark rush you're trying to conceal just beneath."

I'm speechless for a long moment. But I can't say he's wrong.

"I'm so close to solving these cases," I finally say. "So close to putting Jonah away, to exposing Marini for what he really was, to finding out what happened to Miley and to Marie. It's all just right there."

"You'll do it," Xavier says. "You'll figure it out. You always do."

"But that's just the thing. What if I don't? Like I said, what if this is the time it all just crumbles? Everyone around me is always completely confident when I go into a case. There's no question. Except from me. I do question it. I am never one hundred percent positive I'll be able to pull a case off. I have confidence. I know my skills and my track record. And I know I will put everything into an investigation and do all I can to bring it to a close. But I also know things can and do go wrong, and I'm not always in control. There's a point in so many investigations where I worry it's all going to slip through my fingers. And that's where I am right now."

"That's why I know you can do it," Xavier says.

"Because I think I can't and you need to believe in me for me?" I ask.

"Because you still care," he says.

It doesn't have the same kind of epic swell of eighties-movie nostalgia I could sense building, but it hits me harder.

"Of course, I care," I say. "Why would I be doing this if I didn't? Why would I still be with the Bureau after all this time if I didn't care?"

"There are plenty of agents who don't. We both know that," he replies. "And the Emma who joined at twenty-three, even the Emma I met just a few years ago, probably wouldn't now. You wanted vengeance when you joined, and you were like a dying ember when I met you. Powerful and intense, but burning out. You investigated out of anger, or out of a sense of duty and obligation. You threw yourself into everything that came your way and rushed straight into the fire rather than seeing anything but the worst possible scenario.

"You cared, you've always cared, but it was more about the hatred of crime and injustice than it was for the victims. You did it all for yourself as much as for them. You were paying a debt that wasn't yours, but the harder you dug, the more you chipped away at that pain. It was about the battle more than the victims."

"The victims have always been the reason I did this job," I say, starting to feel something I want to call offense so I don't have to admit what it really is.

"No, Emma. The killers have been. Caring about the victims, giving them their voices and their names back, protecting them, crying for them, that has all been there, but you've always thought the worst first. You've been reckless and thrown yourself into the most extreme situation you can because you're fueled by that virulence against the killers. Eventually, that would have extinguished you.

"But you've changed. You've grown. You don't live for the next killer. You live in spite of them. They will come, Emma. And you will hunt them and destroy them. You will stand eye-to-eye with them and defend those they want to hurt. Not because you've put the victims behind you, but because you've put yourself between them and the evil. Because after everything you've gone through, after all this time, you still care. It's what makes you an incredible agent. And it's what will move you forward.

"You are worried you're getting so close to the finish with these cases and will stumble at the end because you haven't been given all the answers. But you can find those answers yourself, Emma. And when you do, you'll be able to release yourself from Jonah. Not because you need him. Because the victims need you. *Find the Cleaners. Find the Truth. Find the Solution. End it.*"

CHAPTER FIFTEEN

I DON'T KNOW WHEN I FELL ASLEEP, BUT I WAKE UP STILL IN THE recliner in front of the window with Sam's hand on my shoulder as he gently shakes me.

"Emma," he whispers. "Emma, wake up."

He doesn't sound stressed like there's something wrong, but my general approach to being woken up out of a steady sleep is that I need to be on guard. Good things rarely come from being shaken awake. My eyes snap open and my hand grips the arm of the chair.

"What? What's wrong?" I ask. I instinctively reach for my gun to make sure it's in my holster when I head for whatever the danger is, not thinking that my pajama pants don't hold up a holster well and my gun is in the bedroom.

"Nothing," Sam says. "What are you doing out here?"

My shoulders relax as the last bits of sleep disappear from the edges of my thoughts and I'm able to fully process what's going on. I pull myself up to sit and shake my head. I look around and notice Xavier draped across the couch, sleeping soundly with his various jars of sour-dough starter babies organized on the coffee table and end table beside him.

"He's a good father," I mutter as I make my way through the living room and toward the bathroom.

Sam falls into step behind me and when I come out, he's waiting in the hall.

"You slept in the living room," he says.

There's sadness in the words, taking them from being just a statement of fact to almost an explanation of something I hadn't asked.

"I didn't mean to," I say. "Xavier and I were talking and I must have drifted off. I'm going to go get dressed."

After dressing and tossing my pajamas in the hamper I need to bring downstairs for another load of laundry, I reach for my phone where I keep it under the pillow. I didn't think to grab it last night when I left the bedroom and I check to make sure I didn't miss any messages or calls since then. There are a couple of spam emails and a message from my father along with a series of about fifty pictures of Bebe from Eric and Bellamy. I'm still smiling over her sweet face and the sense of wonder that she has gotten so big when I get to the last email. Surprise melts the smile off my face.

It's from Gwendolyn Russo. I'm so eager to know what she wanted to say to me I read through the email too quickly and have to go back and read through it again to actually catch what it's saying. It's short and simple, nothing to convey any particular emotion or even why she wanted to get in touch with me in the first place. She introduces herself, mentions she lives in Carlotta, and says she wants to talk to me about Salvador on a video call.

I'm not familiar with the town, but a quick search shows it's less than a two-hour drive from the Breyer Correctional Facility where I'll be meeting with Deandre Wright in a couple days. I message back as fast as my fingers will fly across the frustratingly non-tactile glass keyboard on the phone, telling her I'll be in the area and we can have an in-person meeting instead.

As much as I want to find out what she has to say as soon as possible, I do better with face-to-face interactions with people during investigations. It lets me really evaluate their body language, notice small changes in their facial expressions and voices, and create more of a connection, which can help me get more out of them.

With Gwendolyn in particular, I want to sit down with her and talk face to face rather than through a computer screen. This is the sister of

Salvador Marini, one of the most brutal and disturbing people I've ever crossed paths with in my entire career. I can't help but be curious about the similarities that might exist between the siblings.

I know better than most that these similarities could be slight, if they exist at all. My father has none of the horrifying traits of his identical twin brother, but I know there are characteristics they share. Movements, facial expressions, even the occasional turn of phrase or choice of words that become a vivid reminder that the man I have despised so deeply is so closely linked to the father I adore.

But there are plenty of other sibling pairs that are very much alike, sharing personality traits and tendencies that often stem from their parents or other influences as they grew up. That's what I'm going to look for when I meet her. I'm interested to see if there is any of the intensity, temper, and entitlement in her. Maybe, even more, I want to see her in person so I can gauge if she is trying to manipulate me. It is much easier to detect that when sitting only a few inches from someone than it is through a screen.

It doesn't take long for her to respond. By the time I'm in the kitchen getting the coffee brewing, my phone alerts me to a new message from her. It's even shorter and more to the point than the last message. She agrees to meet with me and gives me the name of a café as well as a time. She at least shares that inclination toward control with her brother.

I confirm the meeting, making sure to note that I'll get in touch with her if I need to change it. She might as well understand right from the beginning that she isn't going to be able to control me.

Sam comes in as I'm putting the phone in my pocket. He stands beside me smelling like warm skin and clean cotton t-shirt. My first instinct is to curl up into him the way I always do, but there's still a twinge inside me from our argument last night. He turns his shoulders slightly, putting his chest toward me like he hopes I'll just not acknowledge the fight and carry on like most mornings.

When I don't, he lets out a sigh that drops his shoulders and turns fully toward me.

"Babe, I'm sorry about last night," he starts.

"I feel like you're saying you're sorry that we fought," I reply.

He looks vaguely confused. "I am."

"So, you're not sorry for anything else?" I ask, pouring my coffee and bringing it over to the table.

"Should I be?" he asks.

I glare at him. "Of course, you should be. Do you seriously not have any idea how out of your mind you sounded last night? How completely ridiculous you were being?"

He nods, relenting. "Alright. Yes. I know. And I really am sorry. I'm sorry I hurt you and I'm sorry I can't get those thoughts out of my mind. I was being unreasonable. I don't know why I suddenly got this flare of jealousy, but it wasn't right of me. I've just been really on edge and what Dean said really hurt me. But I shouldn't have brought up all the stuff about our past. That's ancient history now. I have you back. We're married. I shouldn't care about that anymore, and I don't—but I guess on some level it still bothers me. And I'm sorry for that."

"You don't have to be sorry it bothers you. It bothers me, too."

"It does?" he asks.

"Of course, it does. I was telling the truth when I said how much it hurts me to think about what I did. I hate the way I left things between us all those years ago, and that I hurt you the way I did. It's the biggest regret of my life. And I hate that you felt like Dean became my bigger priority because he became part of my life so quickly. He's my cousin. My blood relative. I don't have many of those. And like I said, I didn't want to have him around just for me. It was for him, too. He should have a family. He went through so much turmoil and lost the only family he knew when he was so young. He didn't deserve that. I wanted in some small way to give him back at least part of what he had lost. A family. And that's what we are, right?"

He chuckles softly. "I suppose so."

"And families fight sometimes. Or they get into it. But that doesn't mean they love each other any less, right?"

Sam opens his mouth as if to respond but I hold up a hand to stop him before he can.

"I had words with Dean last night. He acknowledged that he was out of line. And I told him he's going to need to work it out with you to apologize. I don't want to be put in the middle of it and I don't want you to take it out on me. I love you both so much, but obviously in very different ways. You're not in competition with each other. You're family."

That makes Sam stop and nod thoughtfully. "As always, you're right. I shouldn't have taken it out on you. It's just... cousins have been a sore subject for me lately."

"I know."

"I'm sorry," he says. "Really, Emma. I'm sorry. I love you."

"I love you, too," I smile.

He leans down for a kiss and I smile at him, then jump when I hear a voice from the doorway to the kitchen.

"Is the moment over?"

"Damn it, Xavier," Sam groans with a chuckle. "Can't you put on a pair of tap shoes or something?"

Xavier looks down at his feet. "I don't have any with me right at this moment, but I could bring them with me next time."

He walks past us toward the door leading into the backyard, his arms overloaded with his jars of starter. These look like some of the older ones, which means he's probably going to put them down under the tree and come back for the younger ones.

As soon as the door closes behind him, I look up at Sam again.

"You know that means he has a pair at home, right?"

"You kidding? He probably has like, three."

CHAPTER SIXTEEN

"**A**RE YOU READY FOR YOUR MEETING THIS MORNING?" I ASK SAM over the cinnamon rolls I warmed for breakfast.

"I am," he nods. "I'm really nervous, but I'm actually kind of excited, too. It feels like this means something is finally happening. Like I don't have to think and worry about it anymore, if that makes sense."

"It does," I reply. "And remember, whatever happens, you're going to do what you need to do, what's right for you and for your family. You have my complete support."

"Thank you. That means a lot to me." He pulls off another chunk of roll and swirls it around in the extra cream cheese frosting I poured over them. "What about you? Is everything still set for your talk with the corrections officer at Breyer?"

"Yep," I say. "And I'm actually going to be taking care of some other business while I'm up in that area as well."

I fill him in on the message from Gwendolyn and our planned meeting.

"Do you think she's going to be able to tell you anything import-ant?" he asks.

"I really don't know. It's obvious the two of them were estranged. Probably for a considerable amount of time, since no one around seemed to know he even had a sister. She may not be able to tell me anything new about him, but then again, she could give me insight into what he was like when he was really young. If he had patterns of behav-ior that might have been red flags. She might even have some childhood anecdotes that could tell us how to find more details about what he did. Maybe that'll even lead us to some secrets he might have had, like a place he liked to hide things, or something he might have used as a password."

"You think you're going to be able to access his safes and vaults with the password he had for his treehouse when he was ten?" Sam regards me skeptically.

"It's possible," I shrug. "Maybe not that specific example, but it's possible. The biggest thing, though, is finding out why she wanted to get in touch with me in the first place. She didn't tell the attorney what she wanted to talk to me about, and she didn't give me any indication of what she needed when we set up the meeting. Just that she needed to talk to me about her brother."

"Sounds like it could be good," he says. He glances at the clock, then makes a slight gulping sound in his throat as he realizes how late it's get-ting. "I've got to go. I don't want to leave them waiting for me."

He kisses me again and we exchange our goodbyes before he rushes out of the house. I admire his dedication and commitment. Not many men would be as professional and conscientious as he's being. They'd take the reality that he was elected and not hired, and therefore has no real direct boss, as an opportunity to do anything they want when it suited them. But instead of doing that, Sam is trying to be considerate and responsible, and make sure the town he loves is still taken care of, and that the people in it know he hasn't just abandoned them.

That's just one of the reasons why I love him.

An hour later I've left Dean to his investigating and Xavier to the process of drying out some of the older, bigger starters so he can recon-stitute them if there is ever a sourdough shortage and we all need emer-gency bread. He already has quite the library of these dried specimens built up in one of the pantries at his house, so we'd all be pretty well set if that happens. He told me before I left home that he was planning on doing some baking today, too. As I make my way across town to run a few errands, I'm hoping I'll return home to a batch or two of his sourdough crackers. He makes them with poultry seasoning, which seems like a strange choice but is addictively delicious.

As I'm strolling through the aisles of the grocery store, checking things off of my meticulously planned list, my phone rings. I'm heavily focused on my comparison between two types of raisin bran, so I don't check the screen before answering.

"Hello?"

"Agent Griffin?"

"Angelo?" I ask even though I know it's him. I wasn't expecting to hear from him. "Everything okay?"

I don't want to immediately go to something else going wrong, but considering the only interactions I've had with this man have revolved around Salvador Marini and everything he's done, I have a hard time not going straight there. I find it highly unlikely he's calling to see if I want to get together for tea.

"I was just calling to see if you'd heard back from the lawyer," he says.

Everyone who worked for Marini has their reasons for wanting to know what happened to him, and none of them is because they want to avenge him. These aren't people who are mourning for the dead and needing to fulfill some part of themselves left empty by his death by finding out for sure what happened to him. Quite the opposite, in fact: they need confirmation he's gone and won't be coming back. And I believe there might be a hint of questioning in each of them as to whether it was one of their own who finally decided they'd had enough from Marini and wanted to see him pay the ultimate price instead of heading to prison.

"Actually, I did," I tell him. "But not because he wanted to talk to me. He was getting in touch with me to ask permission to share my contact information with Marini's sister."

There's hesitation on the other end of the line. "His sister? So that really was his nephew?"

"No," I clarify. "At least, not according to anything we found out about him. He has this sister, but she does not have any children. They are the only siblings. If he does have a nephew, it's going to take some explaining."

"Why didn't any of us know about his sister?" Angelo asks. "Not that he would have gone out of his way to introduce us to his family or anything, but I would think a man whose sister was the only member of his immediate family left would have some desire to keep her close. At least have her around for holidays or something."

"I'd think so, too. And, honestly, I don't really know much about her or their relationship. All I know is that her name is Gwendolyn Russo. Does that ring a bell? Ever heard him mention it? Or seen it written down somewhere in the house?" I ask.

"No," he says. "I've never heard that name."

I tell him about the email from Klein and the messages Gwendolyn and I have exchanged.

"We're going to meet up when I am in the area in a couple of days. I get the very distinct feeling brother and sister weren't exactly close, so I'm really curious about why she wants to speak with me about his death. Whatever the reason, I hope she's able to give me something more to go on. That's kind of the theme of the trip. I also think I'm going to stop by Miley's house again."

"Miley's house?" he asks, just the mention of his friend's name making his sound a touch tearful.

"Yes. Her parents have continued paying for it, so it's still accessible. Officially, there is no investigation, but I have their permission to go in whenever I want to. They want to find out what happened to her as much, if not far more, than all of us."

"Good."

His voice sounds tight, like that's all he can manage to say. I knew mentioning going to the house would bring up a wave of emotions for him. This situation isn't easy for Angelo, for a few different reasons. His friendship with Miley was important to him, but there were also unrequited romantic feelings he had to shove down to keep her in his life. I believe him when he says he accepted that she didn't feel the same way about him and that he valued her friendship more than enough to be fine with them not having anything more than that bond.

But that doesn't mean the feelings just disappeared. He didn't find out she wasn't interested and instantly turn that part off. He was just able to package those feelings all up and put them into the back of his mind so he could move on. They made her disappearance even harder for him, compounding the loss.

Usually, this isn't a conversation I would want to have while roaming the aisles of the grocery store, but there are only a couple of other shoppers and I can hear in Angelo's words he needs to talk about this now.

"I haven't given up, Angelo. I'm not going to. Finding Miley and understanding what happened to her is my priority," I tell him. "Wherever she is, I will find her."

"You don't think there's any chance she's alive."

It's not a question. It barely feels like he's saying it to me. It's like he's acknowledging it for himself, making the statement so he can work toward truly processing it. She's been gone a long time now, but coming to terms with something like this doesn't happen quickly. Especially when there are no answers.

I want to reassure him. The part of me that has softened, that has learned to connect again, to feel compassion rather than just focus and rage, wants to make Angelo feel better. I want to tell him that everything is going to be fine and we're going to find out that Miley is out there somewhere, living happily ever after.

But I can't make the words come. I don't know the truth, but I know what I've experienced and what I've seen. And I don't want to build him up just to destroy him later if this doesn't turn out the way he's hoping it will. Instead, I turn it around.

"Do you think that's a possibility?" I ask. "You said you want her to be happy. Whatever that takes."

"I do," Angelo says without hesitation. "I want to think that she's happy. I don't necessarily want to think she just picked up and left without giving me a thought. Or that even after Marini died she wouldn't reach out to me and tell me she was okay, or even come home. I'd want to think she valued our friendship enough that she would want to contact me. But I would much rather think that than think something horrible happened to her."

"But do you think that's a possibility?" I press. "Do you think she could be out there somewhere with the man Marini called his nephew?"

"No," he says in a gush of breath. "Marini would never stand for that kind of betrayal."

CHAPTER SEVENTEEN

"Do you think he's right? Or did Marini just scare him so much he can't think of anyone getting out of his grasp?" Dean asks.

"Or is he asking that because he's embarrassed and doesn't want to think he could have gotten away and never did?" Xavier adds.

"They weren't slaves," I point out. "He *had* slaves, but Angelo, Louisa, and Peter weren't among them."

"You're right. They weren't slaves. He didn't capture them or shackle them. They left the house. But that doesn't mean he didn't have a hold on them. They told you themselves that they were afraid of what he could do. Even when they didn't know what he had done and what he was capable of, his threats were enough to keep them in line," Xavier says. "No one wants to believe that's happening to them."

"What do you think?" Dean asks. "Do you think Miley and the nephew really did meet up and run off together?"

"I don't know. At this point, there isn't anything that proves they even met, much less were a couple. Angelo just said that there was something about her when she talked about him. Miley never mentioned that they were together. She never said his name."

"The guy might have told her not to mention it. Marini was throwing around threats to the people who worked for him. We don't know who this nephew guy was, but I don't think it's that much of a leap to think he had more than a passing familiarity with the way Marini treated people. Angelo said Marini wouldn't stand for that kind of betrayal, right? He wouldn't stand for people leaving him," Dean muses. "The nephew could have warned her that Marini wouldn't look kindly on him fraternizing with someone who associated with his help."

"But Miley knew what he was like. He knew how much Angelo hated him," I counter. "She wouldn't just abandon him that way, especially since they were so close. She would tell him that she was leaving. Or at least get in touch with him now that Marini is dead and they don't have to worry about anything he could do to retaliate."

"You don't know her, Emma," Dean points out. "You never met her. You've only heard about her. Angelo isn't exactly an unbiased source, either."

"You're right. I've spent so much time and energy trying to understand her life and find out what happened to her that it feels like I know her, but I don't. I haven't met her or spoken with her. What I have done is stood in her house, touched her belongings, talked to the people who really knew her. I've seen the way Angelo looks when he talks about her. I want her to be alright. If there was some reality I saw that included her being out in the world somewhere, happy and living her best life alongside whoever the hell this dude is, I'd cling right to it. That's what I want to have happened.

"Is that a problematic solution to all this? Of course, it is. It means I've spent all this time searching around for someone who doesn't want to be found. And it means she didn't care enough about Angelo or her parents, or even Jonah as much as it pains me to include him in the list, to let anyone know what she was planning on doing or where she was. To take all sentiment out of the situation, would make her a seriously shady bitch."

"Better shady than dead," Xavier offers.

"I'd say that depends on the circumstances," Dean says.

"But in this case, I'd rather this girl have just decided to completely disregard everything and everybody else so she could run off and have her happy life than to think Marini got his claws into her, too. I'd really like to think there's someone else who got one over on him," I say.

"I don't know if I would call murder getting one over on someone," Dean says.

"I'm not talking about the Cleaners," I say.

"Then who?" he frowns.

"You."

Dean's eyes darken as he's instantly dragged back into those moments he doesn't want to be a part of. But I have to tell the story.

"You survived, Dean. And not the way the men who were discarded and happened to live survived. They were so broken and destroyed that they're never going to be okay. Ever. That didn't happen to you. He wanted you. He took you. Or at least he had someone take you. But somehow, you got out."

"That's the headliner of my career. I rebelled against the Emperor," he says with an almost bitter huff of laughter.

"It's more than that, Dean. He didn't do these things alone. We know for a fact he had help before Serena, and he was still active after her death. So we have to assume he had help after as well. Once someone like him is accustomed to getting what he wants, he's not just going to let it go. Someone was doing his bidding, kidnapping and destroying all the victims to bring them to the Emperor. And I believe there was more than one accomplice. They used various tactics to capture and keep people. But you managed not just to survive, but to get out without being rescued. We need to know how. And maybe more importantly, why."

"He admitted he chose me because of my link to Jonah," Dean says. "He wanted to show he had the upper hand."

"Because Jonah didn't recognize a rivalry," I say. "He just thought Salvador Marini was reprehensible and wanted to stop him. But he didn't see him as any credible threat to his power. Marini was obsessed with Jonah and with proving himself the better of the two."

"Better what?" Dean asks.

"The superior serial sadist?" I suggest.

Xavier cringes and shakes his head.

"Too many s's?" Dean asks and Xavier nods.

"I'm sorry," I say. I give Xavier a moment for the shiver to move its way from the top of his head down through his shoulders and out of his body. "My point is just that Marini wanted to get his hands on you because he was desperate to prove he had the upper hand, that he was the one who was going to control things. He thought taking you would push Jonah over the edge. If he was going to willingly let you go, it would be ceremonial. He would make a big deal out of presenting you to Jonah or publicly pretending to rescue you. He wouldn't just have you dumped off by the side of the road somewhere. It didn't do anything."

"Good point," he acknowledges.

"You got out somehow. You managed to get through everything he put into place, including anyone who was helping him. We need to figure out exactly what happened. I know there isn't much that you remember, but think hard. Is there anything?" I ask.

"Wait," Xavier says. He runs out of the room and comes back with a notepad and pen. "Go ahead."

"What's that?" Dean asks.

Xavier looks down at the paper like he doesn't know why we'd be questioning it and thinks there might be something else in his lap.

"So I can take notes," he explains. "This could be good for the scrapbook."

"Alright, but I hope you have a lot of stickers or paper cutouts or something, because what I remember would make a really sparse page layout," Dean remarks. He looks over at me and my arched eyebrow. "He's been filling me in on the world of scrapbooking."

"I like it," I say. "Go ahead. What can you remember?"

He closes his eyes and takes a deep breath.

"I got a phone call from my client and stepped outside to take it," he says. "I have a few flashes of the arena, but nothing concrete. I don't remember anybody being there, or anything specific happening. Then the gunshot. And that's it until I woke up on the side of the road. It's not enough to mean anything."

"You needed to get something out of your car," Xavier offers.

"Out of my car?" Dean asks.

Xavier nods. "You got the phone call, but you went outside so that you could get something out of the car."

"What else do you remember, Xavier?" I ask. "He was gone for a long time and you didn't tell anyone. Weren't you worried? Or at least didn't you wonder where he'd gone?"

"I knew he went to his car. Then he didn't come back in, so I thought he might have gone somewhere. But his car was still there. I thought his client might have come and gotten him. Maybe he did say something to me and I missed it. I'm used to things not sinking in when I'm thinking about something else. Then time passed. He didn't come back. I called you."

"That's all you remember?" I ask. "Nothing else? You didn't hear anything strange, or see anything out the window?"

"I heard a couple of car doors close," he shrugs.

"A couple of them?" Dean asks.

Xavier nods. "Each one sounds a little bit different when it closes. It wasn't the same door more than once. It was the front passenger door, then each of the back passenger doors. They were fast, like you were rushing."

"Fast, like there wasn't much time in between?" I ask. "Not enough time to get around the car to open the opposite door?" Xavier shakes his head and I look at Dean. "Why would you open both back doors? I've seen you look for things in the car. You can stretch from one side all the way to the other. You don't need to go in through both sides."

"And if those doors closed that fast, it means it wasn't one person doing it," Dean points out.

"You were taken," I say, confirming the assumption we'd already come to. "You didn't just leave on your own. And you left with more than one person."

CHAPTER EIGHTEEN

"IT MIGHT TAKE A COUPLE OF DAYS, BUT THE PHONE COMPANY IS going to send the records," Dean tells us, getting off a call as he comes back into the room. "They'll show any calls or messages that came in but were deleted from my phone."

"Good," I reply. "I know we looked at them when this first happened, but I don't think we paid enough attention. We were looking for something so specific. We know more about the situation now, so something might stand out to us."

He nods. "Something obviously happened after I walked out of the house on that call. I don't remember what I was going to look for in the car, but if I went out to it, that would explain why Xavier didn't hear any kind of struggle."

That strikes me. "But he heard the doors. If he could hear the car doors closing, he would be able to hear if there was any kind of shouting or fighting. From the very beginning, we assumed there wasn't any kind of fight to get you away from the house because Xavier would have heard it. This doesn't contradict that. It confirms it. Whatever happened after you walked out of that house, it happened without conflict."

"It was someone I went with willingly," Dean says.

"Or they made sure you went willingly," Xavier suggests.

I nod. "We already know there were drugs in your system. It isn't just a blackout that's keeping you from remembering things. They drugged you to make sure they could get you underground without you lashing out and without you knowing where you were. But the doctor said it was a fairly fast-acting drug. You would have been aware again not too long after the dose."

"So I could fight," Dean says. "They used a medication specifically designed to ensure they could take me captive, then release me into the arena just in time for me to come back to my senses and go to battle. Only, I still don't remember."

"The point is, that's how they got you underground," I say. "The question is still what happened in that interval. I can't imagine someone just rushed up on you and injected you, then dragged you to a car. It was broad daylight and that would be a bit more of a scene than I think most people would risk making in the middle of a neighborhood. Besides, you aren't a small man. It would take a lot of effort to haul you into a car once you were unconscious. Which means you probably got in the car with them and then were injected. The question remains how they got you to get in the car."

"What about the other gladiators?" Dean asks. "The ones who have been in any kind of state to talk about what they went through. Have they remembered anything else about how they ended up at the arenas?"

I shake my head. "They haven't been able to give us much. A couple of them have really fuzzy memories, but it's nothing concrete. The problem is, I have a feeling most of them were going through things like Mark Webber. They were out drinking, doing drugs, engaging in all kinds of risky behaviors that would make it far more likely they would encounter danger and not be noticed. And because their minds were already altered, the fact that they don't remember much is not all that surprising. Mark's situation is unique because of the conflicting reports of his driving and getting pulled over that night. We're still trying to figure that out."

"What about Eric, though?"

"Eric is pretty sure he was ambushed. But that doesn't really help because he volunteered himself. He willingly put himself out there in the hopes he would get taken and could gain information that would help with the investigation. Because of that, we can't really assume that his situation paralleled any of the others. It's like with you. It keeps coming back to the fact that you were chosen very intentionally. Not just in the way that Marini chose all of his victims, but because he specifically wanted to make a point with you. So the way he arranged to get you in his grasp is different."

"What about this sister?" Dean wonders. "I know you said they weren't close, but could that be a ploy?"

"You think his sister could have had something to do with it all?" I ask.

"There's nothing anywhere about his parents or any other relatives, right?" he asks.

"As far as I can tell from the information I was able to find, his parents ceased to exist when he was pretty young," I tell him.

"Ceased to exist?" Dean frowns. "What does that mean?"

"Just that. I don't mean that they died, I mean that they don't exist anymore. There's nothing about them anywhere except for his birth records. Completely off the grid. I haven't been able to find anything else. It seems like he put a lot of effort into hiding his family."

"Give me what you have about him," Dean says. "Let me look into his family. I have some resources."

I know he does and I don't ask about them. That's one of the rules I've developed since Dean came into my life. His tactics frequently skirt the line of what's ethical and legal in investigations—and sometimes snap that line altogether, delving right into a very gray area I don't really need to know about.

But we have an understanding. He doesn't need to tell me, and I don't need to know. As long as the information is solid, I don't care. I trust Dean not to compromise an official investigation by resorting to flagrantly illegal methods, and so far, he hasn't failed me once.

After gathering up the information I have about Marini and handing it over to Dean, I settle in the living room with my laptop and a cup of coffee. Talking about Gwendolyn Russo has made me even more curious about her. I intended to meet her and gauge what I could about her in person, but I can't get rid of the little voice in the back of my mind pricking my thoughts and asking questions about her.

"Gacy's sister didn't know."

Xavier comes into the room with his crocheting bag and takes his favorite corner on the couch. He fishes a bundle of green and blue yarn from the bag and plops it onto his lap.

"What?" I ask.

Unrolling the project and finding his hook, he starts stitching without looking up at me. His hands are fast and it's easy to get mesmerized by their movements.

"Gacy. As in John Wayne."

"I'm familiar."

"His sister didn't know what he was doing. He was killing teenage boys right and left and stuffing them under his house, and she had no idea what was going on. And they were really close. She visited him in prison and was with him the day he was executed. She never denied what he did or tried to protest his innocence. But she did say she wasn't afraid of him. There was never a moment of her life when she believed he would hurt her.

"Marini and his sister aren't close. Maybe they were when they were younger, or maybe they never have been. But either way, it doesn't mean she has anything to do with it. Or even knows about any of it. More likely she doesn't know anything. She probably rarely thinks about him at all in her day-to-day life—and now she's finding out all the horrible things he's done.

"And she isn't even being given all the information at once. It's coming to her in little bits because that's what's available. It's water torture but with acid. Tiny drips prolonging the torment rather than immersion that would at least have the mercy of destroying her quickly."

"Do you think that's why she wants to talk to me?" I ask. "To stop the drips? So she can stop worrying about him? Or so she can know who he really was? Or do you think she knows something that might help the investigation?"

"She knows who you are. She knows you know everything there is to know about this and she hopes you'll tell her. It's up to her to tell you why."

When Sam gets home a few hours later I've just finished the platter of snacks we're bringing over to Paul and Janet's house for Game Night. He kisses me on my cheek and goes to the cabinet for a glass.

"Hey, babe," he says. "That looks good. You made those pinwheels."

I nod. "Yeah. Every time I make them Bellamy calls them vintage like I'm using ingredients from a bomb shelter."

"Well, I think they are delicious and she's not here to comment," Sam cracks, snatching one of the coils from the plate and popping it in his mouth.

"Right? She doesn't know what she's missing out on."

"How was your day?" he asks, leaning back against the counter as he sips his water.

"I got a call from Angelo. He sounds like he's coming unglued, but he's never going to admit that."

"I know you're going to hate that I even say this..."

"Yes, I've considered that he might be involved in Miley's disappearance," I interrupt. "And, you're right, I do hate it. I hate even thinking something like that about him, but I wouldn't be doing my job if I didn't."

"And?" he asks with his hands raised out in question.

I shake my head. "I don't think he had anything to do with it. He didn't have to tell me he knew who Miley was or that they were friends. I would have had to do a lot of deep digging into his life to find any indication they knew each other, and I didn't have any reason to do that. He got in touch with me and told me he knew her. There's really no reason for him to tell me that if he did something to her. He doesn't strike me as the kind to get a thrill out of knowing he hurt someone and watching law enforcement run around trying to figure it out.

"And I hesitate to even say this because we both know it means diddly shit a lot of the time, but he really cared about her. They were good friends and he had feelings for her. She made it clear she didn't feel the same way, but that was a long time before her disappearance. If he was going to do something to retaliate against her for that, it wouldn't have taken him so long."

Sam considers it and nods. "Makes sense."

"I did do some research about Marini's sister. The fact that nobody knew she even existed has made me really curious about her. I know I'm going to be meeting with her, but I wanted to know more about her first."

"You want some leverage."

"It's not about leverage. It's about being prepared," I say. "There are things about her that I won't know until I talk to her, but I want to know what I can. Xavier says I shouldn't judge her based on Marini, or assume she's anything like him, but I can't just ignore that this woman is the sister of a master liar and manipulator. She may be nothing like him. And she may be exactly like him. I was curious to see who this woman is."

"And do you know who she is now?" he asks.

"Not fully," I admit. "I do know that she is perhaps not on the total opposite end of the spectrum as her brother, but she's definitely living a different life. Divorced a couple of times. Very much working class. Nothing like the life of luxury her brother led."

"Interesting. I wonder if she ever asked for his help," Sam muses.

"I'm definitely going to try to find out." It suddenly occurs to me that I've been rambling about my own day and haven't even asked about his. "Oh! What about you? How was your day? How did the meeting go?"

Sam smiles warmly. "It went really great. They understood and agreed to grant me extended leave. The deputies will handle everything while I'm gone, and when I get back I'll still have my position without any loss of their support. I trust them and they'll do great."

"That's great," I say. "How do you feel?"

"Better," he admits with a relieved sigh. "I was fine going into the meeting knowing even if they pushed back I was still going to do what needs to be done, but I'm glad to know they don't feel I'm abandoning the town or letting anybody down."

"Of course, you're not," I tell him. "Anyone who knows you would never think that. So, what are you going to do?"

"I still need to talk to Rose, but I'm planning on leaving the day after tomorrow. That's when you're leaving, and since Dean and Xavier are leaving tomorrow morning, it will give us some time together before we both go," he says.

That brings a bit of tightness to my throat and a little sting to my eyes.

"How long are you going to be gone?" I ask.

"I don't know. As long as I need to be. It might be a while," he says.

I nod. "Everything will be fine."

Xavier comes into the room wearing a bowtie and carrying a small velvet bag.

"Is this alright?" he asks. "It's my first Game Night. I want to make a good impression."

"You look great," I tell him. "What's in the bag?"

"Oh. I know I'm usually pretty casual about things, but this I'm kind of particular about. I hope they don't mind if I bring my own," he says, opening the drawstring of the bag.

"Casual?" Sam murmurs to me.

Xavier opens his hand and tips four dice from the bag into his palm. Game Night will officially never be the same.

CHAPTER NINETEEN

D EAN'S INVESTIGATION NEEDS TO MOVE PAST THE STAGE OF research and into actually hitting the pavement, so he and Xavier pack up and leave early in the morning so they can make it back home to the cavernous, several-times augmented mansion in Saltville. That house is what I like to think of as the closest thing to wandering around in Xavier's brain that any of us will ever get.

Treated as a subsection of the tiny town of Harlan, even tinier Saltville is a sprawling rural area dotted with a few neighborhoods featuring everything from little box houses with no more than a living room, kitchen, and bedroom, to estates like Xavier's. Xavier doesn't recognize that his house is as impressive, or confusing, as it is. He explained to me once that his reality is very focused. He doesn't think in possibilities the way others do. Instead, what he's experiencing in that moment is virtually all that exists. He has to put effort into thinking of anything else. I wonder if that's how he thinks of his house. He spends most of his time in the back, roaming between the kitchen, library, and den, so maybe he forgets the rest is there unless he wants to go into them.

I miss them when they leave Sherwood to go back home or I leave them to come back here, but even with the four hours of driving between us, it's good to have them there. It gives them faster access to some of the places we've investigated and people who continue to depend on us even long after their cases have been closed. I know Dean stays in much closer touch with Ava James, a newer agent I was responsible for training in her earliest days. Her first assignment was to a field office near Harlan and she often treats Dean as a touchpoint as she navigates her career.

Sam trundles out of bed just in time to wave goodbye from the front door and I go into the kitchen to start breakfast while he takes a shower. I try not to think about the fact that this is the last morning we will be able to enjoy being together like this for what could be a long time. Over the last couple of years, Sam and I have spent far more time apart than most married couples probably do. Especially couples just barely out of our newlywed stage.

It's hard every time, but we always get through it. And we'll get through it this time. And every time after. But I'll still do everything I can to hold onto the moments we have before we have to say those goodbyes.

I'm prying waffles out of the waffle maker when he comes in. He pulls me into a hug and the sweet smell of fresh, clean Sam takes over the scent of the fried chicken tenders I have heating in the oven. I close my eyes and just pretend this is the only thing I need to think about. I try to be like Xavier. This is my reality and nothing exists outside of it.

But a hungry husband belly grumbles, breaking through the moment. We both throw our heads back and laugh, and he kisses the top of my head then steps back so he can walk around me and peek into the oven.

"Chicken and waffles?"

"I feel like I have to fill you up and sustain you for however long you're going to be gone," I tell him. "By lovingly preparing an intensely unhealthy but delicious breakfast for you. Gear up for lunch and dinner. There's more of this type of thing coming your way."

"Food does exist in Michigan, you know. I'm sure Rose will make sure I don't starve while I'm there," he grins.

I wave the fork I've been using to extract the waffles at him. "Can't you just indulge my wife nonsense for a little bit?"

"Sure," he says with a laugh. "It is my favorite." He tears off a piece of one of the waffles and pops it in his mouth as he heads over to brew coffee. "Want to go to Pearl's for breakfast tomorrow before we both leave? I can sustain you with a big plate of biscuits and gravy that I lovingly purchase."

"I will never turn down Pearl's biscuits and gravy," I tell him.

"Good to know," he says. "I'll make a note of that for when I suspect you might be an evil shape-shifter pretending to be the real Emma."

I nod. "Why do you think I'm always baking your cinnamon rolls? If you say no to those, I'll definitely think something's up."

"I would deserve it, too."

We share another kiss, feeling so happy in the moment despite both of us knowing that it can never last. We sit down for breakfast and his phone immediately chimes. He pulls it out of his pocket, checks the screen, then sets it on the table where it promptly chimes again.

"I'm sorry," he says. "I'll turn off the notifications."

"No, it's okay. Is it about Marie?"

Sam shakes his head, looking vaguely sad and regretful.

"This is our time. I don't want to think about that right now. I just want to be with you," he says.

"I want to be with you, too, but you can't just ignore what's going on. The whole reason you're going to be leaving is so that you can find out what happened to her. And every second counts. I understand that better than most. Tell me what's going on."

He hesitates for a second, then picks up his phone.

"I've been talking to Rose over the last couple of weeks trying to get as much information as possible. She's going to be more influential than me because she's Marie's mother and will be able to access more details. Honestly, I'm not sure how much more professional courtesy I'll be receiving after how it shook out last time I was up there. But I'm hoping I'll have a lot more to go on by the time I land tomorrow.

"It didn't seem like she was going to be able to get a lot because the police department is still officially considering her death a non-suspicious overdose. Thinking of her as just another statistic. But she was finally able to make some real headway. A friend of hers is an attorney and was able to help her get a copy of the medical examiner's report as well as toxicology and crime scene reports."

"Wow," I note. "That's not easy to do. We need more lawyers like that around here."

"I'll see if I can bring him back as a souvenir. She just sent me the reports along with some notes that were with them. It seems the medical examiner isn't totally on board with the idea that her death was an overdose," he says.

"What do you mean?" I frown.

"According to the report, the cause of death determination was done not out of any scientific finding, but presumptively. A full autopsy was performed, but because her remains were in such an advanced state of decomposition, they weren't able to actually find any drugs in her system. Her request for a more advanced analysis of tissues was all but dismissed. The department said essentially they would get to it eventually, but at this point, it wasn't considered a priority because everything else indicated a simple overdose."

"What is everything else?" I raise an eyebrow.

"The location of her remains, her arm was tied, a needle was found next to her body," he shrugs. "The scene had all the hallmarks of someone desperate for their next fix, went somewhere dangerous, and either took far too much or got bad stuff. And because she was in such a desolate area, there was no one around to notice she was in danger and get her help. That's their narrative, and since that is considered an accidental death without any suspicious elements, there wouldn't be a deeper investigation.

"According to them, the only thing that would come of investigating deeper would be proving what drugs killed her. They wouldn't be able to conclusively link her to any dealer since the only information they had was her link to a man who is now dead. It wouldn't matter anyway because she would have taken the drugs herself, so it's extremely unlikely there would be any charges brought against anyone. They don't feel like it's worth their time."

"But the medical examiner doesn't think she died of an overdose," I say.

It's what Sam and I have believed since we found Marie's body, but we've had no proof. Nothing to make anyone listen and care.

"At least she doesn't think the evidence is as conclusive and airtight as the police seem to. Especially considering the damage to Marie's skull. Remember?"

I nod, vividly remembering what her body looked like lying there in the debris of the abandoned warehouse. After many months of lying there unnoticed and seemingly forgotten, her body was severely decomposed. Sam recognized her only by some of the accessories she wore and the color of her hair. It took dental records to confirm it was actually her. While there was no immediate sign of foul play on her body, no gunshot wounds or signs of stabbing, one thing that did stand out was an injury to the side of her head.

"Her skull was fractured," I say. "But there was the piece of the ceiling right there beside her head. The investigators said it had broken off and fallen on her."

"Right," Sam nods. "And that made sense. That building is crumbling. There were pieces of the ceiling and the walls all around her, under her, all over the floor. It's obviously been decrepit for a long time. So it was feasible that's what happened. It didn't look like the correct angle or enough force for someone to have picked up the piece and hit her with it, not with the size of that piece."

"Did the autopsy report have anything about the fracture? Any examination of it to determine when the injury was made?" I ask.

There are many things that should be considered standard in post-mortem examinations of a body, especially in ones where the exact cause and timing of death is technically unknown. Unfortunately, I've learned over my career that just because something seems like it should be automatic, or even compulsory, doesn't mean it actually will happen in all situations. Often corners are cut, people are given instructions to skip elements of certain processes, or conclusions are made without enough supporting evidence, so the real story is missed.

"Yes. She wasn't able to get much information about the skin around the injury, but she examined the bone. There were no signs of cell regrowth and reformation, but there were signs of the inflammation stage," he confirms. "Obviously any true inflammation or hematoma would be impossible to see due to decomp, but the biomechanics of bone healing were present in the fracture."

"But no actual healing," I note. "Which means that injury happened right at or sometime very near her death. If she died of a drug overdose, it would mean she took the overdose, tipped over, and then was hit by a chunk of ceiling."

"Yes," Sam nods. "Which seems like a very serious run of bad luck."

"You need to talk to the medical examiner," I tell him. "Find out what she really thinks. And get as much information about that injury as you can. She could have died because of that injury, which begs the question of why the police are so eager to declare it an overdose and move on. Other than just the fact that they don't want to get tangled up in it."

"Maybe that's the cleanup?" Sam suggests. "The Cleaners didn't do anything to her, but they cleaned up the image of her death? Made it easier and less work for the police."

"Maybe. If nothing else, it's something to go on. A place to start."

CHAPTER TWENTY

L IKE IT ALWAYS DOES, THE TIME HOME ALONE WITH SAM WENT TOO
fast, morning came too early, and before I was really ready, we finished our breakfast at Pearl's and are now at the airport for him to
catch his flight. We pause outside the door that leads to the security
checkpoint separating the main terminal from the gate.

I hate that I can't walk with him right up to the plane, but I'll never
be one to argue with security. I'd much rather kiss my husband goodbye
here and let him go purge his luggage and stroll through the scanners on
his own than worry about the many things I know could go horrifically
wrong if people were allowed to board a plane with nothing but the
honor code controlling their behavior.

He hugs me tight and kisses me. We exchange the usual reassur-
ances and promises of calling and texting, being careful and staying safe,
give one more kiss, and he heads for the labyrinth of TSA. I wait where
I'm standing and watch him through the glass walls for as long as I can.
He takes off his shoes and his belt, empties his pockets, thinks for a few

seconds, reaches in his carry-on for a few things, shows off his plastic bag of liquids and gels, and shuffles sideways beside the conveyor as he waits for his turn through the metal detector.

I can't help but laugh to myself when the guards choose him to go through the full-body scan. They say the scans are random, and I really believe they think they are, but it seems Sam is "randomly" selected nearly every time we get on a plane. We joke that the one time he forgot to declare the bag of hard old-school bubble gum in his carry-on as a food, and had to take every item out of the bag and individually scanned, got him put on some sort of high-security list. They're always on the lookout for terrorists, hairspray, and clandestine sweets.

When he's gotten through the checks and I can't see him anymore, I leave the airport and hit the road. I'm staying in a hotel near the Breyer Correctional Facility for the next few days and will meet with Deandre Wright tomorrow, but my first stop before I check in is Miley's house.

I've been to the house so many times before, but every time I step inside, I carry with me a glimmer of hope that this will be the time I notice something. Maybe this time I'll see something I didn't before, or something will stand out to me with a different meaning now that I know more about her and the case. It keeps drawing me back, telling me it has secrets it's holding onto. Even as I pull up in front of the modest home that's been sitting empty for more than two years now, I can feel the two lives it lived both simultaneously and separately.

The first was Miley Stanford, young and sheltered, given everything by her parents, and brought up to be exactly what they wanted her to be. So much so that it stopped them from seeing who she actually was. She was so lost among the intensely guarded, private neighbors, that no one living around her even noticed when she disappeared and was replaced by a completely different woman.

That woman was the second life of the house. Serena was set in place by Jonah to fill the emptiness left by Miley going missing, something he didn't even know how to explain. Serena was brought out of horror and abuse only to be celebrated for the darkness that existed within her and set in front of the Emperor as bait. He used her even as she used him in return. She isolated his victims and fed them to him, while at the same time working to destroy him.

He got to her first.

The house sheltered both of them and there's still so much of both of them in it.

I wonder how much of the outside of the house changed when Serena moved in. Not that it matters. And at the same time, it does. I don't know how much Jonah told her about Miley and the reason he was having her live in that house. All she knew was that he was protecting her. She earned his favor along with the tattoo on her back. It makes me wonder if this really felt like home to her, enough for her to put her personal touch on the outside. That feels so different than the inside of a house.

Putting her own belongings around the inside of the house is one thing. That was her realm, where she lived on her own. What happened there was shielded from everyone else. The only people who entered the space, who could see anything about it, were the ones she allowed in. But altering the outside of the house would be different. Outward-facing changes meant the neighbors could see. Anyone who went by the house could see. Maybe they would never say anything, but they would notice. And if they noticed, maybe they'd start to wonder. The last thing Serena needed was questions.

Miley's parents had a lockbox installed on the front door to ensure access to the house during the ongoing investigation. They won't come back into the country. As much as it seems like parents would immediately make arrangements to come to the area when they find out their only child is missing, I've come to understand the decision.

There really isn't anything they can do. Even if they were to come back, it wouldn't do any good. Jonah is still in touch with them and says they are just as baffled by her disappearance as the rest of us. They wish they knew something else. They wish there was anything they could tell us that would help guide us to her. But there isn't. Coming back here would only put themselves at risk for no benefit. From a distance, they can ensure I can get inside the house. That I'll keep looking. Other than that, there's nothing they can do.

I punch the code into the keypad and open the lockbox to take out the key to let myself inside. The air in the house feels heavy the second I step over the threshold. The air conditioning is barely on, making the house humid and warm. I go to the unit and turn the temperature down. If it stays hot and muggy like this, it's going to damage the house and everything in it. I don't know why I think that matters.

Standing in the middle of the living room, I try to convince my brain to look around the house as if I've never seen it before. Knowing about Miley's friendship with Angelo and her possible relationship with someone associated with the Emperor gives me a different perspective than the last time I was here. That sets the gears in my brain turning as I consider Miley in a completely different light.

Most of her personal belongings were moved when Serena moved in, but hints of Miley still litter the space. And the lingering remnants of her life were stashed away in a hidden wall storage space that reminded me so much of the secret room in my attic. Pictures, clothing, papers. Letters. Bills. The things she left behind the last time she walked out of her front door, not knowing it was the last time she was walking through the door, are all there.

I've gone through them, read her handwriting, and looked through her mail. I didn't notice anything that stood out to me then, but now that I know more about her, I want to see it all again. I hope that something will stand out with more meaning. Something that has been right in front of me the whole time but only now can tell me its secrets.

Some of the items I found in the storage space have been seized to be used as evidence for Miley's disappearance, as well as the crimes of her parents, but the rest is spread out across the spare bedroom at the back of the house. There's little to no organization. Papers, documents, and random things litter the floor, the window sill, and the top of a dresser pushed against the wall.

I look over them with Angelo's words echoing in the back of my mind. I listen to my memories as he tells me about her wandering haphazardly into the Blue Ridge Backpackers outdoor adventure club, about him befriending her, and how much fun they had together.

I listen as he tells me about Marini's supposed nephew and the way Miley looked at him, and the way he sounded when he said he hopes she's happy with him somewhere, even if it hurts so much to think that she would leave him that way without even saying goodbye.

As the words filter through my thoughts, my eyes fall on a pile of random belongings beside me. It looks like someone was trying to sort through things and had created a mound of jewelry and other accessories. Hidden among the rings, necklaces, bracelets, and decorative belt buckles is an object that doesn't belong. The slightly shimmering metal is a pale, almost pearlescent shade of pink, which I can assume is why it was put in this pile. But a closer look confirms that it isn't jewelry or even an accessory.

It's a carabiner.

The curved metal clip is small and delicate, not the type that would actually be used for rock climbing or any other high adventure activity, which tells me it isn't there for function. This is a token, possibly a gift meant to remind her of something, or of someone.

I separate it away from the rest of the items and take a picture to send to Angelo, asking if he recognized it. Maybe it was something he gave to Miley when they were friends, possibly even as a sign of his feelings for her. I get a response from him within seconds. He didn't give it to her, but he recognizes it. Miley started wearing it on her belt loop a few months before she died. He figured it was just a quirky accessory she was trying out.

That's possible. But it feels like more.

I thank Angelo and put the carabiner back with the rest of the items. Something occurs to me as I look over everything else piled in the room and I take out my phone to call John Waters, the detective who investigated Serena's death with me. He isn't happy to hear I'm at Miley's house again.

"Emma, the case is closed. You need to let it go," he grumbles.

"You've closed Serena's case," I correct him. "You came to your conclusion and that's enough for you. It's not enough for me. And I'm not calling about her anyway. It's about Miley Stanford. She is still missing and I want to know what happened to her. I need to know about the items that were taken from her house."

"They were catalogued as evidence," he says.

"I know. I just need to know about a specific thing. Well, a couple of specific things."

He lets out a heavy breath. It's the kind of breath that tells me I should feel lucky he and I have known each other for years, that I helped him through his son's death and the brutal aftermath in his own personal life. Probably even more that he knows my father and admires him. If all those things weren't true, he likely wouldn't even still be on the phone with me right now.

"What do you want to know?" he finally relents.

"Can you find out if there's a date book? A calendar, an agenda, anything like that? And also if you have any receipts, bank statements, credit card statements. Those kinds of things."

"I can't remember about the calendar. I'll look into that for you. But I know there are a few financial statements. Nothing terribly thorough, but a few things."

"Was there ever a subpoena for more?" I ask.

There's been little official investigation into Miley's disappearance. Even without the possible link to the Emperor, as soon as people realized she was the daughter of major criminals who fled the country and are hiding out in Europe, any true concern about her dissipated. I know that would never be the official statement from the police. Or even the Bureau. No one would want to admit that a missing and extremely endangered person was downgraded in importance because of familial ties.

But it happens. All I can do is stand in the gap.

"I can get them for you," Waters says, sounding resigned and tired of the conversation.

"Thank you," I reply, ending the call without an explanation of why I need the information.

It doesn't matter if he knows. What matters now is I feel like I'm right at the edge of finding the path I need to follow. It's somewhere in front of me and if I keep reaching for the tiny breadcrumbs that show themselves, one of these times I'm going to find the one that leads me there.

CHAPTER TWENTY-ONE

I LOVE THE COLDNESS OF HOTELS.

There's something about stepping into a hotel room for the first time and getting hit by the bracing cold of an air conditioner set far too low while breathing in the combination of chill and bleach that puts me at ease. The novelty of staying in hotels definitely wears off after a while, which is why I've been known to rent a house or an apartment in an area where I know I'll be investigating for a protracted period of time. But when it's only a handful of days, a fresh hotel room, starched white sheets, and the little basket of snacks that's waiting for me at check-in clears my head and helps me focus.

It doesn't hurt that being in a hotel helps me miss Sam less. Not that I stop thinking about him completely, but being away from our home with his smell on the pillow, his shoes by the door, and the random sock I always find under the bed, makes me feel less of the emptiness of not being there. When I'm in a hotel room where space hasn't been carved

THE GIRL AND THE TWISTED END

out for him, it doesn't hurt as much to walk through that space and have him not be there.

After putting in a call to order dinner, I flop my suitcase on the bed and unpack. As I'm putting my clothes away in the dresser under the bed, I call my father.

"Hey, honey," he says when he answers. "What are you up to? Is the air conditioner holding out in this heat? That house can be a bear to keep cool."

I let out a soft laugh and sit down at the end of the bed. After going so many years without having my father in my life, it amuses me every time he takes on the doting, protective dad role. It wasn't quite the same for him. Through all those years when he was missing, he still followed along with my life. His deep undercover work and the occasional stint in custody kept him from being aware of every step I took, but he kept tabs from a distance.

For me, though, his worrying about me is still new. It never fails to make me laugh to think he believed in me enough to sign over bank accounts and multiple pieces of real estate to me at the age of eighteen so I could carry on in life alone, but he is still concerned that my air conditioner isn't working properly or that I haven't gotten the oil changed in my car recently enough.

"It's doing fine," I tell him. "We replaced the entire unit this spring with two different ones to control the temperature in different zones of the house."

"That's a good idea. It will keep you comfortable and save you money on your power bill."

His voice trails off into silence. He knows there's another reason I'm calling and is just trying to stretch out his fatherly advice to fill the quiet until I get to it.

"I'm actually not at home right now. I'm back up near Breyer," I say.

"The prison? Why are you there?" he asks with obvious concern.

There's tension in his voice now. It's no longer the voice of a casually interfering father concerned about his daughter's temperature control and now one of a battle-scarred man well-versed in the dangers of the field.

"I'm meeting with the guard who facilitated Jonah's escape," I say.

The seconds that pass sit heavily in the air.

"You know how he did it?" my father finally asks.

"Yes," I say. "Xavier found out while he was in the prison. He wanted to check the details to make sure it all added up, but he told me a few days ago."

"What are you going to do?"

"I'm going to talk to the guard who helped him. Make sure he understands I know what happened and that it would be in his best interest to cooperate with me."

"Cooperate with you in what? Aren't you going to turn him into the prison administration?"

"Not immediately."

"Emma, what he did is a felony," Dad presses. "He let an extremely dangerous man out into the world after all that effort to bring him in. At the very least, he should lose his job. Not to mention he should be held legally accountable."

"Dad, I know. I know on the surface it's easy for you to say I should just turn him in and have him fired. But it isn't that simple. Especially for me."

"Why not?"

"I want him gone. Jonah. If the story Xavier told me is actually what happened, the situation isn't as easy as a guard helping a prisoner escape. I'm not trying to defend him or say that he didn't do anything wrong, but there's more to it. Enough that it's worth taking advantage of this moment to ensure I can get Jonah out of my life. Out of *our* lives. Once and for all," I say.

"I want that, too, Emma. But I don't want you putting yourself in danger to get it."

"It's the only way to get it. The end of this story was never going to be smooth and simple. If it was, he would have been back in custody a long time ago. I have a choice here. I can either keep going with him out in the world, pretend he's not out there, and keep going until the next time he decides to screw with me. Or I can put myself between him and the world, be willing to face the risk, and take him down.

"I've dealt with a lot from him. I've been willing to go against all of my instincts and everything I know professionally because I thought it was the right choice. There were people who needed help and stories that needed to be told, and the only way to accomplish that was to be willing to let him stay free. I'm done with that. I don't need him to finish what I've started and he doesn't need to complete anything he left when he went into prison the first time.

"I wanted to think I didn't care anymore. I told myself I could go on with my life and if he was ever right in front of me, I'd take the chance to get him, but I wasn't going to devote so much time and energy to him anymore. I stopped communicating with him. I stopped reaching out to him. But it's not enough. Even if I did decide to just go forward, I would always know people were suffering because he was out. People would die. People would be brainwashed. I can stop that."

"What does this guard have to do with it?" Dad asks. "He already helped Jonah get out of the prison. Why would he tell you the truth about that, much less help you put him back in?"

"Because he will know that I know exactly what happened. And I know *why* he did it," I say.

There's another long stretch of silence. "We were close once."

"I know you were," I say.

"When we were in school, kids would talk about him behind his back. They'd say he was weird and make fun of him. Did I ever tell you that?" he asks.

"No," I say. My voice has gone powdery. I hate to hear the pain in my father's voice when he talks about his brother.

He lets out a puff of air that might be a word of affirmation.

"He has always been different. Nothing like he is now, but different. He's brilliant and creative, but there's always been something about the way he thinks, the way he does things, that makes him stand out. Kids call it weird. He didn't fit in, and it made him a target. I did everything I could to defend him. I told him they only did that because they didn't understand him and were intimidated by him.

"They made fun of him because it was easier to react that way than it was to admit they didn't feel secure about themselves near him. It was just the same things our parents said, but I thought he would listen more if I said them. I would never have thought he would turn out this way. I thought he'd tuck his head down and get through school, and eventually, it wouldn't be so awkward for him. But he took it all and internalized it. He took his rage and decided he was going to control everyone who ever hurt him. If they were already intimidated by him, they were going to learn what it was like to fear him."

"It isn't your fault how he turned out, Dad," I say. "You didn't do anything that made Jonah the way he is."

"I encouraged him not to let those people upset him. That he was better than that. Better than them. I believed he *was* better than them. We were so close. We did everything together. I thought he had it in him to do such incredible things."

He draws in a breath. The unspoken truth hangs between us, but he doesn't need to say it out loud. We both know all too well.

"Dad?"

"Do what you have to do."

CHAPTER TWENTY-TWO

I GET A CALL FROM SAM AS I'M DRIVING TO THE PRISON THE NEXT morning.

"Hey, babe," I say toward the phone attached to the cradle on the dashboard. "How was your flight?"

"Good morning. It was decent. A little turbulence, but I kept it together."

I laugh. "How's Rose?"

"Glad I'm here. I'm sorry I only texted yesterday. She got hold of me as soon as I got off the plane and I was going until I fell into bed."

"It's alright. Did you find out anything new?" I ask.

"I was able to talk to the medical examiner a little bit. She was on her way to a hearing, so I was essentially jogging along beside her asking her questions, but it gave me a chance to ask about the skull fracture. She admitted that really bothered her when she did the autopsy, but that she couldn't come to any conclusions about it. If she had to make an expert determination, she would say it definitely didn't come from someone picking up the rock and hitting Marie over the head with it."

"Well, that's something."

"Yeah. Not only is the position of the injury all wrong for a typical place where someone would get hit on the head by an assailant, but like the report said, the force just isn't there. It's not exactly accidental to hit another person in the head with a big chunk of concrete like that. It's something that's done with the specific intent to cause severe injury or death. They aren't just going to give it a little whack and be done with it. And while Marie's skull was fractured, it wasn't completely smashed. It wasn't caved in or totally obliterated. It was a serious injury, but not one she would expect to come from somebody hitting her."

"So, maybe it did fall from the ceiling," I say.

There's a flicker of disappointment in the statement. We've spent so long poring over the details that the realization that the police might have been right all along leaves me feeling antsy and uncomfortable, like someone is whispering behind me.

"Maybe, but she said she wouldn't feel anywhere near confident stating that conclusively. Again, the positioning of the injury doesn't fit what she would expect if a piece of the ceiling came down on someone below. If we're going with the narrative that Marie was shooting up, she would presumably be sitting up against the wall, right?"

"That would make sense," I say.

"Alright. So, if she was sitting against the wall and the piece of the ceiling came down and hit her, she would likely fall over to the side and the piece would be close by her head. Or if she had already passed out, the piece would fall and hit her on the opposite side of her head, then fall behind or in front of her head. I'm going to send you a crime scene picture. Keeping all that in mind, look at it and tell me what you see."

I hurt for Sam as I wait for the picture to arrive. I know how hard it is for him to look at images like this. Marie and him were close, especially when they were younger, and I know deeply how difficult it is to face gruesome images of what's left of someone you love after a tragedy.

The picture arrives and I look at it. I remember noticing the piece of concrete and the injury on her head when we found her, but I didn't take the time to dwell on it. Instead, I deferred to the police actually investigating the case and instead put my energy into supporting my husband. He wanted to be involved in the investigation of the scene and the removal of her body, but I knew those weren't experiences he needed etched into his mind.

Looking at the picture of Marie's body brings back the visceral memories of that day. It isn't just the way a body looks when it's at this stage of decomposition. There's a smell, a taste in the air, a feeling on your skin. I learned years ago to shut that off. It's impossible to let your mind absorb the intense reality of a murder victim lying in front of you, sometimes brutalized, sometimes decomposed, sometimes so perfect and pristine it's like they'll open their eyes at any second, over and over again, and still be able to do the job. Evaluate the scene. Gather the facts. Close the case. Think later.

That's what I do now. I cut off the emotion, stop myself from thinking of Marie, my husband's cousin, and think only of a victim of a death without a satisfactory explanation. It lets me focus in on the uneven piece of concrete beside her and the position of the injury on her head.

"There's something off about where the concrete is," I note. "It doesn't look like it would have fallen there. And look at the blood. There isn't much, but you can see there's a more saturated area."

"Like a point of impact," Sam replies, confirming he's on the same train of thought as me.

"Exactly. Then look below it. I'd expect to see some trails if there were drops of blood, but they look almost… smeared. I'm no blood spatter expert, but I've seen enough blood evidence to piece a few things together, and the direction of the blood doesn't look like something that fell onto a stationary person," I continue. "If that were the case, I'd expect the blood to be moving in more of an upward direction away from the point of impact."

"What do you think it means?" Sam asks.

"I'm not sure. But if you were looking for more evidence to confirm there's more to Marie's death than just an overdose, I think you can consider it found."

The next morning I'm already in the prison office when Deandre Wright comes in. He looks confused, but there's also hesitation around the edges of his eyes, like he knows there's something behind my visit and is trying to figure out what he's going to say and do before I even tell him why I'm there.

"Good morning, Officer Wright," I start, gesturing at the chair across from me. "Have a seat."

He glances around the office like he's expecting someone else to be there. I'm going to take care of that for him in a few seconds, but first, I want to talk.

"Good morning," he replies.

"Agent Griffin," I tell him and he nods.

"I know who you are," he says. "The Warden told me you were waiting for me."

I give him a hint of a smile. "I figured he would, since he's the one I contacted to set up this meeting."

"What's going on?" he frowns. "I don't understand why you wanted to talk with me."

"I came to talk with you because I need something done and you're the one to do it for me."

His eyebrow cocks. "And why is that?"

With my fingers folded together as my hands rest on the table in front of me, I lean toward him so he has no choice but to look at me.

"A good friend of mine spent some time in this facility recently, and he brought back a really interesting story for me. He wasn't here because he did something wrong. He was here because there was a question that had been bothering me, and he thought the only way to get the answer to it was if he came here and got to know the prison and the people inside. You see, he wasn't the only inmate here who I have a connection with."

A knock on the door makes Wright jump slightly. We both look over and see another guard leading an inmate in. His hands are cuffed in front of him and he has the same kind of confused, worried expression on his face.

"Oh good," I smile. "Our other guest has arrived. This is better. Now we can all talk." I look at the guard who brought him in. "Thank you, Nabil. I appreciate it."

"Absolutely, Emma. Let me know if you need anything."

"I will."

He sounds almost hurt, or at least annoyed, and I understand the reaction. I've worked with Nabil before and I trust him, but I also don't want to put him in harm's way. He doesn't need to know the full details of our plan. The official word from the Warden for anyone who asks is that I'm on a special case and need cooperation from selected members of the staff and prisoners. As far as any of the other guards know, I have asked that Deandre Wright and Benson Mandeville take part in a highly classified sting operation, and they won't be able to give any details. It's actually skirting right there along the edge of the truth—more true than not, actually —and it works perfectly to deflect attention from the staff as well as from the Warden.

Nabil leaves and Wright makes eye contact with me.

"Emma?" he asks. "Emma Griffin? You're Emma Griffin, the FBI agent?"

I gesture to another chair across from me. "Come on, Benson. Join us." He sits and I smile briefly. "You don't mind if I call you Benson, do you?"

"It's better than my inmate number," he grumbles.

His voice matches the rest of him. Much too young to be here.

"I would think so. No one has ever tried to refer to me by my badge number," I say, rattling off the number. "It has kind of a ring to it. But it's a bit cumbersome."

"You are Emma Griffin, from the FBI," Wright says again.

I finally give a single nod. "I am. And by that look on your face, I'm going to go ahead and assume you know exactly who I'm talking about when I say the other inmate I'm connected with. And if you know that, maybe you can piece together why we're all together."

They exchange glances, but neither of them says anything.

"Alright, then I guess I'll just keep going," I say. "Benson, this place isn't exactly the most comfortable living situation, is it?"

"Fuck no. It's like hell in here," he says.

"But there are things that can make it a little better, right? Commissary, phone time, maybe some perks for your cell?"

He shifts a bit, but his expression doesn't change. He's defiant, not wanting to give up anything.

"If you can get them," he says.

"And you can, it seems." I pull a piece of paper out of the folder in front of me and slide it across the table toward him. "This is a list of all the money that's been put on your books as well as packages sent to you over the last year and a half. It looks like you've been very well taken care of."

"I've got people on the outside," he says.

"Were they out of town for a really long time a couple years ago?" I ask.

He looks at me quizzically. "What?"

"The prison keeps thorough records of things like this, and before November the year before last, you didn't have much in the way of creature comforts around here. A couple of dollars here and there on your books, maybe, but for the most part, you were living off what the facility gave you and indigent supplies. That must not have made for very pleasant living for the first … looks like six years of your sentence."

"I dealt with it. It's what we do," he says.

"You don't really have a choice. But I bet you're liking this life a lot more. Which is why it makes sense that if someone offered to take care of you and make sure that you would always have everything you could possibly have here, you'd take him up on it," I go on.

"I don't know what you're talking about," Benson scoffs.

"I think you do. You went from having absolutely nothing to being at the top of the food chain around here. At least in terms of the little luxuries in life. And if I don't miss my guess, there are some other perks that go along with it, too, because the person helping you is making sure you stay safe while you finish out your sentence."

He stiffens up, but he's not budging. He doesn't want to give anything away, and I completely understand it. The benefits he's getting are worth everything to an inmate in a prison like this. It means he can get extra food whenever he wants it. Toiletries, clothes. Even a TV in his cell. He gets care packages of food, books, and other goods. Everything that's allowed in these walls, he has access to. And I know exactly who's supplying them to him. I just need him to admit it.

"Like I said, I have a friend on the outside," he says evenly.

"No, you don't. You have someone paying for your silence and your cooperation. You have someone named Jonah Griffin. He is no one's friend."

"What does this have to do with me?" Wright asks.

I go into my folder again and take out another piece of paper, scanning it to make sure I get the details exactly right.

"You've worked here for five years, right?" I ask.

"Yes," he confirms.

"And before that, it looks like you weren't having the easiest go in life," I tell him. "You bounced around the foster system a bit, had a few run-ins with the law. Nothing that would disqualify you from corrections, obviously, but enough. Looks like you were homeless for a little while. Things weren't great for you."

"How do you know all that?" he asks.

"I'm with the Federal Bureau of Investigation, Officer Wright. I can know anything I need to about anybody I need to."

"So what if I had a rough start? It happens. I went through some hard times, but I'm here now. I'm making it."

"Yes, you are," I nod. "You have a good job. Benefits. A nice salary. You even have a little one at home, correct?"

"My son."

"He's a little over a year old now, right?" I ask.

"I worked hard to pull myself out of a shit start so I didn't end up behind the bars in this place," he says through gritted teeth. His voice has dropped to a growl that sounds like a wounded animal.

"I know you did. That's obvious. And it's why you wouldn't want anything to happen that might compromise that position or the benefits from it." I take out another piece of paper. "You have an exemplary track record for attendance and are constantly picking up extra shifts, doing overtime, volunteering for work other people don't want to do. Your file has note after note about your work ethic and how dependable you are."

I frown and tap on a particular line on the page.

"But here in November of the year before last, there's a note that says you came back from a transport over an hour late. There was no disciplinary action, but it was considered an anomaly. Do you remember that happening?"

"Yes," he says. "I was doing a medical transport and the procedure took longer than expected."

"In fact, you were doing a medical transport for two prisoners, weren't you? Inmate Mandeville and Jonah Griffin. And then you did another one just a few weeks later, but you came right back exactly when you were supposed to. And it was only for Benson."

He draws in a breath. It's obvious now they aren't going to be forthcoming about this. I think both realize I'm getting closer and that I probably know what happened, but neither of them is going to be the one to break. They're going to hold out until the very last second until they're forced to bring down the walls and tell the truth.

"Aren't my medical records private?" Benson demands. It's his Hail Mary, his last-ditch effort to derail the conversation and stop me from getting any closer to what they did.

"Not in prison," I clarify. I close the folder and lean closer to them again. "I want both of you to listen to me closely. I'm not here because I want to bust you for something. I'm not trying to get on your asses and cause trouble. I'm here because I *know* what happened. I know both of you were very much involved in my uncle's escape from this prison and that you are continuing to benefit from the escape. But I also know both of you had your reasons and they make sense to me."

The two of them share a glance and I know I've got them.

"Officer Wright, you got a raw deal starting out in life and you had just started climbing up. Things were good, you were expecting a baby, and everything looked like it was finally going to work out for you. No one knew about your seizures. You hadn't had one in years and you didn't think they'd come back, but you knew if the prison found out about them, it could impact your job. So, you didn't say anything. Only they did come back. While you were driving the prison transport van with Benson and Jonah."

"I'm fine," he insists.

"I'm sure you are. But that one incident changed everything. You can't drive if you could have a seizure behind the wheel. Especially when you are responsible for prisoners. But if no one knew what happened, they couldn't take your job from you. And they would keep quiet, in exchange for a favor. You would transport two inmates, but only sign out one. And the inmate you signed out would live in comfort as long as he never spoke a word."

"How do you know any of this?" Wright asks.

"Remember a few months ago when a preacher in the community outreach program was arrested in the chapel?" I ask.

They glance at each other again and I reach into the bag at my feet to pull out a scarf crocheted from glittery pink and silver yarn.

"Son of a bitch," Benson mutters.

CHAPTER TWENTY-THREE

Sam

EVEN WITH THE WARM DAY OUTSIDE, THE CUP OF STEAMING TEA set beside his hand was comforting. Sam looked up at his aunt and offered a hint of a smile.

"Thank you," he said.

Rose looked different. Older. Paler. Like she was fading and might soon become transparent. It wasn't unexpected. He was honestly surprised to find her still standing and functioning when he arrived in Michigan. She'd been carrying on with strength and determination that astonished him since the day she called him to tell him her only child was missing. But she couldn't withstand it all unscathed. It was chipping away at her and each day was getting harder.

She wasn't just carrying the burden of her child disappearing and then being found dead. That was painful enough. It destroyed her world and sent her reeling. But she'd taken on even more than that. It hurt her deeply when the police told her Marie was a drug user and living a double life away from the family who loved her. She couldn't imagine that was something Marie would do.

It wasn't that Marie was an angel. She'd had phases in her life when she'd made bad decisions and did things she later regretted. Like most teenagers, she rebelled against the rules put in front of her. She went through rough patches with her mother. She drank, had questionable relationships, told her fair share of lies, and put herself in situations more dangerous than Rose ever wanted to think about.

But she'd gotten through them. And she'd gotten through the hard times she hit when she got older. She'd rebuilt her life and was making something of herself. It didn't make sense that she would give all that up for a high. A relapse wasn't impossible. She was human. She could have made that mistake. But she wouldn't hide it from Rose. She wouldn't let herself deteriorate in the shadows and not reach out to claw herself back to safety.

Her mother was there for her. Sam was there for her. Marie had known that about both of them. She'd known she wasn't alone and never had to be ashamed of what she'd been going through. They would be there for her. They would do anything she needed. She didn't have to hide.

And Rose knew she didn't. It wasn't just protecting herself from the thought. It was a mother's heart knowing her child. And she'd picked up the cause to battle for Marie. She was going to do anything she could to make sure people knew the truth about her daughter. She wanted Marie's story to be told and she would give everything in herself to see it done.

She'd done just that. There wasn't much left of her. When Sam looked at her, he felt like she was disappearing right in front of him. Working to prove Marie didn't go out to that warehouse and inject herself with enough drugs to kill herself was no longer just about knowing the truth and holding whomever was involved accountable. Now it was also about saving what little was left of Rose, too. It was to keep her from fading away completely.

"You said you were able to get more information off her computer," Rose said.

She sat down in the corner of the couch, gripping her own cup of tea. She didn't drink it, just held it close to her face like she was breathing it in.

"Emma had some people at the Bureau look into it, and her cousin Dean did some investigating as well. Whoever went into her apartment after she died went to some pretty extreme extent to try to destroy everything on the computer so that no one would know what she was doing. But the cyber forensic investigation was able to reconstruct some of the fragments. Marie was doing really extensive research into a company called Alfa-Corps. Did you ever hear her talk about that?"

Rose shook her head. "I've never heard of it. What did the notes say?"

"Since they weren't able to put together the notes in their entirety, I can't tell for absolute certain what she was looking at exactly, or why she was doing it. Right now, the notes are essentially just lists of words and questions to herself."

"What kind of questions?" Rose asked.

"Just things like: 'Did they know?'; 'How many of them?'; 'How about the children now?'; 'Compensation?'" he told her.

"What do they mean?"

"I don't know. But I'm talking to some people, including the police, tomorrow. Hopefully, I'll find out."

The next day Sam walked into the police department knowing the officers wouldn't be happy to see him. They had made it very clear they wanted him to stay out of what they considered to be a closed case. They offered him access and cooperated with him in the beginning, but when he started asking questions and not blindly following along with everything they said, walls went up.

But those weren't going to stop him. There were answers out there, and he would do whatever it took to find them.

By that night, he felt closer than ever before.

Hearing Emma's voice over the phone always had a comforting effect for Sam. Even with her unpredictable, often chaotic personality, he felt like she anchored him. She was the soft spot where he could fall, the reminder of who he was deep at his core when he started getting too into his own head. She was bold and blunt, sometimes intense and abrasive. But it was exactly what he needed. She made sure he saw things for what they were, and he did the same for her.

"It's a shell corporation," he said when she answered.

"What is?" she asked.

"Alfa-Corps."

"The company Marie was researching?" she asked.

"Yes. I went to the police department today and told them about the evidence we've found that points to there being much more to the story than Marie just dying of an overdose. Specifically what was found on her computer. She was researching something. Very intently. She wanted to know what was going on with that company, but why? And what was it that she had found? So I asked around. Not surprisingly, the detectives weren't particularly receptive. They think I'm wasting time and just need to let this whole thing go."

"Either that or they know that you're getting close to something they don't want you to know," Emma said.

"Very possible. But before I left, an officer who doesn't have anything to do with the case came out to me. He had overheard me talking about the company and suggested I look into something called Everbright International. So, I did. And I discovered they are the same entity. Everbright International is an umbrella that is over more than a dozen smaller companies. They don't seem to have much of a connection at all. Different fields, different demographics, different locations. And some of them don't seem to have anything going on at all."

"Like Alfa-Corps."

"Like Alfa-Corps," Sam confirmed. "That company was just started about two years ago. But the thing is, it didn't really start a company. It was just a name that was registered. No actual business was ever done. Then a little more than a year ago, a very secretive deal was drawn up to merge it with an existing company known as Exceed Ventures."

"I feel like I've heard of that," Emma said.

"You probably have. They manufacture a huge number of industrial goods and products. Very very deep pockets. Big names, bigger paychecks. Which begs the question of why they would want to have a different company take over. Some more digging gave me that answer and possibly the one we've been wondering about this whole time."

"Why Marie was researching them," Emma said.

"It turns out all that manufacturing wasn't nearly as environmentally friendly and progressive as they wanted consumers to think," Sam explained. "Not only have several of the products they produced been taken from the market because of labeling concerns, but their plants have been linked to several instances of water and land contamination. People living in the areas where these have happened have reported decreased fertility, high frequency of birth defects, soaring rates of cancer and other diseases, and other chronic health problems."

"If all that is happening, how have they not been shut down? Or at least sued into submission?" Emma asked.

"It seems there's a strange pattern of people not bringing the company to court, or pulling out of the case before it can get anywhere. And rumor has it that everyone who has ever had anything to do with any of these cases has immediately been issued a gag order so they can't talk about it. There's no real way of proving that, of course, but there are enough rumblings I can't help but believe they're true."

"That's all definitely something the company would want to keep under wraps," Emma noted. "But why would Marie care? Did she live anywhere near one of the affected areas?"

"No," Sam said. "I think it has to do with her freelance writing. Rose said she had only really been writing occasionally and it was mostly fluff pieces, but she was really hoping to progress into more intensive subjects. But I already talked with the publications she'd done pieces for and none of them had her under contract for anything, much less something about Alfa-Corps."

"But she could have been writing for someone else, even on spec," Emma mused. "Maybe those companies weren't willing to give her more hard-hitting assignments, so she decided to go find something for herself. If you can find out who she was hoping to sell the piece to, maybe they can give you more details on what she knew."

"And that's my search for tomorrow."

CHAPTER TWENTY-FOUR

NY THOUGHT THAT TALKING TO GWENDOLYN RUSSO WOULD BE an emotional conversation supporting a woman through the death of her estranged brother was pretty much blown out the window the second I saw her. Because of the research I've already done, I knew what she looked like before she strode through the door of the café where she told me to meet her.

I left the hotel early to make sure I wouldn't be late if I got turned around in the unfamiliar town, but ended up arriving at the café almost forty-five minutes before the appointed meeting time. I've been sitting here working my way through a shockingly strong black coffee and I have just started my second croissant when the door flies open and Gwendolyn enters.

The expression on her face isn't angry. She isn't storming in like she's on some sort of mission to avenge her brother. But there's definitely a no-nonsense look in her eyes. She's here for a reason and I doubt there's going to be a lot of small talk happening between us.

I stand as she approaches the table and extend my hand to her.

"Agent Emma Griffin," I introduce myself.

"I know who you are," she says without shaking my hand. "I'm Gwendolyn Russo."

I nod and we sit. A waitress materializes beside the table and takes her order for a heavily sweetened and flavored drink along with a chocolate chip muffin.

"I'm sorry for your loss," I say when the waitress has walked away from the table.

It's one of those sentiments Xavier considers compulsory language. It doesn't necessarily mean what it sounds like it's supposed to, but there's a place for it in these situations and you just have to say them. He both has little patience for them and is a strict adherent to the practice.

"Let's just get this all out in the open right now, Agent Griffin. I'm not here because I want to cry over my brother's death and wax poetic about all the time we lost and all that bullshit. I hadn't talked to Sal in almost twenty years when he died, and when I found out, I didn't shed a tear," she replies. "He was always looking out for himself. When our parents died and we got dumped in foster care he didn't particularly care too much about me. And the second he turned eighteen, he disappeared and left me there to take everything the monster married to our foster mother wanted to dish out to me—and Sal's portion, too.

"I didn't even know what happened to him until I started seeing his smug face showing up on the news, talking about his philanthropy and all the wonderful things he does for people with the money he made stomping on the heads of the little people who end up in his path. Be very clear when I tell you I am not a sister in mourning."

"Got it," I tell her.

Her face changes slightly and she rolls her head to the side like she's cringing at some internal pain.

"Shit." She drops her head down into her hands for a second, then looks up at me again. "Shit. I shouldn't have put it that way. With that girl he..." she can't even bring herself to say the words, that he killed Serena, "...and everything."

"Don't worry about it," I tell her.

"All I meant is that he has only ever thought of one person in his life, and that's himself."

"I'm not going to argue with you on that," I say. "From the very brief interactions I had with him, and what I know about him, I can't say I disagree with you. But you got in touch with me. Why don't you tell me what you want to talk about?"

It's taking everything in me not to talk about Marini's alter ego as the Emperor and the horrific crimes he committed in that persona. Technically, he hasn't been officially linked to the string of horrific tortures and murders. There isn't a single actual doubt he committed those crimes, but I have to be careful in how I talk about them. Until I am more familiar with her, I can't talk freely about something that is still in the eyes of the law only alleged.

"I want to know what happened to the money," Gwendolyn says firmly.

I blink at her a couple of times. That wasn't what I was expecting. I didn't really have an idea of what I thought she was going to say, but I know that isn't it.

"The money?" I frown.

"*His* money," she specifies as if that actually clarifies anything. "I am his only living relative and that means I inherit everything. At least that's what his lawyer said," she says. "He didn't have a will giving it to anyone else, so it's mine. But the papers he gave me with the amount of money that should be in the estate and what the banks are telling me are wildly different. A shit-ton of money is missing."

I shake my head at her, bewildered by the conversation that's unfolding.

"I'm still not sure why you want to talk to me about this," I say. "As I told you, I barely knew him. I talked with him only a few times before his death."

"But you've been investigating him," she points out. I try to stop the look on my face before it changes, but she sees the flicker of surprise. "Yes. I do know who you are. I've been following the case. He killed that girl and you were the one who got him for it. Which means you know more about him than you want to say. Like where he might have funneled money before he died."

"I don't know anything about his finances," I tell her honestly. "I'm an FBI agent. I was investigating a missing person and a murder when I encountered Mr. Marini as what I thought was just a friend of one of the victims. He was never on my radar for any other reason. I know nothing about his money or what might be missing."

She looks at me like she doesn't believe me.

"The lawyer said you're still digging into the circumstances of his death. You don't think that it was just a heart attack."

"That is common knowledge," I reply.

"Then who do you think did it?" she presses. "It stands to reason the same person who offed him is the one who took all his money. Probably why they did it. He was going off to prison, right? He was going to rot for killing that girl. What would that mean for his estate? I would have inherited it because he wouldn't have been around, right? And whoever it is knew that, so they made sure the money was gone so I couldn't have it."

I shake my head. "That's not how it works. You wouldn't have inherited anything just because he went to prison, even if he was in there for a long time. He would have had to go through a legal process to transfer his possessions to you. Did he do that? That lawyer, Mr. Klein, would have paperwork he filled out to that effect and signed."

She shakes her head, starting to look angry now. "He didn't say anything about that. Just that I was responsible for the estate now and that he could help execute and file everything. I said no because that just sounds like he's grubbing for more of the money. But then I looked at the papers he did give me and I contacted the bank and they don't add up."

"Do you have the papers?" I ask. "Would you mind if I looked at them?"

She reaches into her bag and pulls out a thick folder that she hands over to me. "Have at it. The stuff from the bank and everything is up on the top."

I look over the papers and immediately notice the discrepancy she's talking about.

"This is strange," I note, then shake my head and look up at her, "but I don't know what it means. I have no idea why any of the money would be missing or where it went. I've been trying to get permission to search his mansion and other properties as well as access his personal records to get more information about his crimes and his death. This is all information I haven't seen."

"I tell you what. I don't give a damn about his reputation or anything you find out about him. All I want is the money. I plan on selling that house and everything in it, and finally getting a life that doesn't mean struggling every day just to get by. You can look through anything you want and do anything you want as long as you help me find my money."

I nod. "I'll do what I can."

CHAPTER TWENTY-FIVE

"REMEMBER THAT TIME WE WENT TO THE FAIR AND XAVIER GOT stuck in the house of mirrors?" I ask the next day when I get back to the hotel, cradling the phone between my neck and shoulder. I toss my bag onto the bed and kick off my shoes, happy for the feeling of the air conditioner on my hot feet.

"How could I ever forget that?" Dean asks.

"Well, it was like that," I say, plopping down onto the bed. "Except there weren't reflections anywhere and he wasn't crawling on his hands and knees in front of us to find his way out. But it seemed almost as twisted. It's a huge house, obviously. So I knew there were going to be a lot of rooms and probably hidden spaces since that's something eccentric wealthy people like to do."

"We should probably not normalize referring to savage serial killers as 'eccentric wealthy people,'" Dean points out.

I switch the phone over to my other ear so I can reach into the nightstand table and get out a menu for an Indian restaurant I saw down the block.

"Fair enough. My point is, I expected to wander around, open a lot of doors that didn't really lead to much, maybe find a couple of closets with false walls and hopefully a couple of safes full of all the information I could possibly ever need to prove Marini was the Emperor, identify all of his victims, and get them back to their families."

"So, nothing ambitious. You were coming in cool and casual," he says.

"Exactly. But when we got in there, it was ridiculous. Not Xavier's house ridiculous, but hallways that had fifteen or twenty doors along them, but only two or three could be opened. The rest were locked. A couple of them seemed like they were sealed or maybe never opened at all."

"Like he was trying to make himself look more impressive than he actually was?" Dean asks.

"Could be. Or he wanted it to be as confusing and frustrating as possible. Like it amused him to think about someone not being able to find their way around the house. There was a room that you went into through a door in the hallway, but then that door didn't have another doorknob on the opposite side. So you couldn't open it to leave. You had to go to the other side of the room, through the bathroom, and use the door leading out of that one in order to make it out of the room."

"That's sick," Dean replies. "I know you said Angelo and Louisa never saw any signs of Marini committing any of his crimes at the mansion, but I can't help but imagine him releasing some hapless girl into that and watching with some sort of messed up hidden camera network as she runs around desperately trying to get out."

The image is graphic and disturbing, but extremely close to what I was already envisioning. We still don't have a clear idea of exactly when Salvador Marini began to take on his persona of the Emperor. I highly doubt it was like flipping a switch. The kinds of things he did only come after escalation. And I've been wondering if the creation of his underground lairs, complete with gladiator arenas, prisoner cells, and other implements of torture, were built as he fantasized about capturing and killing, or if he had already begun his reign of brutality and decided to indulge himself further by making his own hedonistic playgrounds where no one would be able to find them.

My first instinct was to believe he kept the two halves of his life separate. There was Salvador and there was the Emperor, and he kept them apart. Some of the people he encountered in his regular life thought he was charismatic, generous, dynamic, and influential. Others saw him for the controlling, elitist, demanding man he was. It was when he morphed into the Emperor that he indulged his cruelty and decadence.

Allowing the two of them to overlap would be dangerous. It would put him at risk of being caught and his way of life being brought to an end. He was very aware of the people working for him, always in his house or around him. If he were to bring his intended victims to his home and then they were discovered dead, one of his staff might recognize them. But there was also the element of keeping those activities isolated and special in their own sick way. If he kept it hidden away, he got to enjoy the feeling of no one around him knowing what was actually going on. He got to feel a sense of yearning and excitement building up before his visits to his lairs.

But now that I've seen more of his mansion, it doesn't seem as unlikely that he brought at least a couple of his victims there. Somehow that makes the story even more disturbing. I hate to think of Louisa and Angelo working there, spending their days in that very house, not knowing anything that could have happened. A shudder runs through me at the thought of Louisa being forced to clean up, not even knowing what she was doing.

"We found a couple of safes, but they didn't have anything particularly interesting in them," I say. "There are a few locked rooms and some furniture that has locked doors and drawers, so Gwendolyn is going to have to find the keys to those, or find someone who can break through them to find what's inside."

"Do you think the money that's missing will be in one of them?" Dean asks.

"I guess it's possible, but I don't understand why he would take his money out of a bunch of different accounts just to keep it at the house."

"Then what do you think happened to the money?"

"I have no idea," I admit. "It does seem really strange. But Gwendolyn is very motivated to locate that money, so I'm sure I'll find out everything about that mansion soon. I did get a chance to look through some of the paperwork the attorney gave her and noticed a few things. She has the deeds to a couple of the pieces of property where we found his underground lairs. It's right there, legal proof he owns the land."

"What about the new one we found?" he asks.

"No. That's not in there. And neither are a couple of other ones that we have confirmed. But then there's paperwork for pieces of commercial real estate and business ventures no one knew he had anything to do with. A couple of them are partnerships with the same person. Kerrigan Moyer. You ever hear of him?" I ask.

"No," Dean replies.

"Neither had I," I tell him. "I'm going to do some research and see what I can find out about all that. We need to track this missing money. That's key. It could point to a motive for the Cleaners to be called in."

"Do you have it in you to look over a few more papers?" he asks.

"I can always find the strength," I tell him. "Why?"

"I got the copies of my phone records. Because it's me requesting them rather than going through the police or a lawyer or anything, I was able to get them emailed to me. I thought you might want to give them a glance."

"Absolutely. Send them my way. Did you notice anything about them when you looked through them?"

"I don't want to say," he says. "I want you to read through them and let me know your thoughts."

"Sure." I wait for the records to show up and pull them up on my computer. "Okay, I have them up."

"Go ahead and isolate your own phone number and Xavier's and remove them. That will clear the list up for you so it's easier to see everything else."

Dean isn't one to carry on social phone calls with many people, so removing those two phone numbers cuts out a good portion of the list, leaving his clients and a few scattered outliers. It makes patterns easier to see and it takes only a few seconds for me to notice something.

"You didn't get any other calls on that day," I note. "Not until later when Xavier and I started calling you. It's just this same 8431 number."

"That's my client," Dean explains. "The one with the most intensive job I was working at the time. That's who I was talking to when I went outside that day. It was a nasty divorce case. The husband hired me to collect evidence against his soon-to-be ex-wife to show marital misconduct and that she was trying to conceal assets during the divorce."

"That sounds unpleasant," I remark.

"It happens," he says. "Being a private investigator can't always be all sunshine, puppies, missing people, and murder. I vaguely remember starting that conversation. You'll notice he'd already called several times that morning, so the conversations all kind of blend together. But now that Xavier has mentioned me going out to the car, I'm wondering if I'd left my notes out there and needed to get them. A lot of times in cases like this, the client will ask me to take pictures and I like giving them hard copies with notes on the back rather than just digital versions. It gives them something tangible to show their lawyers and possibly bring to court.

"I'd just gotten a few pictures printed for him and I must have left them in the car and went to get them. The case didn't feel like it was really going anywhere. A lot of what I was doing seemed to be just running around following a car and taking pictures of a house. But this guy was insistent, so I did what I was hired to do. Now, this brings us right back to the same question. How did I get from stepping outside on a call with a client, headed to my own car, to getting into a car with apparently at least two other people?

"I didn't get another phone call while I was outside. I didn't get any texts. I went back through my email and I didn't get any messages from around that time. There's still that piece missing. What got me into that car without a struggle?"

"You only talked to your client during that time," I say. "By the way you describe him, it seems like he took up a lot of your time and attention. Maybe you were so distracted by the phone call you didn't notice someone had come up behind you until they already had you. What happened with that client? Are you still working that case?"

"No. He was pissed when I got in touch with him from the hospital because apparently, I missed an important moment he'd wanted me to photograph, but when I explained what was going on, he lightened up a little. It's not like he had much of a choice. I was half-dead in a hospital. I wasn't exactly primed and ready for a photography session. The whole thing dragged on for another couple of weeks after that, then it was done. He didn't call me with an update after, but he sent me a bonus, so I'm assuming it worked out for him," Dean says.

"Hm… what if you get in touch with him?" I suggest. "Ask if he remembers talking to you that day. If you were on the phone with him when whoever it was got a hold of you, maybe he heard something. A voice or your reaction. Something that could give us more of an idea of how the whole thing went down."

"Good idea," he says. "Alright, I've got to go. Xavier's package of scrapbooking supplies arrived and I've been conscripted into sorting stickers. Apparently, they all have to be in their place before we leave tomorrow morning."

"How long are you going to be gone?" I ask.

"A few days at least. There have been a couple of possible sightings of Thomas and Mila Auden and some tips about their movements I need to follow up on. I'm heading to Georgia tomorrow and then Texas."

"How's that frequent flier program working for you?"

"By the end of this case, I'm going to be able to bring the entire crew to the moon."

"Benson is supposed to have his visit with whoever Jonah sends to do his bidding the day after tomorrow. I'll let you know how it goes," I say. "Travel safe."

"Talk to you then."

I end the call and muster up the energy to order dinner, then drag myself into the shower where I contemplate Marini's mansion, his bitter sister, and the sheer volume of stickers Xavier must have ordered.

CHAPTER TWENTY-SIX

BENSON MANDEVILLE SHIFTS IN HIS SEAT, HIS EYES DARTING around the room, and I want to shout at him to sit still. He can't look nervous. He can't look like he's not the one in control. If there's even a hint that someone, especially me, has put him up to this, the entire plan will go to hell before it can even start. He needs to keep it together. He needs to get through this with an attitude and force that will convince the person he's meeting that he's serious. Serious enough for them to bring the message back to Jonah and ensure it's well heard.

I pace back and forth a couple of steps, then stop to look through the window again. I want to walk out into the long, narrow space where Mandeville sits on a cold, scuffed metal stool, waiting on one side of a piece of glass for someone to show up on the other. If I could get out there, I would be able to coach him again. I could talk him through exactly what he needs to say and how he needs to say it. But I can't.

I have to stay out of view. There are people in this prison who know who I am and who wouldn't be thrilled to have me around. They wouldn't hesitate to spread the word I was hanging around again. And I know for damn sure whoever is going to show up on the other side of that glass and pick up the phone to talk to Benson would recognize me in an instant. That would end everything. The second they saw my face, the plan would be done for. And it's very possible Benson would be, too.

That's something I didn't mention to him when we were going over what I need him to do. He knows the job I gave him is important, and that I've promised him immunity in his complicity in Jonah's escape if he goes through with this. But we never talked about the personal danger I know I'm putting him in. I'm essentially asking him to play a trick on the Devil and get out of it with his soul intact.

If Jonah gets word that Benson is trying to manipulate him, or that he's met with me and is helping me, it will paint a huge target right on the young inmate's back. Jonah might not be in the facility anymore, but that means very little for Benson's safety. We could do everything in our power to protect him and keep anyone from getting to him, but I know well enough that those efforts are all but futile if Jonah is truly determined to have his way. He's already proven his ability to get out of and into high-security facilities without detection, and despite what some would consider a downfall after being arrested and imprisoned, he maintains a complex and ravenously loyal network of followers willing to do anything for him.

The most dangerous are the ones he has only just nurtured, the ones seeded in the jails and prisons where he's expanded his empire. Those on the outside have been seasoned, but also largely identified. We know about the elaborate sea monster or mermaid tattoos they earn through devotion and service to Jonah. The new ones are still raw and compulsive, jumpy and eager to display their commitment to the leader who was once a legend and is now a visceral reality. They aren't tattooed. There's no marking to identify them among the rest of the inmates.

He could easily declare hunting season on Benson, sit back, and watch the mayhem unfold.

Even without mentioning it, I think Benson is aware that he's in danger. Maybe not of the extent of it, but he knows he's putting himself out there. Just before today's meeting, when he contacted me to confirm he'd reached out to Jonah through the coded lines of communication they established before his escape and that remind me of my own convoluted way of getting in touch with him, Benson asked what was going to happen to Jonah when this was over. He wanted reassurance he wouldn't be brought back to this facility.

The decision isn't up to me. I can't determine where someone goes to serve out their sentence, but I can make recommendations. And I fully intend to speak to whomever I need to speak to and do whatever I need to do to keep Jonah away from this prison and the relationships he has cultivated here. Part of it is to keep Benson safe, but another part of it is to keep others safe from Benson.

Right now, all the young inmate is thinking about is the possibility of retaliation from Jonah. He knows what Jonah has done and what he is capable of doing. He knows he holds the secrets of Jonah's escape and believes the only thing that's keeping him alive is his cooperation and agreement not to say anything.

What he doesn't understand is, that alone isn't enough to keep Jonah from eliminating him. There's a much higher chance he's alive not because he knows Jonah's secret, but because Jonah sees something in him. He wants to recruit Benson, to turn him into one of his own so he can use him to do whatever he wants to be done in or out of the prison.

He'll twist him and brainwash him. Convince Benson he has a special quality very few have and that he can be a part of something incredible. His prison sentence is just a testing ground. He's there to learn and to grow, and when it's time, they will go out into the world and rebuild Leviathan, controlling the population through the gospel of chaos. He could weaponize him without Benson ever knowing it's happening.

Jonah has told me he's done with that. He doesn't care anymore about the philosophy he once lived by. He has no intention of carrying on with the horror he meted out on unsuspecting people in the name of creating a better world. And I don't believe him for a second.

I think he's stepped back. I think he has slowed down on his destruction. And I also think it's building up inside him at a terrifying pace, building up pressure ready to explode at any instant. He's never going to walk away from his hunger for dominance. Inside him is still that broken child his brother had to stand up for. The rejected young man who watched that same twin brother marry the woman he was obsessed with. He'd never let himself feel those things again.

Benson's visitation time is disappearing as he sits there with no one on the other side of the glass. My stomach twists as I wonder if somehow Jonah has found out what I'm planning. Maybe I was too quick to believe Deandre Wright was a victim of his circumstances, a man who made a bad choice and would be willing to make up for it. He could be gaining more from the transaction with Jonah than just being able to keep his job because of the agreement not to talk about his seizures. Jonah could have already gotten to him.

I'm about to call off the plan and go into crisis aversion mode to get Benson out of the facility when the door to the visitor section of the room opens and a guard escorts a woman I don't recognize down the narrow space and to the cubicle across from him. I step up closer to the window that looks down over the meeting area. Usually, there are only guards here, supervising the visits happening below. Even with no contact between visitors and inmates, a lot can happen when the prisoners communicate with someone from the outside world. Not to mention the conflict that can unfold between the inmates themselves.

I'm only thinking about Benson and the woman sitting across from him. She doesn't look familiar, but I try to dig back into my mind to sift through my memories and look for her face. It would be easier to think this was someone who was already following Jonah before he went into prison rather than yet another life he has taken over. But I can't bring her forward. I don't remember her in any of my interactions with Jonah's followers or in any of the footage of his horrific plans being executed.

They each pick up a receiver and lean toward the glass as they talk. Even from this distance, it's obvious they are keeping their voices low to keep their words away from the others on either side of them. As he talks, his body posture relaxes. He's settling into the ruse and looking more at ease. It takes some of the tension out of my neck, but I know I won't be able to relax completely until this is all over.

The woman lifts her hand and presses her palm to the glass in front of her in the same gesture countless other women repeat every day in this space. From them, it's a sign of longing and connection. From this woman, though, it means something else. Benson looks at her hand for a moment, then rests his against it. The shared sentiment lasts only a second before she stands and leaves.

"What was that?" I demand. I look back at the guard there with me. "What was that?"

He doesn't know the real reason I'm here. The Warden and I agreed it would be safest to share the details with as few people as possible. Everyone else would either get the cover story from when I first met with Benson and Wright, or not get any explanation at all. They didn't need to know.

"It looks like they were saying goodbye," he says.

"I sure as hell hope not," I mutter, stalking out of the room and down the secure staircase.

I get to the empty classroom seconds before Officer Wright leads Benson in, his hands cuffed behind his back like they usually are when walking through the prison. He closes the door and releases the cuffs. The guard's eyes meet mine and he gives a single nod.

"Her information is on the sign-in form," he confirms.

"Good. Who was she? Have you ever seen her?"

Both men shake their heads.

"No," Benson says. "He's sent a couple people before, but never her."

"What was that thing at the end with your hands?" I ask. "What did it mean?"

"She had a message from Jonah written on her palm to prove he sent her," Benson explains. "I'm supposed to have the same thing written on my hand when he sends someone else next week."

"Draw it for me," I say. "We'll make sure it's done. Did she say anything that makes it seem like he's suspicious?"

"No," Benson says. "He told her to remember my message and get it to him in full. Then she reassured me Jonah heard I had concerns and is waiting to fix the situation however he can."

"Alright, perfect. Next week you'll meet with whoever he sends, tell them there's someone on the outside you need him to take care of, and we'll go from there." I look at Deandre Wright. "Have you talked to the Warden yet?"

His face is stiff, but he gives a single nod. "I asked to take on new responsibilities and he agreed to take me off of transport."

"Good. It will be better this way."

"As long as you tell him I did what you asked of me and put in a good word for a better placement," he presses.

"When this is done, I will," I say. And I'm being completely honest.

I know I'm walking a fine ethical line with my decision not to turn him in for helping Jonah. I'm sure there are plenty of people who would say I'm doing something wrong. That he should be prosecuted, not rewarded. I know what he did was wrong. But I am also a strong believer in restorative justice. Wright made a choice based on the circumstances he was facing. He did what he felt he had to do. And he likely saved his own life doing it. There's a reason discretion exists. As of the moment I found out what happened and he agreed to help me, I consider both of these men informants for the FBI. They've earned forgiveness.

CHAPTER TWENTY-SEVEN

M Y PHONE RINGS AS I'M LEAVING THE PRISON.

"Agent Griffin," I answer after seeing an unfamiliar number on the screen.

"Agent Griffin, this is Julian Ruiz. I'm a friend of your cousin Dean."

"Yes. I remember him telling me about you. How are you, Officer Ruiz?" I say, climbing into the car.

"I'm doing well. I'm calling to let you know that Jason Hoyt, the owner of the property that we've been investigating, is back in the country and is willing to meet with you when it's convenient."

"Does he know I want to go down into the underground structure?" I ask.

I stop myself short of calling it a lair. I know that's what's behind the hatch, beyond the small area that was photographed. I know that when I'm allowed to, I'll walk into a manmade cavern of rooms and alcoves, designed for one purpose and one purpose only: to imprison human beings and make them do the bidding of a man who thought of himself as an all-powerful ruler. They weren't people. They were entertainment.

But Marini was never named an official suspect in the crimes. He was never investigated. The case is still considered open. I have to tread carefully to avoid tainting the investigation and possibly having it closed and access cut off before I can get all the answers I need. Dean told me his friend with the department recognized the details of the space as being similar to the case he was looking into, so they know it's being unofficially linked to a serial killer. We just have to bide our time and ensure we aren't going on assumption, but actual fact.

"Yes," Ruiz confirms. "He's aware that's what you intend to do and he's open to it, with the condition that he meets with you first and can accompany you."

"Do you think that's a good idea?" I ask. "This could be a critical piece of evidence in a massive serial murder investigation."

"And it could be nothing. The reality is, this is still his property. Until it's been declared a crime scene, the chief has determined that whatever is under there is accessible only by permission from the owner of the property. The judge hasn't issued a search warrant, so we're at the mercy of Jason Hoyt. He can withdraw permission for anyone to be on the land and block access to whatever is down there whenever he wants, and then we'd have to go through the hassle of getting warrants and proving probable cause."

"You're right," I say. "It's better to have his cooperation. I just don't feel comfortable with someone no one knows being so up close and personal to the investigation."

"I'll make sure that's noted. Do you want me to tell Dean?"

"No. I'll call him. Thank you. Please give Mr. Hoyt my contact information and let him know I will be in town tomorrow. I'm ready to meet with him whenever he's available."

The call ends and I immediately dial Dean. I'm surprised when he answers so quickly.

"Hey," he says. "You caught me right at lunch."

"I was wondering why you answered. I figured you'd be busy and I'd need to leave a message. I can let you go so you can enjoy your break."

"No. Go ahead. I'm just sitting here with a box lunch while Xavier goes over the kidnapping case from last year," he explains. "There are a lot of conflicting feelings about that whole situation. I want to know what he thinks of it."

"Always a good move. I just got a call from your buddy Julian," I tell him. "Jason Hoyt is back in town and ready to meet with me. He says I can go underground and see what's going on down there, but he insists on going with me."

"I thought you expected that. To ensure no one plants any evidence and that he's aware of everything going on with his property," he says, referencing the last time we talked about the possibility of Hoyt wanting to be involved in the investigation.

"I know. It made sense to me then, but now that it's actually happening, I feel strange about it. He's a wild card. And we have no idea what we're going to find down there. We know what *could* be there. Both of us have been in more than one of these lairs. But how is he going to react if he sees evidence of one of the Gladiator fights? Or what if the body of one of the women is still there? We know there are victims that haven't been accounted for. A civilian doesn't need to go through that."

"It's his choice, Emma. You can't stop him. But you can do what you can to protect him. Go in first. Make sure he doesn't wander away from you and stumble on anything. Make sure you emphasize to him how important it is that he doesn't touch anything or move anything. It is his property, but he could really compromise the investigation if he doesn't follow your instructions," Dean says. "You know. Standard practice."

I chuckle. "Listen to you sounding like an agent."

"I have my moments. When are you going?"

"I told Julian to let him know I'll be in town tomorrow. I'm not sure if you can be able to meet me then, but he said whenever it was convenient, so I might. Is there any way you would be able to get there and meet me?"

He mutters a profanity under his breath. "No. I'm completely slammed for the next couple of days. I really wanted to go in there with you."

"I know. But I don't think I should delay it. If Hoyt's giving me permission to go in now, I think I should take advantage of it. Especially considering he could just wander down there by himself and I don't think anybody wants that."

"No, you're right. You need to go. I just wish I could be there."

"I do, too. I'll take pictures and video if I can," I reply.

"Thank you."

I know the gravity of this situation for Dean. It's personal for him even more than it is professional. He refuses to call himself a victim, but he is one of the men who'd been taken and abused by the Emperor. He survived, but there's a gnawing memory in the back of his mind, a gunshot at close range, that makes him wonder if there was someone else there with him who didn't.

Knowing I'll need to spend a night or two near the wooded lot where the lair was discovered, I gather up the clothes I wore over the last couple of days and stuff them into a laundry bag. There are no laundry facilities in this hotel and I've always felt strange about using the full-service laundry option for regular clothes. I might have a suit or dress dry cleaned while staying at a hotel, but it feels needlessly lazy to toss my socks and jeans out in the hallway so they'll come back folded and starched.

A quick internet search of the area shows a coin-operated laundry a few blocks away, so I load up the laundry, my messenger bag stuffed with work files, and my computer, and head out. It's still early enough in the day for the sun to beat down through the windshield as I take the short drive. I'm glad for my dark sunglasses and the air conditioner that doesn't quite rival the hotel room but still creates a distinct chill around the edges of my face.

The laundromat is in a little shopping center anchored by a gas station on one end and a tiny ice cream shop on the other. It's one of those very Southern destinations designed to pack as much function as possible into little pockets of businesses.

I haul everything into the laundromat and stake my claim on a back corner. The building is quiet at this time of day, but there are a couple of other people scattered among the rows of washing machines and dryers. The air is heady with the blended smells of several different types of detergent and fabric softener, and the soft tumbling sounds are almost hypnotic.

I buy a packet of detergent and get my load washing before settling into one of the cream-colored molded chairs bolted to the linoleum floor to the side of a folding station. Digging the folder of papers Gwendolyn gave me out of my bag, I spread it out on the chair beside me so I can read through the individual papers one by one.

The missing money is a strange wrinkle in Salvador Marini's ongoing story; one I didn't expect. His name was synonymous with exorbitant wealth and he was well-known for being a savvy businessman. The idea that his accountants got his worth that far off seems extremely unlikely. There's the possibility he was hiding money. Maybe in an effort to evade taxes. Maybe because he could feel us breathing down his neck and needed to fund a new life away from his crimes. But if that were the case, it seems he would be smart enough to make the adjustments with his lawyer so the discrepancy wouldn't be so easy to detect.

Easy to detect, yet impossible to explain so far.

I'm reading through the records of a few transactions that happened in the weeks before Marini's death when I hear the lid of the washing machine ahead of me open. My chair has me close to the dryers and a dozen or so feet away from the washer, but I know the exact one I used. And there's a man standing in front of it with the lid up.

"Excuse me," I say, putting the papers aside so I can stand up. "That's my washer."

The man looks up and an expression that shifts from startled to embarrassed to confused crosses his face. He looks back down at the paused load and then at me.

"Oh. I'm sorry. I thought this one was mine."

He closes the lid and steps back. As he walks toward the next aisle of washers, I notice he's gripping a bag of laundry close to his leg. He walks slowly along the row of machines, glancing over at me until I sit back down. Keeping my head down as I pretend to read, I continue to watch him. He opens the lid of another washer, only a few inches this time, and I see his hand move quickly toward the lid and back down. He closes the machine and then moves on to the next aisle. He repeats this a couple of times, seeming to avoid the machines closest to the people focused on their own laundry.

It takes a few seconds to realize he's slipping individual garments into the machines that are already washing. A flicker of sympathy goes through me and I turn my attention fully to the paper in my lap. I'm interested to see how he manages to reclaim the laundry he's piggybacking on others' loads, but I'm not going to say anything.

By the time my laundry is done, I've made some notes about some of Marini's transactions and business moves, but I don't feel any closer to knowing what happened to the missing money, or if it has anything to do with his death.

As I walk out of the laundromat, I leave a folded pair of shorts that aren't mine on the edge of the folding table.

CHAPTER TWENTY-EIGHT

Sam

Sandra Cooper
Merritt Randall
Melissa Toland
Christine Jarret
Lisa Huckabee
Linda Smith
Corrine Dreyer
Perry Samson
Gus Vanderbilt

H E COULD HAVE KEPT WRITING, BUT SAM STOPPED AT THOSE NINE. He'd chosen them because they lived close enough to Rose's home for him to travel to easily, at least according to the information he'd found online. If he didn't get what he needed from them, he could continue on. There were plenty more victims of Alfa-Corps for him to find.

Discovering the sordid reputation of the company Marie had been researching in the weeks leading up to her death energized him. He was already motivated when he came here, enough that he'd left his life behind in Sherwood to focus completely on bringing this chapter of his life, and his family's life, to a close. But it was the kind of motivation that came from just knowing something had to be done, not necessarily knowing how it was going to get done.

But all the little nuggets of data salvaged from the computer changed that. It turned the picture from a vague outline to a definite shape. Now he felt like he wasn't just gazing into the distance in the right direction, but starting to move that way.

But there was still so much to figure out. Marie's writing career was something she'd wanted for a long time. Even when her life was derailed by her poor decisions or just the circumstances she'd found herself in, that had been the one thing she'd held tightly to, the biggest dream she'd been working for. She didn't always talk about it. Sam knew it was because she didn't think anyone would actually believe in her.

"Everyone thinks they can be a writer," she'd once said to Sam when they were younger. *"And yet, so few can actually do it."*

But she held onto that determination. She fueled it with journals and scribbled notes. It wasn't the kind of forlorn, melodramatic poetry and tortured short stories people would probably expect from someone living through the challenging life she was. Instead, she took news, ideas, and issues from the world around her and distilled them into words.

She wrote out her opinions. She recorded important moments. There were even rants about famous crimes and verdicts and how she thought the cases should have been handled. It was clear her passion wasn't just writing. It was informing.

And she'd gotten the opportunity. But the only work she could find was for magazines and websites that wanted to push out cheap clickbait garbage. She didn't care about celebrity gossip or gardening tips. Human interest pieces could be more interesting, but they still fell short of her desire to dig deep and create the kind of news that would catch people's attention and not let go.

And looking at the bits of research that they'd recovered made it seem like she'd gotten there. They just couldn't figure out who she was doing it for.

But for right now, he needed to focus on what he did have, rather than wondering about what he didn't. And what he did have was names of victims who had suffered because of the reckless business practices of Alfa-Corps. Sam hoped talking to them might shed more light on what they'd done. Maybe one of them would have even spoken to Marie and would be able to push him further in the right direction.

With his list of names and the few identifying details he had about each of them sitting beside him, Sam opened his computer and pulled up social media. His steps to contact the victims would start there.

CHAPTER TWENTY-NINE

"AGENT GRIFFIN, IT'S GREAT TO SEE YOU AGAIN," SAYS JULIAN Ruiz.

It's not something I'm used to hearing from a person I've only seen over a video call, but I suppose these are the times we're living in. The video call was to give me more information about what they have so far and to give me directions to the property so I would know how to access the area easily. But it's different seeing him in person. The officer in front of me has a bright smile and the kind of sparkling eyes that always surprise me in people who have chosen this field. Sam has those eyes. They've lost some of their light recently, but I know it's still in there.

"Call me Emma," I tell him. "Any friend of my cousin Dean's is a friend of mine. And that is one of those sentences you don't actually think you will ever say in real life until you hear it coming out of your mouth."

The words all blend together and he laughs.

"I guess they wouldn't be cliches if they weren't ever actually said. You can call me Julian." He looks behind me and frowns. "Dean isn't with you?"

"Unfortunately he isn't able to make it today. He's working a pretty intensive case and it has him going all over."

"Adding up those frequent flier miles," he says.

"He told you that, too," I reply with a laugh. "He really wanted to get the chance to go inside, but he wasn't able to make it back here in time and I didn't think we should wait. If Mr. Hoyt is willing to cooperate, it's probably best to jump on it while we have the chance before he changes his mind. Or decides to embark on his own personal investigation."

"I agree," Julian nods. "And so do the detectives."

"Are they here?" I ask. "Did they already go down?"

I try to keep the disappointment out of my voice, reminding myself this isn't technically my investigation. Until this is truly and officially linked to the Emperor case, I'm in effect a guest of the police department responding to the property.

"No. Jason Hoyt was very specific that he wanted who he called 'the feisty FBI agent investigating the serial killer.'"

"How did he know about that?" I raise an eyebrow.

"When Detective Mitchell spoke with him, he used your theory about the underground area to help Hoyt understand how important it is for the space to be officially investigated as quickly as possible. He didn't give any details, just said you believe this could be connected to a network of other similar crime scenes linked to multiple murders. Hoyt seemed fascinated by the idea that the FBI wanted something to do with his property. I guess he looked into your career."

"Yeah, that's not the first time that's happened." It takes me a beat for what he said to sink in. "Feisty? Did he seriously call me feisty?"

"That was the word Mitchell used," Julian chuckles apologetically.

"I'm not a fan of that. Anyway, if he only agreed to me being here, why are you here?" I ask.

The slight upturn of the corners of his mouth makes me realize my tone, but I don't bother to correct it.

"Detective Mitchell figures you would find a way to do this by yourself anyway, so he isn't going to get in your way. He said by your reputation, you can handle it just fine and call him if needed. But personally? I know for a fact that Dean would string me up if he knew I let you do this without at least backup in the vicinity. So, here I am."

I laugh. "Well, thank you for your dedication. Detective Mitchell is right. I tend to favor immediacy and efficiency over protocol, but as

I've recently been informed, the older and wiser version of myself recognizes and values the importance of thinking things through and making good decisions. Considering my gun my backup is not one of those good choices, so I appreciate you being here."

"Absolutely."

"I am going to ask that you stay up here on the surface unless Hoyt invites you down," I tell him.

Julian's lips press together and he gives a single, resigned nod. "Yep."

"Agent Griffin?"

I turn around toward the sound of the voice and see a man coming toward us through the trees. Julian was waiting for me several yards away from the traces of bright yellow tape still clinging to the trees near the entrance to the underground space. Because of the controversy surrounding the actual ownership of the land and the inability of the police to simply go in, the tape they'd put up was taken down and searches of the area were suspended. Depending on what we find today, they will start again soon.

"Hi," I say, extending my hand.

He takes it, meeting my eyes with an unwavering, green-flecked hazel stare. He looks several years younger than me, but there are still bits of peppery gray at the temples of his dark hair. His clean-shaven face shows off a friendly smile that reminds me this man called me 'feisty.' It sets me slightly on edge. I want to be here because he wants to help the investigation, not so that I can amuse him.

"Jason Hoyt," he introduces me.

"Mr. Hoyt, thank you for agreeing to meet with me and give me access to the structure," I say as our hands fall away from each other.

"Jason," he insists. "I appreciate you coming."

He seems to glance behind me like he's scrutinizing Julian. I gesture at him.

"This is Officer Ruiz. He's here to secure the area and provide assistance as needed," I tell him. "The potential danger associated with this discovery really shouldn't be underplayed."

Jason nods. "I understand. Officer, thank you for being here."

That lessens my concern that he may have already ventured down and discovered there was nothing and was now just wanting me here for fun.

Heat is prickling on the back of my neck and sweat rolls in beads down my spine. I wish we'd agreed to meet somewhere else before coming here. As eager as I am to get down into the lair and find out what's there, we need to talk first.

"Why did you ask specifically for me to be here today?" I ask.

"When I was told about law enforcement wanting to investigate my property, your name came up. I had heard it before and I was curious why you might be involved. The detective I spoke to explained your thoughts on what was found and I believed you were taking the situation seriously. I looked into the other details of the cases you believe are linked and I feel the same way. I think if this space really is what you think it is, you are going to be the one who will carry the case through."

"You know no official suspect has been named in the case," I tell him.

"Yes," he says. The smile is gone from his face now. "But, as I said, Agent Griffin, I know who you are. I know you wouldn't be so fervent about pursuing this case if you didn't believe you could prove your suspicions. And if something horrible happened on my property, I want to know it will be handled with the respect and determination you will bring to it. If what you're saying about this place is true, this is way bigger than anything a local PD can handle, and I trust your extensive expertise with the Bureau to finally put an end to this. I just want to do my part to help any way I can."

"Thank you, Jason," I say. "This is an intense situation and a very personal case for me. I can assure you I will put every resource at my disposal into closing it. Can you tell me more about the property? Why you bought it and what else is here. I heard you invest widely in a variety of businesses and real estate. What about this piece of property specifically drew you to it? How much time have you spent on it?"

Jason nods. "Sure. This particular property, I purchased after receiving a tip from an associate who believed the land had good potential for development. There used to be a school here, but other than that, it hasn't been used for much. The woods are largely untouched and there is a tremendous amount of space that can be utilized for any number of projects. The original plan was for a multi-use development. There's an area that could easily be cleared for residential use and another that could fit a shopping center or an outlet mall. I was planning on starting basically a self-contained little suburb out here.

"But after purchasing the land and actually seeing it, those purposes didn't seem to fit anymore. At least not at that moment. It's beautiful here and I feel like there is potential that hasn't been considered. And so, I honestly haven't quite figured out what I want to do with this area. I just can't bring myself to bulldoze this place down and pave it over. And because I've been focusing on my other investments, this one has just been on the back burner for a while."

I can't find fault with the answer. He's right. The area is beautiful and it would be a shame to decimate the trees to pack in houses, roads, and stores.

"I understand you want to be present while I search the space," I say.

"Yes. I want to know what's found in real time," he nods. "I don't want to be uninformed."

"Do you have any questions?"

"Why do you think this is linked to the serial killer you are investigating?"

I should have expected the question, but it's bold and blunt, like a barrier he's putting up.

"The pictures I was shown have indications of this underground structure being structurally similar to other locations we've confirmed are related to the crimes. We've also done research into the history of this property and found no records of there being any kind of structure built here when it was operating as a school. If it was built for school use, like a bomb shelter or storage, it would be on the plans for the area. But it isn't. Which means it was built either before the school opened and went unnoticed, or after the school closed.

"In my opinion, it is extremely unlikely something like this would never have been found when this place was active as a school. The materials used for the hatch and the areas that we have documented are not consistent with building materials and methods of the time before the school. This means it must have been built after the school closed and the land was abandoned. But so far there isn't a conclusive timeline for it."

Hoyt nods. "If you do determine this is connected to your killer, what will happen to the land? Will it be seized?" he asks.

"No. It's your property. We'll need access to it for investigation, but it won't be taken from you. After the investigation is done, it will be up to you to decide what to do with the actual underground structure."

"Alright," he answers simply.

"Okay. Before we go down into the structure, I need to ask you if you are completely sure you want to go. I can absolutely understand your curiosity, but I have no way of knowing exactly what's down there, and what I've already witnessed has been difficult for even seasoned officers and agents to digest. You may see some horrific things. I need to know you are prepared for that."

"Yes. I want to see it."

I nod. "Then I'm ready when you are."

CHAPTER THIRTY

T HE OFFICERS WHO INITIALLY RESPONDED TO THE DISCOVERY OF the strange entrance hatch didn't really step into the space beyond it. At the time, they didn't have any idea what they were looking at. All they saw was a hatch that opened to a set of steps leading down into the ground. It was suspicious and scared the hell out of the teenagers who'd stumbled on it in the first place, but there was no actual probable cause that would allow them to search it. People are allowed to do just about anything they want with the land they own. Including digging down in the ground and building elaborate structures if they please.

Until the police have reasonable suspicion that modifications like that are related to something criminal, they don't have the right to go in and search without permission. It's the same rules as a person's home. They can't just demand access or go in on a whim. There has to be some sort of clear and reasonable suspicion that a crime has been committed or is presently being committed in that space.

My gut tells me this is another of Marini's lairs. It fits the hallmarks of the others and the description from the one boy who was courageous, or dumb, enough to open the hatch when they first found it has stayed with me since I heard it. There were only two descriptors used. Two things that stuck out to them enough that they fled the area and contacted the police, even though they were on the land illegally.

It was dark.

It had a terrible smell.

But assumptions aren't enough. Oddity isn't enough. Not even the bad smell is enough. If one of the officers who responded identified the smell as decomposition, they might have had grounds to enter, but none of them pressed that issue. They decided to follow protocol and take the easier route of waiting for permission.

Now I am finally getting the chance to find out the true extent of what's really down here. The officers took a few photos of the entrance but didn't go any further. Even those small glimpses were enough to ignite in my belly and draw me here.

"I'll be waiting right here," Julian says as I follow behind Jason to the entrance hatch.

He's really saying it as much for Jason's benefit as for mine.

"I'll let you know if we need you," I say.

The hatch was closed again after the police took pictures, and I don't wait for Jason's permission to open it. He might be insisting on coming down with me, but Dean's words were absolutely correct. It's up to me to protect him while I am searching whatever is down there. I need to try to limit his exposure to any gruesome trademarks of the Emperor's work, so he doesn't have to have them seared into his mind forever.

But I'm also very aware of the need to protect myself and the integrity of the investigation. Even with another officer here, this type of search presents inherent risks and dangers. I have to be aware of my surroundings and aware of Jason at all times. Stepping back from the now-open hatch, I take out my phone and start a recording.

"I'd like to document this search if I have your permission," I say.

I don't turn the camera toward him. Preserving the privacy of people unwittingly linked to crime is critical, and the way he takes a step back as if trying to keep himself from being recorded tells me he feels the same way.

"Yes," he says quickly.

"Thank you." I document the date and time and describe the property and circumstances that brought me to it. This creates a record of the evidence, which will come in handy once we get everything documented and set up in court. "I'm going to ask that you go in first, and once we are both down there, please do not get behind me. Stay to my side and please do not touch or disturb anything."

I step to the side and have Jason go through the hatch first. I know from the pictures that there is nothing horrific just inside, and I am not going to put myself in the potentially dangerous situation of going underground with someone I don't know behind me operating the hatch.

The smell hits me before I'm fully inside. It's a stomach-turning combination of damp, putrid, and stale. A heaviness of dirt in the background isn't the rich earthy smell I'd imagine, but dry and dusty.

Staying right at the entrance, I pull the black metal flashlight from my belt and turn it on. The beam sweeps across the area around me, showing that we're standing in the small vestibule-like area the police photographed the first time they came. Ahead of us is a door standing partially open. Walking up to it, I position my phone to record the complex locking mechanism along the inside edge.

"There's no sign of the lock being broken. It seems it was unlocked and then not put back in place. Earlier photographs show the door is in the same position it was during the preliminary search."

My eyes slide over to Jason and I watch him examine the lock from a few steps away. He leans slightly forward, like he's trying to get a better look without getting in the way of the video. I take a step forward and he comes along, staying beside me and in my range of peripheral sight just as I asked. I'm aware of his hands and the positioning of his feet as we move through the doorway. As soon as I am inside, I turn so I am facing him directly, ushering him with the movement to come around so I am standing near the opening of the door rather than him.

I sweep the beam of my flashlight across this new space. It's a curved corridor with large windows cut out of the gray stone forming a wall in front of us. I know this space. It looks exactly like the corridors we've found in each of the other lairs we've uncovered. Which means I know what is beyond those windows, through the thick, unbreakable glass.

This is what Julian was talking about when he told Dean they saw something that looked like an underground arena. They didn't go beyond the wall, but they could see inside. I walk along the corridor, staying close to the wall looking for the entrance.

"Does this property have electricity?" I ask Jason. "The school obviously had it, but do you know if they removed the transformer when the building was taken down?"

"When I bought it, the agent said it was utilities-ready. It was a big selling point that it would be easy to get any new buildings connected."

"But you don't have anything connected, so you haven't been paying any bills for it," I say.

"There isn't any development on the property," Jason points out. "No buildings that would need to use electricity."

I nod and continue my search for the door to the arena. Finally, I find a hook in the wall where a heavy chain is coiled and tied in place. Just like the other lairs, this chain is attached to a gate-style door that lifts up and out of the way, rather than swinging in or out of the space beyond the wall. I make sure to record the entire area and then release the chain.

It takes some effort to work the mechanism that lifts the gate, but it finally moves out of the way and I'm able to step into the gap in the stone wall. Stretching out ahead of me, further than the beam of the flashlight touches, is a massive dirt-floored arena.

I draw in a breath and continue forward slowly, illuminating the ground in front of my feet before every step. A second later, I notice a set of footprints.

"Stop," I tell Jason. "I need to mark where you are."

Showing only his feet, I record where he's standing in relation to me and the position of the door. Then I move the phone up slowly to show three interlocking trails of footprints crossing the open dirt area.

"Is there any way to tell when the prints were left here?" Jason asks.

"Not just by looking at them," I say with a shake of my head. "Casts could be made of them to try to get more information about them, but that will be the size and type of shoes, and if there was more than one person. It's unlikely they can be dated."

It isn't the presence of the prints that is bothering me. I expected to see signs of movement down here. It's the placement of them in combination with the unlocked door and hatch. The dirt of the arena had been refreshed like it was being prepared for another fight. But I don't see Marini being careless enough to leave this place unsecured. Either he had to abandon this lair suddenly, or someone else had access to the space and went in—likely after his death, because they didn't care about making sure it was locked when they left again.

I go to the edge of the arena and start following the wall, pausing when the flashlight falls on blood splattered across the stone. I make sure there are several seconds of footage recorded to show the aftermath of what was likely a brutal blow. It's confirmation that this is one of Marini's underground buildings and that it was used for one of the horrific gladiator fights that claimed so many lives.

There's more of the staining several feet ahead and I take a breath, knowing this is only going to get worse from here.

Remembering the layout of the other lairs I've already searched, I follow along the edge of the arena until I find a door. Like the others, it's unlocked and I'm able to pull it open. The steps leading up are narrow and I have Jason go up ahead of me so I don't have him at my back. They lead to the boxed seating area where the Emperor would sit and watch the fights unfolding below. If this lair is like the others, there are more of these suites positioned around the curve of the arena, accessible from different corridors and rooms.

This seems to have two purposes. The different rooms gave him a variety of angles to choose from so he could customize his viewing experience. This fit in with his unquenchable need to have everything exactly as he wanted, when he wanted it. Having just one option wasn't enough for him. He wanted *options*. He wanted to be able to control every second of the narrative.

But I think there's another reason. The fact that the other rooms are accessible through various points in the larger underground complex tells me he wanted to be able to get to them quickly and easily. This main box allowed him to watch from the prime position and go down into the carnage if he pleased. It was for when he was prepared in advance for the fight. There's a ceremonial quality to it. The others are still luxurious, but smaller. It tells me there were times when he was surprised by a fight and rushed to the nearest room to watch. I can only imagine these were used when it took some time for a victim to arrive. As soon as they did, he'd take his place and watch as the servant he called Charon ushered the new fighter into the arena and released his opponent into battle.

I'm staring through the glass at the front of the room, tinted to prevent anyone from being able to see in, when a sudden burst of light temporarily blinds me. I jump back from the counter along the wall under the window and wait for my vision to return.

"What the hell?" I demand.

"I found a light switch," Jason says.

"I told you not to touch anything," I snap.

"You needed light."

"Don't touch anything else." I look down again and see the full horror of the arena, the blood on the walls, weapons on hooks ready to be grabbed and used, metal grates that lead to the holding cells where the fighters waited until they were forced out and into war. "Oh, my god."

I hold up my phone and record the scene dutifully, holding in my horror as best as I can as I zoom in on the dried blood on the axes, maces, chains, and other implements of torture on the walls.

"What now?" Jason asks.

I straighten, lowering my shoulders and setting my jaw.

"Have you had enough? Do you want me to bring you back to Officer Ruiz and I can see the rest myself?" I ask.

"No," he says.

"Then we keep going."

CHAPTER THIRTY-ONE

"**L**OOK AT THAT THING," DEAN SAYS, WATCHING THE RECORDING on my shared screen as we video chat. "It's even more elaborate than the other ones. This has to be his primary lair."

He sounds almost excited as he says it and I understand why. We've assumed from the beginning of the investigation into the Emperor and his crimes that while he had several underground hideaways, we would eventually find his favorite. It would be where he felt the most comfortable and indulge himself most lavishly. More importantly for us, it would likely be where he kept personal items that would identify Marini as the Emperor and possibly confirm the identities of more of his victims. We've been searching for it, and now it seems we've found it.

"I thought the same thing while I was going through it. Look at the pictures of the rooms with the beds. There are at least five of them. In the other lairs we've found, there were one or two of that kind of room, but this one had an entire wing."

It's not intentional, but as I talk about them, I find myself carefully choosing the words to describe what felt like a high-end bordello when I was walking through it. Each of the rooms is different, themed and decorated down to the most meticulous detail. It only furthers the sense that this is a valued space to him. This is where he brought the girls he was most intrigued by, the ones he wanted to keep for longer than just a couple of hours.

"I can't believe how many rooms there are. It just keeps going," he says.

"I don't even think the video does justice to it. It's mind-boggling how big this thing is. The arena alone is massive, but then there are the cells, the bordello rooms, his private observation rooms, at least two lounges, and what look like bedrooms for guests he might have invited to enjoy his twisted festivities with him, which I don't even want to think about. How does something this massive get built underground and no one knows?

"I know several teams of contractors were used so that none of them knew what was going on in full, but this is an undertaking I can't even wrap my brain around. This would take months, if not years to build something like this. I just don't understand how it could be done without more people noticing."

"What I don't understand is the woods," Dean adds. "How is this place under all those trees and it looks like none of them have been disturbed?"

"I don't know," I admit. "It's not like it's an area of new growth. Those are not young trees or things that just kind of grew up over the last few years. This is an established area. They aren't huge, towering species, but they are definitely big enough and with enough undergrowth to show they've been around. And only a couple hundred yards from the hatch is where the schoolyard used to be. All the structures and modifications like parking lots and things were torn out a long time ago, but the space is fairly open. Some young trees, bushes, that kind of thing, but definitely enough area for this thing to be under it and for those things to have grown up over any disturbed ground after it was put in."

The presence of the hatch in what seems like a fairly dense wooded area is strange. I know from going into the lair that the hatch leads directly into a smaller vestibule area but then goes into the main section of the structure. Constructing something like that would require extensive excavation of the area, but the trees, undergrowth, and rocks scattered around the entrance are undisturbed. It illuminates why this particular lair, possibly even more so than the others, has gone undetected for the many years it has to have been there.

This is not a new structure. It was not just put into place soon before Marini's death. The age of the space sends a chill along my spine. It means he was likely active even before we thought. How many victims do we not know about? How many people were brought through those trees and into the hatch never to see sunlight again?

"What about the guy that owns the property?" Dean asks. "What kind of vibe did you get from him?"

I let out a breath and shake my head slightly. "Jason Hoyt. I'm not sure about him. There's something that didn't sit right with me from the first moment I saw him. He was really friendly. Like he was excited to have me there."

"He probably was," Dean offers. "I'm sure finding out a serial killer might have built a murder complex under a piece of land he owns was a bit on the unsettling side. But a big-time businessman like him could easily rake in the profits on that story. Practically build a kitschy Emperor-themed tourist trap. It's distasteful, sure, but these things happen all the time."

I shake my head. "No, that's not the vibe I got from him. It was more like he was really excited to help me solve the case. And not that I don't welcome that. But it felt off."

"How did he react to what you found inside?" Dean asks. "You didn't show him on the video."

"I thought it would be better not to have him be documented as linked to any of it. He was stoic through most of it. I tried not to say too much or bring too much attention to some of the details because I didn't want to make it traumatizing for him, but there were things he couldn't exactly avoid. He saw the blood and the weapons. The cells for the fighters. The tools in the darker bordello rooms. There was no way he didn't start piecing things together about what happened in those spaces. He didn't say anything about them. He was very quiet. Emotionless."

"How would you have wanted him to react?" Dean asks. "Scream and run? Cry? Laugh?"

"Well, I don't think laughing would be the right choice there."

"It would make you feel better about being suspicious about him," he says.

"I'm not suspicious of him. I don't have a reason to be," I clarify. "We know Salvador Marini was the Emperor. But Hoyt? I don't know. Something just put me on edge about him. Like he might have gone down there by himself before telling the detective he was willing to meet with me."

"What would be the point of doing that and not telling you about it? It's not like he was under orders to stay out of there. It's still his property and he can do whatever he wants. What would be the point of not telling you that he'd already checked it out? Or if he had gone down there and saw those things, why wouldn't he get in touch with the detective and let them know?" Dean points out.

"To deflect suspicion?" I suggest. "This place still hasn't been officially linked to any of the other ones or to the murders as of yet, and Salvador Marini hasn't been publicly named a suspect in those deaths. Until the investigation catches up, he could worry people would think he did these things." A thought pops into my head. "The lights. I can't believe I didn't even mention it. He turned the lights on."

I scroll back through the video and show Dean the moment when the lights in the observation box as well as the arena below burst on. "When that happened, I paused the recording because I didn't know what was going on. But he's the one who turned them on. He said he found the switch and thought it would be helpful to have some light even though I told him specifically not to touch anything."

"So, you think he knew where that switch was already?" Dean asks.

"Not necessarily. He showed me where it was and it was pretty obvious. My flashlight was shining right near it, I was just looking at other things and didn't see it before him. That's not my point. The point is— who's paying for the electricity? I asked Jason if there was power to the property and he said it was advertised to him as being ready for utilities, but since there aren't any buildings or anything on the land, nothing is hooked up. He certainly hasn't been paying for any electricity. At least, he says he hasn't."

"That's easy enough to check," Dean notes. "I can call the power companies in the area and see if I can get them to tell me who has been paying the bills for that property. If they won't, we'll need to get the police department to get a court order."

"Unless Eric will do it," I say.

There's a half a beat of silence.

"You're going to officially bring this to the case?" Dean asks.

"The Bureau is already involved in the Emperor case," I tell him. "But I think it might be time to push it further. I'm going to talk to Eric about including this into the investigation and officially declaring Salvador Marini the primary suspect."

"The public doesn't like big investigations into dead men," Dean points out. "And showing your cards about this could tip off the people he had helping him. We know there are at least two, maybe more. If they feel like they're getting squeezed in, they could destroy evidence. Close ranks. It could make it a whole lot more difficult for you."

"I know it could. But I'm done waiting for something to happen. I'm done sitting around hoping there's going to be some magical moment when everything will fall into place and we'll be able to tie everything up in neat little bows and present it without any conflict or question. This case is fucked up. That's the only way to describe it. Why should we think the investigation is going to be any different?"

CHAPTER THIRTY-TWO

G WENDOLYN ANSWERS ON THE SECOND RING.

"Hello?"

"Ms. Russo? This is Emma Griffin. Are you still at Salvador's house?"

"Did you find out something? Do you know what happened to my money?" she asks.

Her single-mindedness might be understandable in the context of her life and her relationship with her brother, but it makes me cringe. She doesn't know the full extent of what Marini did, but she is aware that he killed Serena. She knows he took someone's life in a cruel, brutal way that left her frozen to the ground for nearly a year. I would hope that would come to her mind at least for a second when she thought about him rather than just her self-righteous anger about not being able to access what she believes is rightfully hers. Especially considering the FBI isn't exactly her personal treasure hunter.

"Not yet. That's not why I'm calling. I need to speak with you."

"Go ahead," she says.

"This isn't something we should talk about over the phone. I'd really prefer to be able to talk to you in person. There've been some changes in an investigation and there are things about your brother that will be coming out in the media. You need to hear them before then."

There's a pause. "I'm still at the house."

"Alright. I'm a few hours away, but I'll be there tomorrow morning."

My phone alerts me to an email almost as soon as I end the call with Gwendolyn and set it down. The message is from John Waters from Breyer, and it's just three words.

Here they are.

I set my phone down and pull my email up on my computer again so I can open the attachment on the message. Scans of Miley Stanford's financial records fill my screen. He'd prepared them for transmitting in non-official email, redacting some of the details, but there's still plenty visible for me to dive into. Hopefully, I can track some of her movements in the months leading up to her disappearance.

At first, not much stands out. It looks like any young woman navigating independence and adult life except for the regular deposits I know are from her parents. Though, there are plenty of adults who have that on their financial records as well.

There are trips to the grocery store, orders of takeout food, a hair salon, and clothing stores. Bill payments. I notice the first time the Blue Ridge Backpackers club shows up in the transactions. This gives me a little tingle. I know that marks the moment that she first met Angelo, making her life and the life of Salvador Marini first overlap.

I use the highlighter feature to mark each of the transactions that don't fit into the pattern of basic daily expenditures. There are more payments to the club, presumably for dues and the costs of activities. She went to an outfitter and spent a considerable amount of money on the gear she would need for her new hobbies. I remember the way Angelo laughed under his breath when he described her having the expensive clothes and tools, but seeming so out of place and with no idea of what she was supposed to do next.

Nothing looks out of place until a couple of months after that first meeting with the club. Sprinkled in among the trips to the store, eating out, and continued activities with the club is a series of withdrawals of cash. Nothing huge. No trips multiple times a day or massive withdrawals. That's the kind of behavior I've seen on the records of people with gambling addictions or drug habits. Instead, these are small to moderate amounts, taken out at completely irregular intervals, but significantly more frequently than before that point.

I pull up a notepad on my computer and type in a couple of thoughts before going back to the records. A few weeks after the withdrawals started, I notice a transfer with a notation on it. *Rent.* That immediately strikes me as odd. First, because it's the first one in all the records that mention rent or any kind of housing payment. And second, there is no reason for those types of payments to appear on her records because Miley's house was owned and paid for by her parents. And third, because it was paid out on the seventeenth of the month. I know that not all people necessarily pay rent on the first of the month, but the seventeenth seems like just such a random date that it raises my eyebrows.

I scroll forward to the next month and see another payment in the same amount, and a third the next month. Just like the first, these were also processed on the seventeenth of each month. This continues until the month before her disappearance, when there is no payment. And in the month she disappeared, her transactions keep going on as normal—until they suddenly cut off, once again on the seventeenth.

Opening the notepad again, I type the name of the person associated with the payment, CC DIVE, and a single question to myself.

Was Miley being blackmailed?

I've gone back to the beginning of the records to see if any of the transactions I initially thought were completely normal stand out at all with this new information when my phone rings. I glance over at the screen just enough to hit the button to answer the call and then the speaker phone button.

"Agent Griffin," I say.

"Hi, this is Jason Hoyt."

Surprised, I pick up the phone and take it off speaker so I can hold it to my ear.

"Hi, Mr. Hoyt. What can I do for you?"

"Jason," he insists.

"Jason. What can I do for you?"

"Would it be possible for us to meet again? Some things came to mind since we were down in that coliseum, and I'd like to talk to you about them," he says.

"Absolutely," I say. "I have a meeting out of town tomorrow morning, but I would be able to meet you there possibly in the evening or the next morning."

"The sooner, the better," he says. "I appreciate it."

"I'll let you know when I can be there."

My mind is spinning a little from all of the new information and everything that needs to be done. Taking a breath, I start researching flights. There's no way I'm going to be able to drive to all of these locations in enough time without completely burning out. Fortunately, I'm able to book tickets that will get me to my meeting with Gwendolyn and then back to meet with Jason tomorrow. It's going to be exhausting, but the familiar fire is burning in the pit of my stomach. It's that moment when everything seems unhinged, like the tangles are only getting tighter. But that means I've gone past the beginning. I'm deep in it and getting closer to the end. I can't stop now. Whatever it takes.

I pack my bags again and take a shower, ordering an early dinner so I can hopefully get at least a couple of hours of sleep before heading to the airport. Sam calls as I'm sliding under the blanket. He tells me about the people he met, who suffered various injuries and ill-effects from the activities of Alfa-Corps. Most were reluctant to open up to him, only sharing a little about what they suffered.

A few did say they were contacted by representatives from the company. They were forced to sign paperwork that acknowledged the company wasn't responsible for what they were going through in exchange for a small monetary settlement. None would go into detail, though, saying they were told they weren't legally allowed to talk about the details.

This infuriates me. I hate that people in power can take advantage of people like this, especially after they've already caused them so much harm. Sam doesn't even have to give me any details about the victims for me to be able to intuit who they are and what their lives are like. I could be wrong, but chances are these are people of lower socioeconomic status. Maybe getting by, maybe struggling, but certainly not equipped to handle the massive impact these kinds of injuries, illnesses, and tragedies could have on their lives.

And because they don't have the legal or financial power to fight back against a faceless mega-corporation, they feel helpless. They don't know what they can do and are terrified that if they go against what they're being told, they'll be in even worse circumstances. They are desperate for the money the company is offering, and even though the compensation is egregiously small, they don't want to risk not having it at all.

It makes my skin crawl and makes me even more determined to help Sam in any way I can.

"Marie had something on this company," I tell Sam. "She knew what happened to those people and what the company was still doing to them."

"And maybe she'd decided she was going to stop them."

"So they stopped her."

CHAPTER THIRTY-THREE

M Y FLIGHT LEAVES BEFORE THE SUN HAS EVEN HIT THE SNOOZE button and I'm on the ground right as the craving for coffee and eggs kicks in. The little restaurants near the gates are thankfully open, so I grab a coffee and breakfast sandwich to go before making my way to the rental counter to pick up the car I reserved.

The pre-dawn flight gives me the advantage of not having to rush as I make my way toward Marini's mansion. Gwendolyn has been staying there since Nathan Klein gave her the keys, ostensibly to go through his possessions and determine what she's going to do with them. I have a feeling some of the pleasure of living in the lush surroundings is rubbing off and she's more interested in soaking it in for a while than she is in liquidating the estate and moving on.

Her fascination with the money and finally being able to experience, if only on the surface, the kind of status and lifestyle her brother had, could end up going a couple of different ways.

She might get completely wrapped up in it. Swept away by the new world laid out in front of her. It could feel like now that she has access to the money, the house, the cars, and everything her brother left behind, she could have the life she was denied. She could latch on to it and try to be a part of that world, making her way through it and hanging on as tight as she could for as long as it would last. And maybe she would make it. Maybe she'd meet the right people, say the right thing, stumble her way into actually living that life.

But more likely, she would be like a grease fire, flashing hot and intense and burning out just as quickly.

The chances are so slim that she would ever really be able to fit into that world. No matter how hard she tries, she will always be on the outside. It's far more likely that she would suffer cruel humiliation and lose everything as abruptly as it came into her life because she was trying so hard for it to work.

Corruption runs deep in places used to a life bolstered by infinite money. It isn't a hard and fast rule, and there are plenty of wealthy people who avoid it, but the temptation is there. The pits are deep and it's far too easy to fall into them. Everything about Marini's life is steeped in it, and it could claim her before she even realizes what's happening.

Or she could recognize it now. She could know it wouldn't be as easy as just moving into his house and using his money. That it would be much more difficult to maintain than she imagined and that she would be better off selling everything and using the money to live a comfortable life. To pursue her dreams without a single worry in the world.

I hope she does the latter. For all she went through, Salvador owes her that. It might have taken his death for it to happen, but it's finally time for him to be her big brother and take care of her.

There are already two cars parked in front of the house when I pull into the driveway. The door is standing open and I can almost hear my mother's voice yelling at my father when he ran out of the house to flip burgers on the grill and came back in without shutting the door behind him.

"We're not air conditioning the whole neighborhood."

Dad didn't talk much about my mother for a few years after her death. It was like just the thought of her was too painful to even fathom. There were always reminders of her around, but they existed, and he existed, and they didn't come together. He was drowning in his grief, and not talking about her seemed like the only way he could get enough air to survive.

But then we were watching TV and he heard someone say that phrase. He laughed and told me that was my mother's favorite American saying, the first colloquial turn of phrase she learned when she came here from Russia.

After that, he could breathe.

Gwendolyn opens the door for me before I get to the top of the steps leading onto the porch.

"Oh," she says. "I thought you might be the art guy. He was supposed to be here twenty minutes ago."

"The art guy?" I raise an eyebrow, following her into the house.

"I'm getting all of this stuff appraised," she says, fluttering her hands around her as if to indicate everything in the house. "I want to know how much it's all worth and make sure the insurance inventory that attorney has isn't missing anything."

She says it with a distinct surly edge like she's decided to assign blame for the missing money onto Nathan Klein, even though we've already discussed that he didn't know about the missing money and likely had nothing to do with it. I decide not to argue with her. There's really no point. Until she's able to figure out exactly what happened to that money, she's not going to listen to anyone.

And right now there are far more pressing things she needs to know.

The conversation with Gwendolyn is painful and slow. The words feel sticky and hot as I try to choose and deliver them as carefully as I can. Even though she says she and her only sibling had no relationship, and she seemed to simmer with animosity every time she spoke about him, I know hearing about his crimes isn't easy for her.

I remember what Xavier said to me while we were sitting in the living room staring out the window at the house across the street. The fact that I'm still angry about Jonah shows I haven't put him out of my mind and that I'm not over him, much as I wish I was. The fierceness of this woman's fury toward her brother tells me she's carrying not just anger and bitterness about his success, but also a tremendous amount of hurt. He left her in a situation that scarred her, and while I know that makes her sad for herself, I'm aware of the pain she might be hiding not about Salvador himself, but about what he could have been.

No matter what, Salvador Marini was still her brother. They had a bond that they didn't choose and that they didn't have the option to dissolve. It existed because they both did, and though it might not cause her to feel any fondness toward him, it did create an inescapable link. A link that has the power to put the burden of these murders on her shoulders, even without her knowing a single detail about them before now.

I know what that feels like. I know what it is to carry the guilt, responsibility, and torment of someone else's horrific misdeeds just because they share the same blood. There isn't a single day that I don't ache for the people affected by everything Jonah did, and everything the members of Leviathan did in his name.

I think about Greg and the brother he didn't have a chance to be close with as an adult, but who cried at his grave. I think about Lydia, who could have been the next chapter of his life and who I hope is with him now. I think about Mary, the young woman who lay dying on the floor of the bombed bus station as her camera captured the carnage around her.

I think of my mother and father, both simultaneously dead and alive because they breathed for each other. When she died, she drew his heart down into the grave with her, and he brought hers up to beat in his chest.

I did nothing to harm any of them, and yet I still grieve for them with a heaviness that comes from knowing it was my uncle who destroyed all of their lives.

There's a chance Gwendolyn won't feel that way. She might be so hollowed out and toughened by the life she had to live that she doesn't care what others have gone through or that her brother is the one to have done it. But I can't make that assumption. I know this is a conversation we need to have. She needs to be prepared for what's coming.

We don't know each other well and I would hesitate to even say I like her, but I still believe hearing these things from me is the best thing in this situation. No one deserves to find out something so horrific and unsettling by watching TV or reading the news online. At least this way I can answer any questions she has and give her facts she knows are true because they're coming from an investigator working through the case.

She reacts to everything I tell her with horror and disgust, alternating between crying and shouting. I stay with her for as long as I can, but by the time I need to leave, it seems like she's ready to be by herself. As I'm walking toward the door, she stops me.

"Hold on," she says, striding away with heavy determination and leaving me alone in the foyer. She comes back with a box in her arms and shoves it toward me. "Take these with you. I don't want to look at him."

Taking the box, I look down into it and see it's full of pictures.

"Where did you find these?" I frown.

"All over the house," she says. "He had a deep appreciation for himself."

"Did you take any of them out of anything? Like were they hidden?" I ask.

"Some were in drawers," she says.

"If you find any other pictures or anything like maps, drawings, diaries, please don't throw them away. Put them aside and I'll come get them, or have them shipped to me."

Her arms crossed tightly over her chest, she shrugs and steps back from the door like she's separating herself from him by getting rid of the pictures. I can only hope there's something in these pictures she didn't notice, something significant that could give us the pieces to the puzzle we've been looking for.

CHAPTER THIRTY-FOUR

DRIVE AWAY FROM THE HOUSE WITH THE BOX SEAT-BELTED INTO the passenger seat beside me, so it doesn't slide and dump the pictures on the floorboard. I glance over at it a few times, wondering what's in there. It isn't a small box and I doubt it would meet the dimensions required for a carry-on, so I detour my trip into the parking lot of a big-box discount store. Very aware of the time of my flight ticking closer and feeling the essence of Xavier panicking because it's within three hours of takeoff and I'm not in the airport, I run inside and buy the first duffel bag I see with a tag proclaiming it to be compliant with all major airline guidelines.

I'm thankful for the ease of mobile car reservations as I pull into the assigned parking spot and jump out of my rental. Slinging my backpack onto my back and my messenger bag on my shoulder, I grab the pictures out of the box by the handful and shove them into the duffel as fast as I can. When the box is empty, I stomp it flat so it will fit in a nearby trash can and take off toward security.

I cut it so close that it feels like the plane is taxiing down the runway as I'm buckling my seatbelt, but I made it. When we hit altitude, I yank the bag out from under the seat in front of me and open it on my lap. It isn't a long flight, but I can't just leave the pile of pictures untouched. Gwendolyn described the stash of pictures as evidence of Marini's obsession with himself, which isn't a surprise. Anyone who ever crossed paths with that man would have no question of the esteem in which he held himself. But I'm curious to see what he thought was worth preserving.

Pictures are an interesting thing. I never really thought of them as much when I was younger. Even as an adult, they were just something that was around. They were nice to have. I treasured the ones of my mother and my grandparents after they died that let me remember good times that might have faded away from my memory if I couldn't look at them every now and then. But I never really considered the significance of them. Then we brought Xavier to a corn maze.

The entire story of that morning, afternoon, and early evening quickly devolves into a spiral that ends far from where we began, but tucked in there was a comment about Pilgrims wearing black that led to my perspective on something as seemingly simple and widely taken for granted as pictures. A picture can capture a moment as it is actually happening, or it can be manufactured, designed to show exactly what the subject wants it to show. Portraits painstakingly painted over hours and days evolved into snapshots taken in a fraction of a second, but that reality has never changed.

We can take pictures that are true to life and let us remember things in a tangible slice of time, like my father asleep with me as a newborn also asleep on his chest, our faces in the same expression, or Dean staring blank-faced at the camera while wearing a rainbow polka-dotted cone hat on his birthday last year. Or we can plan and orchestrate the pictures so they create any image we want others to see. Some act almost as a historic record rather than a memory, like formal shots of weddings and proms. Others shape history and change others' views, like the popular image of what Pilgrims looked like.

These manufactured images can be sometimes silly and sometimes strange, but they can also be damaging.

Everybody looks back at their prom pictures and cringes a little at the way the photographer posed them with their date, but remember the fun they had the rest of the night. But the Pilgrims got all their portraits done in their finest clothing because it was the only visual record of their lives and they wanted to look their best. And now, centuries later, everybody believes Pilgrims always wore black and a whole lot of buckles.

Salvador Marini lived in a fantasy world of his own making. He didn't have to keep anything around that he didn't want to, or that made him uncomfortable or unhappy. That means every one of the pictures now stashed in my duffel bag was intentionally kept by him. I want to know what he thought warranted being kept. I want to see the narrative he was trying to create.

I want him to have made a mistake.

In the short time I can look through the pictures during the flight, I see a lot of pictures of Marini peacocking for the camera, alternately trying to look cool and charming with a cheesy grin, and powerful and intimidating with a brooding stare. Patterns become obvious, showing his fairly limited range of poses, which result in him hitting the same posture when standing on the beach admiring the waves, showing off an industry award at some dazzling gala, and visiting a genocide memorial.

Most of what I've gone through are just useless snaps meant to fluff his ego and boost his image. I can imagine them placed strategically around the house so he was never far from an opportunity to gaze at and admire himself, and remind himself how impressive and amazing he was. But I've sifted out a few that seem more interesting because they are so different from the rest of them. These ones I've taken and separated into the outside zipper pouch on the side of the bag so I can look through them more carefully when I have the time.

One shows Marini with his back to the camera, sitting in an inflatable pool ring at the top of a snow-covered hill. In another he's standing next to a tent, posing with what looks like hiking gear, but to the side of the frame is a very visible segment of pavement that he clearly intended to be seen. A third was taken fairly close up so it's difficult to see anything around him, but he appears to be sitting on the ground next to a large boulder, which is dressed like a table with a full picnic spread of grapes, cheese, and bread. He has one hand wrapped around a wine bottle and the other held up giving the thumbs-down signal even though his face is sporting its usual grin.

They might mean nothing. It could just be strange little jokes Marini thought were hilarious so he put them on display, or moments he genuinely wanted to remember. There aren't any notes on the backs so I don't know when they were taken or who took them. But they're strange enough for me to want to look at again. Maybe I'll run them past Xavier and see what he thinks.

Dean calls right as I'm heading out to pick up my second rental car of the day. It's getting late in the afternoon at this point and I'm a good distance from that breakfast sandwich from the airport this morning. I'm considering what I could pick up fast when I pick up the phone.

"Cucumber avocado sushi rolls or a big salad with crispy chickpeas and quinoa?" I ask.

"Is this a password situation? Are you in danger?" he asks.

"Just hungry. I just got off my third flight of the day and I haven't eaten since right after the first."

"That's not great decision-making," he says.

"Well, Gwendolyn Russo, Marini's sister, is still at his house cataloging things and figuring out what she's going to do with his estate. And hunting for lost money."

"Is she a pirate?" he asks. I explain the discrepancies in the paperwork. "That's strange. Not totally off-brand for Marini, though. I can imagine there are a lot of things about his assets he wasn't exactly upfront about."

"This is true. But anyway, I thought it would be best if I talked to her in person about the Emperor's crimes before the Bureau makes any statements and everything explodes in the media. I'd rather keep as much of it as possible off the airwaves, but this kind of case is going to catch popular attention like a fucking summer blockbuster and people are going to forget that it involves real victims," I gripe. "I thought it would be better if she heard everything from me and didn't start collecting the little shreds of details and false information from backseat detectives and TV crime reporters. Then Jason Hoyt called and asked if we could meet up again to talk about some things he noticed underground. So, here I am. Jet setting. And hungry."

"Okay. Well, first of all, cucumber avocado sushi is not food. So you can just go ahead and count that option out. The salad actually sounds good."

"Thanks," I say, altering the destination in my GPS to bring me to a restaurant I discovered last time I was in the area. "Anyway, what's up with you? How's your case going?"

"I'm not making a ton of progress," he admits. "Most of the leads so far have been dead ends. One of the places I visited was a hotel where the manager was positive they'd seen Mila, Thomas Auden's wife, check in, but it ended up being a different woman. I saw the registry and watched the security footage. There was a resemblance, but that was about the most action I've had recently. I'm starting to form the official opinion that they either vaporized or are really just figments of popular imagination and never existed at all."

"Both worthy considerations," I crack.

"That's not why I'm calling, though. I wanted to let you know I looked into the electricity bill at Hoyt's property. Apparently, there isn't one," he says.

"How is that possible?" I ask. "I was standing there when the lights came on."

"They didn't have an explanation for that. Just that there are definitely utilities available there, but they haven't actually had anything there in years," Dean explains. "In fact, they said whatever agent described the space as being utilities-ready wasn't exactly forthcoming about the actual condition of the powerlines and everything. They're still technically there, but they are outdated and only really go around where the school was. Any new construction would likely require completely new wiring."

"Could it be from a generator?" I ask.

"That's possible," he replies. "Most generators capable of powering that large of a space would still require electricity, though. And if not, they'd need solar panels attached to batteries that could store the power they generated until use."

"But either way, we're not getting any kind of extra identifying information from a power bill," I say with disappointment.

"Something is out there, Emma. You're going to find it."

"You, too. Talk to you soon. Tell Xavier I say hi. Kiss all the starters for me."

CHAPTER THIRTY-FIVE

JASON IS PACING BACK AND FORTH SEVERAL FEET IN FRONT OF THE hatch when I arrive. He looks up at the sound of my footsteps coming toward him, something distrustful and sharp around the edges of his eyes. It fades when he meets mine.

"Thank you so much for coming," he starts. "I know you're busy."

"I was actually meeting with someone else about the case I believe is linked to this structure," I tell him. "It's my primary focus right now, so I am grateful for any further information I can get."

"Is your cousin following another lead there?" Jason asks.

I'm a bit surprised by the question. I don't think I've mentioned Dean to him.

"My cousin?" I ask.

I search his eyes as he nods, looking for any sign that he made the comment involuntarily, but his expression is clear. There's nothing to hide in the statement. He said it completely intentionally and without thought it would be strange or unexpected.

"Yes. Dean Steele is your cousin, right? He was on the news with you after the last case you investigated together, and in an interview, you mentioned the two of you work together frequently. I thought he might be working with you on this case."

I have the tendency to be immediately suspicious and sensitive when it comes to people asking personal questions about my life or seeming to venture into too familiar a space with me. I'm protective of the people I love, and I've encountered enough situations where our lives have been threatened by people who seemed harmless until they'd gotten too close.

I talk myself down from that reaction now. Jason's explanation makes sense. Anyone who has seen any news footage or read anything about my cases in the last couple of years will have heard about Dean and the work we've done together. There's a fascination about the family element and the intrigue of us not coming into each other's lives until adulthood. We haven't told the full story despite frequent offers from TV networks, reporters, and even true crime writers hungry for a fresh angle.

It's our story. The public knowing some details of it is unavoidable, but we'll guard the rest.

"Yes, Dean is my cousin. He's helping me with this case, but he is a private investigator and is working on one of his own right now," I explain.

"I'm sure he'll solve it. He thinks quick on his feet," he says.

I give a single nod. "Well, he was disappointed to not be able to be here to see this place for himself. But what is it that you wanted to talk to me about?"

The question makes Jason straighten slightly, like he's remembering why I'm standing in front of him.

"After going through this location, is it safe to say you are fairly confident it is linked to the serial killer you are already investigating?" he asks.

I give him a slightly quizzical look. "Yes. As I mentioned, it features the hallmarks of the other locations. And though I haven't been able to conclusively track the movements of the primary suspect to this area, there are some cold case murders and missing persons cases that have enough similarities to the other established victims that this location is very likely part of the same thread."

"And when those other victims were found, were they near the other locations like this one?" he asks.

A tingle starts at the base of my neck and starts moving up to my skull. My hand moves slowly closer to my body so my wrist rests against my gun.

"Jason, why did you ask me to come here?" I ask, speaking calmly and evenly to ensure he's paying attention and understanding me, and that I have control.

"I think I found something."

His voice is tight and his intense blue eyes don't move away from me.

"Where?" I ask.

Jason starts walking and I fall into step behind him, my hand still ready to take hold of my weapon if I need to. We move away from the hatch and deeper into the wooded area. I pay attention to my surroundings, glad for the longer stretches of sunlight during the summer months. Today is not the day I'd like to find myself in unfamiliar woods in the dark.

The ground feels soft underfoot, like heavy rain has soaked into the dirt and made it spongy. I look at the trees as we go past them, still trying to figure out how they could still be standing with the construction underneath. We walk for a few minutes until Jason stops.

"When we were down there, I saw an inscription on one of the walls. You recorded it. It was a row of numerals."

"I remember," I nod.

"It didn't seem to have any kind of purpose. But I couldn't stop thinking about the things we saw down there and I had to come back here and look around more."

"You shouldn't go down there by yourself," I tell him. "It could be dangerous."

"I didn't," he says. "I was trying to walk the area of the structure on the surface, trying to figure out how far it extends on the land. Then I saw this."

He points down, and at first, I don't know what it is he's gesturing toward. It looks like he's just pointing down at the mossy coverage at his feet. Then I realize there's a carving in one of the roots. It almost blends in with the roots around it, and when I bend down to look closer, it seems there was something rubbed into the carving to darken it.

I run my fingertips across the symbol.

"It's a Roman numeral," I murmur.

"Seven," Jason says.

I take out my phone and pull up the footage, scrolling through until he tells me to stop. It takes a few more seconds before the screen shows a section of one stone wall and the carvings of Roman numerals across it. They're evenly spaced, but don't seem to be placed on the wall in a particular arrangement. They aren't centered or highlighted in any way. Instead, they are offset to one side, like the person carving them started in one spot and added to the inscription over a long period.

What were they counting?

"There are ten numbers here," I say. He nods. "Are there more? Did you find any others?"

He shakes his head. "This is the only one I've seen." He hesitates for a beat. "Do you think it could be a grave?"

"I think I need to make some phone calls."

The body comes out of the ground wrapped in a piece of fabric like a shroud. It's little now but bones and matted hair and has obviously been there beneath that tree for a long time.

"This wasn't a quick, hurried burial to dispose of a body," one of the investigators tells me. "This was carefully planned. The grave is almost perfect dimensions and several feet deep. It looks like it was made well in advance without the need to rush."

"I know it's a longshot, but any kind of identification with the body?" I ask.

He gives me a face that says that was a question he didn't want to hear. "You can ask the medical examiner if he knows something I don't, but from what I saw there isn't much in there but the bones and the sheet. No clothes, wallet, phone, anything like that."

I nod. "Thank you."

He nods in return and walks away, returning to the crowd of investigators and technicians who have swarmed the woods. I go over to the medical examiner and wait while he finishes speaking some notes into the recorder on his phone. He offers a tense smile as he notices me.

"Agent Griffin," he says.

"Hi, Dr. Arnett. What have we got?"

"The remains are fully skeletal, so there's not much I can tell right now, and it might be difficult to determine cause of death. What I can tell you is it appears to be a young female. Probably twenties. She wasn't just rolled up in the sheet. It looks like she was placed on it, her body positioned and wrapped."

"Ritual?" I ask.

"I don't know. It's possible."

"Was there anything else with her?"

"Two bracelets. Very simple, unadorned metal cuffs."

I nod. "Alright. Please let me know as soon as you have any more information about her."

"I will. Do you think this is what it looks like?" he asks.

"Different MO, same SOB. We're going to be searching this entire area. If I don't miss my guess, you're going to have a very busy schedule soon," I tell him.

"You know where to find me."

"Thank you."

I walk by the grave as I make my way out of the area marked off by vibrant yellow tape. Looking down into it, something pricks in the back of my mind. There's something off about what I'm seeing, but I can't place it.

"Agent Griffin."

I look up and see one of the officers tasked with guarding the perimeter of what is now an official crime scene coming toward me.

"Yes?"

"Supervisor Martinez is here. He'd like to see you."

I walk faster toward the front of the wooded area. Eric looks up as I approach and walks away from the officer he's talking with to gather me in a hug. It feels like forever since I've seen him.

"How was your flight?" I ask. "You got here fast."

"Used private. It's so good to see you," he says, giving me an extra squeeze.

"Not the best circumstances," I say.

He looks around. "No. Catch me up."

I fill him in on everything and watch as he nods, listening and thinking. Eric has been one of my best friends since college and is now my supervisor in the Bureau. It's a position many assumed I'd take on when Creagan left the position in truly brutal, dramatic form. But that isn't for me. Not right now, anyway. I'm glad he was given the honor, even in an interim capacity. He's a good agent, a better man, and truly an asset to the Bureau. It helps that he doesn't try to lord over me and knows exactly how I do things, so he's rarely surprised by my sudden tangents and unconventional investigative style.

"This is one body," I start. "But if that numeral carved in the tree really does coordinate with the inscription in the wall, there are nine more still left to be found. This is the Emperor's primary palace of the fucking damned and there's more down there and among these trees than any of us know right now. It's what we've been looking for and I know there are answers here. This is where we're going to find what we've needed. I can feel it."

"I'll put together a team for you and set up a news conference," he says. "Do you have anything new on Miley?"

"Maybe," I say. "We can talk it through over dinner once you're ready to go."

"Just let me check in with a few other people and let them know this is a Bureau case. I haven't checked into the hotel yet, so why don't I call you when I get there?"

"Alright. See you then."

He walks further into the fray and I duck under the tape to go to where Jason is standing as close as the officers guarding the space will let him.

"No one will tell me anything," he says. "It's a grave, but what was in it?"

"Skeletal remains were recovered. They appear to be female. That's all the medical examiner can give us right this second."

His face is pale and his breathing seems shallow.

"That's it?" he asks. "There's no identification? Nothing with her?"

He's getting agitated and I try to step in front of him so he'll stop craning his neck to see what's going on. I'm trying to gauge his reaction to the situation, to understand why it's affecting him this way. It's a shock, so I can understand him being unsettled, but there's something more to his heightened emotions.

"Jason, you need to calm down."

"You want me to calm down? They just dug a girl's body out of the ground on my property and it could be…" His voice trails off. "The detective said I'll probably be brought in for questioning."

"It's standard," I say. "As you said, this is your property."

"But you already have a suspect," he says.

"Yes. But he's just that. A suspect. Right now there isn't enough information to conclusively prove this death is linked to the others. There is circumstantial evidence and I believe she is a victim of the same killer, but there's a process to murder investigations. We can't just assume things. We need to document things like when you bought the property, who had access to it before and after that, and when this woman died so we can zero in on exactly what happened," I reply. "Cooperating will make everything go more smoothly."

"What happens now?" he asks.

"This area is now a crime scene. It will be investigated and as much evidence as possible collected, particularly from the grave. My supervisor at the Bureau is assigning me a team and when they arrive, we'll take on investigating the underground structure itself. You can go home. You'll hear more when we need you."

He doesn't move. He looks angry, anxious, and confused, staying in place like if he just didn't go anywhere, something would change. I'd have more information for him or maybe the whole thing would turn out to be a mistake.

One of the officers comes up beside me.

"Is everything alright, Agent?"

"Yes," I nod. "But we might want to arrange a ride home for Mr. Hoyt. This has been a lot for him."

"No," Jason protests, seeming to come back into reality. "I don't need a ride."

He backs away for a few steps, then turns and jogs to his car.

CHAPTER THIRTY-SIX

Sam

CHILDREN ARE CONSTANTLY TOLD TO CLEAN UP AFTER THEM-
selves. It's one of the first things they're taught, and it's drilled into
them every day that it's an unavoidable part of life.

But here's a secret. Adults don't always clean up after themselves.
Even cops.

If they did, Sam wouldn't be seeing the frayed fragments of crime
scene tape fluttering from where they'd been knotted around structure
beams, clinging to bits of debris like mummified skin. They were left
there after the investigation was complete and conclusions were jumped
to. The officers didn't care enough to truly do their jobs. It shouldn't
have been a surprise that they didn't clean up the site, either.

To them, it didn't matter. This was just a dumping ground. It wasn't
somewhere pristine and orderly, kept beautiful for society to keep up

appearances with. It was a place for the dark underside of society. An abandoned scrap heap, scattered with refuse and the fragments and fractured pieces of lives broken apart here. And at least one life lost.

They didn't need to put any effort into treating the space with respect because that wasn't the kind of environment it was. If anything, maybe the lingering crime tape would get the attention of other people wandering into this space and act as a reality check. It could make them recognize the gravity of what they were doing and change their ways.

At least, that was what the officers might have thought. But Sam knew that idea was nothing but nonsense. It didn't make sense and it didn't work. Seeing the world around them degrade and descend into crime didn't make people want to do better. It didn't put a mirror up to who they were and convince them to suddenly alter their lives and make a fresh start. Not for most.

There might be the occasional person who is startled into a better reality by seeing the aftermath of crime. They're brought back from the brink by the forced realization of just how deep the ravine on the other side truly is. But for most people, the more of these reminders they see, the more they give up on having any kind of life outside the world that seems hopeless to them.

Sam never wanted his cousin to feel that. Marie was bright and full of light once. He knew she'd stumbled, but he never wanted her to face that moment when there was nothing left but the oblivion that seemed to have chosen her. He would have fought for her. But it really seemed like even when she hit the bottom hard, she managed to get back up and climb even higher than she'd been before.

He knew she'd never let herself crash like that again. Not because she was better than anyone or because she somehow deserved the second chance more. Because she'd worked so hard and had seen the look of anguish in her mother's eyes when her life had fallen apart and had promised herself that she'd never do it again. And because she'd found something that was far more important to her than even saving her own life—advocating for people who had been wronged.

As he stood feet away from where he'd found her body, remembering what she looked like lying there, broken and unrecognizable, he had a settled sense of peace in his heart knowing she'd found that purpose. All that research into Alfa-Corps wasn't just idle curiosity. It wasn't just some lurid question about the company and its strange amorphous existence, where it could take on a new name and keep going even as people cried out for recognition and justice.

It was a desire for the truth. For justice. Just like him.

Marie was determined not to let the people who pigeon-holed her and tried to hold her back stop her from having the career she wanted. Stop her from making a difference. Whatever it took, she was going to tell the stories that needed to be told. And she set about doing just that. Finding a way to speak truth to power and make the world a better place. That was her commitment.

And that commitment ended up costing her her life.

Someone out there had caught wind of what she was doing. Someone had something major to lose if she went public with what she found out. But knowing that, and knowing what happened to end up with her crumpled and decomposing among the rocks and trash, were very different things.

Sam wasn't going to let it go. Marie's name was important. There were times in her life when it had been all she had. It was taken from her the day she took her last breath there at the abandoned warehouse. He wanted to get it back for her.

CHAPTER THIRTY-SEVEN

E RIC HAS A ROOM AT THE SAME HOTEL WHERE I'M STAYING, SO rather than going out somewhere to eat when he finishes at the crime scene, he comes to my room and we order a pizza. I have everything about the Emperor case spread out across the table and end of the bed, and we go through all the evidence and information while we eat.

It takes all the way until Eric's nursing the crust of the very last slice before we're able to sift through all the data, reconstruct everything we already know about the case, and then integrate the new lair and victim into it. The details of these discoveries fit into the rest of the case seamlessly, like they've been there all along, even with the shift in how the body of this victim was treated compared to the others.

Eric points that out as we look at a row of pictures of the other female victims and an image on my phone of the grave from earlier.

"Why is this one buried like this?" he asks. "Most of the others were posed. Or at least just found in the open. They definitely weren't wrapped and buried so carefully."

"I don't know for sure, but if I have to make a guess, I would say it has to do with how Marini looked at his victim. All the female victims we've found so far fit into his fantasy narrative of appealing to a specific goddess and having that goddess deliver a hand-picked woman to him. Remember, Serena used to change her name and aspects of herself so that she could assimilate into groups and find the ideal woman to bring back to him. And those victims were each found in environments that fit in with the goddess that Marini and Serena had chosen for them. But this woman must be different. She wasn't chosen because of her link to any of the specific goddesses or gods. He saw her in a different light, which is why she was treated differently upon death."

Eric considers that for a moment. "I wonder if that means she wasn't one of the victims chosen by Serena. Of course, he likely had another accomplice before her, so his methods may have changed over the years. Given what we know about him, it's not necessarily implausible, but I'm actually not sure that's the case. Marini had a very specific philosophy and MO that he seemed to have stuck to. I don't know that he would have changed his patterns so drastically."

"What if she's a more recent victim?" I ask. "After Serena's death?"

Eric nods. "That's possible as well. But that still leaves the question open of why her body was treated so differently from all the others. In any case, we'll have to wait until the medical examiner can make a determination on how long she's been buried there."

I nod. "I'm interested in these bracelets that were found with her body. She wasn't wearing any clothing and there were no other possessions with her. But there were these two cuffs around her wrists. I haven't been able to do a lot of in-depth research about it, but from what I'm finding, those cuffs could have represented chains."

"Like the shackles that would be on a slave," Eric notes.

"Yes. The other female victims were very likely murdered within hours of Serena picking them up and bringing them to Marini. He had a specific plan for them and carried it out quickly. But we already know that at least some of the male victims were kept for a considerable length of time. They were used in multiple gladiator fights. That's why the cells are positioned around the arena. They weren't just to keep the new captives. In fact, the newest fighter was most likely just brought directly into the arena right after being captured."

"That was what happened with me," he tells me. "My memories aren't totally clear because of the drugs they administered, but I know I came to in the arena. When my brain woke up and I could process what was going on around me again, I was already in the midst of the fight."

"But Mark had been held captive for a good while. He had sustained injuries in several fights. It was why he was so willing to attack so aggressively. He knew that this was a fight to the death. If we are working within the understanding that this structure really was Marini's primary lair, maybe we need to be thinking about how he treated his victims differently. If this was his favorite space and one where he liked to indulge himself the most, I would think he would like to be able to take his time. He would come here not just to fulfill immediate fantasies, but to relax and take time away from the stress of his regular life."

"Like his favorite spa or a vacation house," Eric says.

It makes me sick to my stomach to even think that way, but if I'm going to understand the Emperor's motives and what could have led up to the death of this woman, as well as the others I believe we will find on those grounds, I have to try to think like him. I have to try to put myself into his mindset and go through the same thought processes he would.

"He had a very high stress and high-pressure job," I postulate. "He, and please pardon the pun here, had a massive business empire. Regardless of what he did on the outside of that, if you only look at his regular life, you can understand how he would experience stress and tension."

"Makes sense. High-stress jobs and lifestyles tend to really create a pressure cooker. A lot of men in these positions either turn to addictions: substance abuse, gambling, sex—which Marini definitely might have as well—or they try to find some way to blow off steam," Eric says. "As I said, they might go to a spa, or the gym to play racquetball. Some own motorcycles or sports cars. And the richest ones have full-time vacation homes ready for them to drop in at a moment's notice."

"That's just what I was thinking," I reply. "This wasn't just a quick stopgap for a quick fight or to use a woman for a night. This was his vacation home. This is where he would come when he really wanted to enjoy himself. An extended stay, as opposed to just a trip to ride on a motorcycle or workout at the gym. And so it would be maintained, with all the amenities he could ever ask for, so he could drop in at a moment's notice without having to prepare too far in advance."

"In the footage you shot, there's a kitchen. I know that there was some basic cooking equipment in a couple of the other locations, but this one is a lot more elaborate," Eric says.

"Elaborate enough to prepare a banquet. And support multiple people living there full-time," I confirm. "This girl was a slave. She wasn't just treated like one for a night or two like the other victims. She was kept for whenever he wanted her. There's a level of respect in the way she was wrapped and buried. Which tells me he didn't just get tired of her and kill her off. She could have died accidentally. There might have been a ritual that involved her death. Or she could have killed herself."

Eric takes the baton and voices my exact thoughts. "I just hope the ME can find the cause of death at all. The body is so decomposed it's going to be hard to find any evidence."

I know that my reply will already be on his train of thought. The two of us have worked together long enough that it's like we have the same instincts when it comes to investigating crimes. I'm grateful to have the full trust and backing of Eric, which is far more than I could say about my previous supervisor.

"For now, there's enough evidence just in the way she was handled at death and in the fact that she was wearing those cuffs, to make me comfortable making the determination that she—and likely any other victims we may find—were kept here for extended periods to maintain this lair."

"And that they were possibly shared with, or at the very least exhibited to, other high-powered men in his circle. We need to find out who came here with him," Eric adds. "Find out what they saw. And we also need to be looking for who was keeping them. Someone had to be there to stand guard over them. To threaten them into all that horrific work. To make sure they couldn't escape."

"To dig the grave," I say.

My mind goes back to the grave and the medical examiner's comment about how carefully it was prepared.

CHAPTER THIRTY-EIGHT

"I WISH I COULD STAY LONGER AND HELP MORE WITH THE INVESTI-
gation," Eric remarks the next morning as he's preparing to leave
the hotel to catch his flight back to Northern Virginia.

"I know. But you aren't a field agent anymore. We have a lot to handle back at Headquarters."

"We miss you around there. Have you thought any more about getting more active again?" he asks.

The circumstances of my life over the last few years have pulled me
away from the FBI to a degree. Moving to Sherwood obviously put the
physical distance between me and the headquarters where I used to
be on a daily basis. But I was able to continue working in the field and
picking up cases when they arose. Then I took a further step back to
focus more on my life outside of the Bureau. To figure out who I am
beyond Agent Emma Griffin, FBI. I learned there is no beyond those
three letters.

That is who I am.

But I am also Emma Johnson. I'm gradually learning to balance both sides of my life. It hasn't been the easiest thing in the world, but I'm trying.

Everything I went through during Greg's case and my coming face-to-face with a nightmare I thought was long dead in the form of the Dragon pushed me to my limit. I decided to take a step back and become a consultant rather than working in the field and participating in official assignments for the Bureau. It was the right choice for me at the time. It gave me the opportunity to rest my body and my mind. It helped me to heal. And it put me in the position to help with other cases that weren't being investigated by the Bureau.

Recently, though, I've been feeling like I'm ready to go back.

"Maybe," I tell him coyly.

"I'll keep your office warm for you," he says.

I laugh and nod. "Thanks."

"I've put in the assignments for your team. They'll be arriving later today," he says.

"Dean and Xavier are coming back today, too," I tell him. "When Dean discovered another body was found, he couldn't stay away anymore. He can only be here for a few days, but he wants to be a part of the investigation as much as he can."

"I know how much he wants this resolved," Eric notes.

Though Dean is far from an official FBI agent, his incredible investigation skills have led to him being used as an official consultant in several cases. Eric has already authorized utilizing him not just for his investigation techniques, but also because of his unique personal experience. The two men share that. Both have first-hand knowledge of what it was like for the people who fell into the hands of the Emperor.

Though their circumstances were different and they were both able to get out alive, what they went through affected both of them deeply, and shaped the way they see this case and others. I know how much it means to both of them to see every victim found and identified, and Salvador Marini exposed for who he really was. Even though it will only be done posthumously, the victims and their families deserve his name and his reputation.

"Tell Bellamy and Bebe I love them," I say.

"I will. We'll see you soon."

"You better," I insist with a grin.

"Trust me, Bellamy has been champing at the bit to come visit. I'll keep you updated."

"See that you do, or I'll have her sick the Killer B on you."

Eric throws back his head and laughs. "The Killer B? Now that's a nickname I haven't heard in years."

We finally make our goodbyes, and he gets in the car waiting for him outside the hotel and drives off. I make my way back up to my room and get in the shower. It's where I do my best thinking. The sound of the water and the heat on my skin blocks out everything else so I'm able to focus and let the broken little bits of thoughts lingering around the edges of my mind come together and congeal where I can understand them.

Xavier says he likes to think of that as "thought Jello." I prefer not to.

My skin is stinging with the intense heat of the water by the time I get out, but my mind is also racing. Thoughts are tumbling around so fast that it's all I can do to open my notepad back up and type out reminders of everything so I don't forget them.

Dressed and with a fresh cup of coffee beside me a few minutes later, I pull up my search engine to start researching. It doesn't take very long for me to find what I'm looking for. Or, more accurately, not find what I'm looking for.

Jason Hoyt seems to be a shadow.

"I can't find a single picture of his face," I tell Dean and Xavier when they arrive later in the morning.

They've brought breakfast and we're sitting in the seating area of the room going through all the notes I've taken since Eric left.

"Nothing?" Dean asks. "No social media, company profiles, anything?"

"Nothing. There are social media profiles under that name, but none of them seem to correspond with the details I know about him, and most of them have pictures that are definitely not him. His investment company has a website, but on the About Me page where it should have one of those boring corporate headshots of him, there's a stock photo of mountains. No explanation. Just mountains."

"Do you think maybe he isn't the actual Jason Hoyt?" Dean asks.

"I don't think so. What would he gain from that? I think he purposely keeps his face from being seen."

"Have you searched for his face?" Dean offers. "Rather than just looking for instances of his name and his face being linked in results, you could take an image of him and put it through a search to find more instances of that face, or at least similar ones, in internet photo files."

"I don't have a picture of him," I say. "I didn't put him on camera while we were going through the lair." My eyes open wider. "Call Julian. He responded to the call about the grave. Find out if the crime scene photographer got any pictures of Jason. Julian has met him; he knows what he looks like. If there are pictures, send them our way."

Dean nods and gets up to make the call.

"What's this?" Xavier asks, sliding closer to me and pointing out a page scribbled with numbers and lists of names.

"Details about the property," I tell him. "I wanted to know exactly when it was purchased and who owned it before that, and if there's any record of the deed transfer. The medical examiner hasn't released any information about how long the body has been there, but I wanted to know if he owned that land when the body was buried."

"How long has he owned it?" Xavier asks.

"Well, that's a bit unclear," I admit. "It looks like there were some mistakes in how the property was transferred from previous owners."

"What mistake?" Dean asks, coming back. He holds up his phone to indicate the call he just made. "Julian's going to look into those pictures. What mistake?"

"I looked into the property records for that piece of land." I pull up the records. "Here is when it was owned by the organization that ran the school there. It wasn't a public school, which is why the state didn't retain ownership of the property when the school closed and the buildings were removed. That organization went defunct and abandoned the property. It was then bought about ten years ago by a real estate developer who only owned it for a couple of months before selling it to someone named Vlad Cressida."

"Vlad?" Dean raises an eyebrow. "As in the Impaler?"

"In this case, it looks more like Vlad the Homesteader. The property tax information shows he made improvements to the land that increased its value quite a bit. I'm assuming that was removing the last of the signs of the school, the parking lots, those kinds of things that would get in the way of someone wanting to build there. I searched the permit filings in the area and saw that he did file a permit to build a house, but the zoning wasn't for residential use at the time. Apparently, he didn't want to go through the effort of having the zoning changed or he decided he wanted to find somewhere else because he sold it within a year and a half of buying it."

"Seems to be a real hot potato," he muttered.

"This is where the mistake comes in," I go on. "Vlad off-loaded the property to a company called Central Enterprises. They then sold it to Jason a couple years later. Only, if you look, a few years ago, ownership transferred again… to Jason Hoyt. There was no financial transaction, just filing of a transfer of ownership."

"Why would that happen?" Dean frowns. "That doesn't make any sense. He already owned it."

"That's what I thought, too. But if you look at the tax records, the first purchase is under Hoyt's name, but as a business. Then the second time, it's acquired by an individual."

Xavier shakes his head. "That's not a mistake. Real estate purchases aren't simple transactions. There's no way to accidentally attribute a purchase of a piece of land to a business when it was actually bought by an individual. And you said Jason Hoyt is a real estate developer."

"Yes," I confirm.

"So, wouldn't he have purchased the property as a business on purpose? Under his company's name rather than his own?" Xavier points out. "Even if he did purchase it under his own name but as a business investment, why would he then have it transferred out of that name and under his own as an individual if he intended for it to be used for development at some point?"

"He told me that he had planned to develop it, but then those plans changed when he couldn't settle on exactly what he wanted it to be. Maybe he wanted it listed under his name as a private owner because of that. But that doesn't explain why it would have been purchased as a business under his name rather than his company name to begin with," I say, realizing the crack in my line of thinking.

"When you were researching him, did you find anything about a company trading under his name?" Dean asks.

"No. All of his property is listed under his companies. He has two. One he started when he was really young, about fifteen years ago, called RedBird, which only has a couple of small holdings now, and then the current one, 404 Investments."

"Not found," Xavier chimes in.

"Not found?" I ask.

"The computer error," Dean says. "404. Not found."

"Maybe for people who are trying to get rid of property they thought had potential and then realized it didn't," I muse, searching for some kind of meaning in the name.

"What about Central Enterprises?" Dean asks. "Did you look into them at all? That's a pretty generic name."

"I did. It's essentially the name of a group of angel investors. It was set up so that everyone involved can invest in startups and small businesses anonymously, which I suppose is why they chose a nondescriptive name. It's listed as a nonprofit organization rather than a business. That's not all that unusual. A lot of times these investors want a layer of anonymity just in case there's an issue with one of their companies. Helps to insulate them," I say. "They might have wanted to snatch it up to raise capital for their other ventures. We could find out who was hit with an income tax for the proceeds from the sale to Jason, but that would take legal action."

"I'm guessing it's safe to assume no permits of any kind were filed to build an underground complex during any of these ownership periods," Dean notes.

"That is safe to assume," I nod. "Other than the house permit, there haven't been any permits for development on the property."

"What about that one?" Dean asks. "A house could mean a lot of things. What do we know about Vlad?"

CHAPTER THIRTY-NINE

B UT A DEEP DIVE INTO THE FORMER OWNER OF THE PROPERTY HAS turned up absolutely nothing of note.

"Just a person with a somewhat unfortunate name," Dean groans. "I was hoping it might have been another alias for Marini or something."

"No, it would be a bit of a stretch to mix historical references like that," Xavier tells him. "The Emperor was obsessed with Romans, Vlad III was Romanian. Salvador Marini wasn't sloppy enough to make that kind of mistake." His eyes open slightly wider and he tilts his head to the side like he's processing a thought that just came into his mind. "Though they did both have an affinity for putting people's heads on pikes..."

Dean's eyes snap to Xavier, who holds up a fisted hand like he's holding the aforementioned pike.

"Thank you, Xavier," I say. I look back at the computer. "So, somewhere in here, Marini was able to bring a construction crew apparently comprised of magicians and ghosts to build a massive underground lair without the owner of the property noticing and without disturbing all the trees."

Something flickers through my thoughts and I rush to pull up the pictures of the grave.

"What?" Dean asks. "What is it?"

"Look," I say, pointing at the grave. "What do you see?"

"A grave," Dean says.

"Right. A very deep, very even grave. So, what *don't* you see?" I prod.

He stares at the picture for another second, then shakes his head.

"Roots," Xavier says.

I nod. "Roots. A tree this large should have a deep established root system that would have been disrupted by a grave like this. It would have been really difficult to dig this perfectly, and it looks like someone was able to just dig right down into the ground and form the hole. Now, look at the carving of the numeral on the tree. It's right at the bottom of the tree. Almost on the ground."

"So?" Dean asks.

"Trees grow," I point out. "This tree is big, but it's not a fully mature tree. It should be growing more than a foot a year. The remains were skeletal, which takes time. Assuming she was buried before her body started decomposing, she's been there for at least a year, likely more. If the numeral was carved in the bottom of the tree when the body was buried, it would have been higher up off the ground. The carving would move up as the tree grows."

"I'm still not following you," Dean admits.

"I'm saying something stopped the tree from growing and kept it from having the root system it should have," I explain. "Xavier, do you remember that documentary we watched about the theme park that needed to create a jungle in the middle of a field? They wanted it to be as accurate as possible. They didn't want to build fake trees."

"So, they transplanted them," Xavier says, his expression surprised.

I nod and search through internet images until I find one of a large tree in the bed of a truck. I point to it.

"It takes a lot of effort and very careful skill, but landscapers can pick up large trees from one location and move them to another. It's a great way to fill in an area and create mature landscaping without the actual growing time, but it's really hard on the trees. Sometimes they go into shock and it takes a few years for them to come out of it. Growth is dramatically restricted and roots can take a long time to fully re-establish."

That seems to finally click the light on in Dean's eyes. "That must be how this area is still wooded even though the lair is under it. The tree was transplanted there."

I nod. "Right. All this undergrowth grows extremely quickly. It's the kind of stuff that shows up in the cracks of a sidewalk or along a flower bed that isn't weeded regularly. It would fill in naturally within a matter of a few months, especially if some was transplanted to help it along. The trees would need to be brought in, but someone with considerable resources could make that happen. Particularly if they already own the trees and don't need to arrange to purchase them and access private land to retrieve them."

"Marini definitely had that kind of money," Dean says.

I go to my duffel bag and pull out the picture of Marini pretending to camp next to the parking lot.

"And access to trees," I add, tossing the picture down in front of them. "Remember when we searched his real estate portfolio to see if he owned any of the land where we found the other lairs? None of the property was listed as his, but there was that one massive tract that turned up not having anything developed on or under it. It had been largely cleared."

"We thought he might have been preparing to build something there," Dean mentions.

"But what he was doing was harvesting. He had those trees on that land, and he needed them to replace what was ruined when it had to be dug up to construct the lair on the school grounds."

"We're still ignoring the fact that no one seemed to notice any of this happening. That kind of undertaking is massive, not to mention the construction of the actual underground building," Dean points out. "That's not going to happen on privately owned land without some-one realizing it. Even if the owner is just some disconnected investor, I highly doubt they wouldn't notice when someone rolls onto their land and spends months ripping it apart, building a giant complex under-ground, then covering it all up and transplanting trees over it."

"And we still haven't been able to find a construction company will-ing to admit they were a part of building any of the lairs," I add. "An operation like this would have had to be massive. Not just something a single contractor could pull off."

Xavier makes a slight face.

"What?" I ask.

He looks at me with widened, questioning eyes. "Hmm?"

"You made a face," I say. "I said we haven't found a construction company willing to admit they were a part of building any of the Emperor's lairs and you made a face."

"Oh," he says. "I didn't mean to. I tried to keep it in."

Dean and I look at each other.

"Why did you make a face, Xavier?" I ask.

"I don't like that you keep saying 'lair,'" he says. "But I'm not going to tell you how to speak."

He holds up a power fist.

"Why don't you like it?" I ask.

"It's just… serial killers don't really have lairs. Not in the real world. They do in movies and TV shows. They also decorate with rolls of thick plastic that they never change even when they're covered in blood and believe dismembered body parts can be easily ground up in the garbage disposal, which is not a plumbing appointment I would want to try to explain. There are clearly killers who have dungeons or killing rooms, but it's not like they're all going around building entire structures just for use as a killing ground."

He looks down at his shoeless feet and narrows his eyes at his socks. "Emma, do you have an extra pair of socks I can wear? These are unevenly stretched out."

"Building entire structures just for the use as killing grounds. Exactly what Marini did," I point out, continuing the conversation ahead as I go to the dresser and take out a pair of socks.

"Yes, but a lair just sounds like a dark gloomy place where a killer lurks around in a cape. It's where a wild animal lives. It doesn't exactly fit with what these structures actually look like or their purpose," he says.

"What should we call it then?" Dean asks.

Xavier reaches out and takes the socks from my hand.

A word materializes in my mind and my breath catches in my chest.

"The Coliseum."

CHAPTER FORTY

CAN FEEL THE COLOR DRAIN FROM MY FACE AS I OPEN MY NOTEPAD of information about Miley and put it beside the one about Jason, then open a new one.

"I guess that would be accurate," Dean says.

"No," I say, shaking my head and cutting him off before he can say anything else. "No. That's not what I mean. I know how he did it."

A quick search engine search gives me another detail that was right in front of me, had come out of my mouth and I didn't even know.

"Who? Marini?"

"Jason," I clarify. "He was the one helping Marini. There's been something that's bothered me about him since the first time I saw him and it just clicked. His eyes changed color."

"His eyes changed?" Dean asks. He sounds incredulous, like he's not sure whether he should take what I'm saying seriously.

"Not in a dramatic, poetic way. I mean physically. His eyes changed color. When I first saw him, he had brown eyes. I remember noticing them. Hazel. But then the second time I saw him, they were blue. He was wearing colored contact lenses."

"Some people do that," Dean shrugs.

"Of course, they do," I say. "But it got my attention. Why would someone put on colored contacts to meet an FBI agent in the midst of a serial murder investigation?"

"Yeah, that is weird," he admits.

"And now that we're thinking about it, there were a few other things that were just off about him. A couple of times he would say things that were just slightly off, slightly different than I would think someone would say them. Or he would start to say something and then change his mind and say something else. Like when he was pointing out the carving of the numeral on the tree, he said he 'saw' it. Not that he found it or noticed it, but that he 'saw' it."

"Like he already knew it was there," Dean says.

"Or thought it might be," I nod. "When he was talking about the grave he started to say it might be something, but he stopped himself. He was extremely agitated about not being allowed closer to the excavation and then the detectives telling him they would probably call him in for questioning.

"But what you just said reminded me of something he said while we were first going through the structure. He referred to it as a coliseum. I didn't think much of it at the time because that's a description that, as you just pointed out, makes sense. It's accurate. A big, elaborate arena used for gladiator fights."

"Which is exactly what it is," Dean says.

"But he didn't know that," Xavier cuts in.

"Right. I didn't tell him any of the details about the Marini case," I go on. "When I spoke with Julian Ruiz before Jason was back in the country, I told him specifically not to tell him anything about the case. I didn't want any assumptions, and since we hadn't gone public with Marini's name or the concept of the Emperor, I didn't want anything leaked and possibly making it to the media."

"I didn't even tell Julian about the Emperor," Dean confirms. "I just told him that I'd been investigating a case that involved hidden underground buildings."

"So, how would Jason know to call it the Coliseum?" I close my eyes briefly, giving a disclaimer before they can argue with me. "Yes, I understand he had already been down there and he saw the arena. He saw the weapons and the cells. But I very carefully did not say the word "gladiator" or "emperor." I didn't describe anything in a way that would make that connection. I was very aware of him being there and didn't want to give away anything more than I had to. It's possible he just made the connection himself and that was what he decided to call it. But that seems unlikely.

"And that's not the only thing. We've been trying to figure out how Marini was able to build these things on property he doesn't own. They aren't in his portfolio and in a lot of cases, finding the actual owner of the property has been a really roundabout situation. Pretty much every time has risen more question marks. Either the land is officially listed as abandoned, technically public-owned land that was rarely used, or it has a private owner like Jason. It doesn't make sense that he would be able to do all these things on so many properties that weren't his and not ever be noticed or stopped. Unless there was some connection to all of them."

Dean starts pawing through the property records. He passes me a few papers and Xavier a few more and we quickly spend the next few minutes rapidly scanning before starting to make the final connections.

"I've got two here with Central Enterprises as a former owner of the property," Dean reports.

"I've got one with C.E Holdings," Xavier adds. "Seems to be part of the same entity. They owned it but then just abandoned it."

"Good, guys. Look at these three here," I point at my own stack. "These are the ones with private owners who are either dead or not in the country. Those are the ones that bother me the most. I couldn't figure out how to tie them together."

"Marini was a smart man and devious as hell. I wouldn't put it past him to be able to find distressed properties and unscrupulous owners so he could buy property that would go undetected," Dean points out.

"But there was no link to him," I complete the thought. "Now there is. Jason."

My mind whirling, I turn to Xavier. "Xavier asking me for socks reminded me of going to the laundromat a few days ago. There was a guy there who was going around slipping things into washing machines that were already going. He would wash and dry with other people's loads and then when they were folding and found things that weren't theirs, they just put them aside and he went and picked them up. People accidentally leave things in the washers and dryers all the time, so it's not that big of a deal to find a wayward sock or a shirt that was stuck to the side of the machine or something. People don't even think about it.

"But he was able to get his entire load done by piggybacking on others. That's what Marini must have done with these properties. Central

Enterprises is anonymous because it was either him or some of his cronies. Wouldn't surprise me if it was the same men he would invite to his arenas to enjoy his 'entertainment.' They would invest in a business purchasing the property, sometimes using a person's name so that it would at first glance look like a private owner. It would enable Marini to control property without it being linked directly to him."

"And I would bet these men were all too happy to sign over that control to him—and their money—in return for being able to partake in his twisted games," Dean says. "Being in that position would mean he probably held pretty substantial blackmail over them as well, to keep them in line. It was a mutually beneficial agreement—as long as Marini was on top."

I nod. "Exactly. Then after he died, Jason took advantage of the situation. He already had inside knowledge of all of this, and likely had access to his accounts as part of Marini's inner circle. He had the property transferred into his personal possession and used the shell company to take money out of Marini's accounts and filter them into other holdings. That's where the missing money is."

"His laundry made you realize Jason was laundering money," Xavier remarks. "He laundered laundry."

Dean's mouth opens but closes without any words coming out. He turns to me.

"He's got a point," I shrug. "Now, look at what I found in Miley's financial records. A few months before she disappeared, she started making fairly large payments to something called CC DIVE and noting them as rent. Miley didn't pay rent. She never had. Her parents paid for the house. So, what was she paying?"

"CC DIVE," Dean murmurs, trying to process it through and understand what I'm seeing. "Credit Card dive?"

"That's what I thought at first as well, but I don't think it makes any sense."

"It's a monogram," Xavier says. "Not a traditional one, clearly, but that would be very challenging to do on a computer. And with mixed alphanumerical coding. It's a valiant effort. Though it does come across as a somewhat smarmy PI. No offense, Dean. Ooooh, or a torch singer. Though that would also be historically problematic."

Dean looks at him for a second, then snaps his eyes to me. "What?"

"CC DIVE. C-C-D-I-V-E." I go to the drawer beside the bed and pull out the notepad and a pen. I draw a large C and E, then write CDIV in between in smaller letters. "C. E. Central Enterprises. CDIV. It's Roman numerals. Like the ones on the wall, like the one on the tree.

They appear in many of Marini's businesses. These represent a number I think you'll recognize."

I type the letters into the search engine and ask for the translation of the Roman numerals.

"404," Dean whispers.

"Hoyt was blackmailing Miley. She was paying him off for something. Then the month of her disappearance and the month before, there was no payment," I say. "Maybe it was right around the time Emperor was looking for a new slave."

"Do you think the skeleton is her?" Dean asks.

"I've been afraid of that," I admit. "We won't know for sure until the ME can confirm it."

"What would he be blackmailing her about? And how would he have even found her?" Dean asks.

"She spent time around Marini's house with Angelo. And if she really did have something going on with this guy he called his nephew, she may have been more involved in his world than Angelo even knows. Neither Angelo nor Louisa know who the nephew was, but they said he was around him a lot and Marini introduced him to very important people. He was clearly someone he had at least some relationship with. But now that I know more about his family history, it could make more sense.

"Marini's sister told me they were raised in foster care and it was pretty horrific. That's the big reason she has so much bitterness toward him. When he was old enough to go out on his own, he just did. He left her and she suffered major abuse from the family. She didn't mention anyone else being in the house, but it makes me wonder if they had foster siblings. If there were other foster children, or even biological children, in the house, it's possible he developed a closer relationship with one of them," I say.

"And if that person had a son, Marini might have considered him his nephew," Dean says.

I nod. "If she spent any time with Jason, she could have gotten comfortable enough to reveal the identity of her parents or other information sensitive enough that it would warrant blackmailing. Angelo has told me a few times he's afraid Marini killed Miley and the nephew because they tried to betray him. He could have expressed a desire for Miley and forbade his nephew from pursuing her. But they decided to do it anyway. They had a secret relationship. Maybe Jason was blackmailing both of them. Jason got tired of not getting his money, so he turned the betrayal around on them, serving them up to Marini for his own pleasure."

My phone rings and my stomach jumps when I see the screen. It's Jason.

"Agent Griffin," I answer.

"They won't let me on my own property," Jason says without greeting. "They're saying I have to stay away."

"It's a crime scene," I tell him. "It has to be isolated and formally processed. You won't be able to access it without authorization until after the investigation is closed." I lift my eyes to Dean. "Why do you want to go?"

"It's my land. I want to be a part of finding out what happened there," he protests.

"I am planning on visiting later this afternoon. My cousin is back in town and would like to see it. I can tell the station officer that you are authorized to be there when I'm present."

Jason lets out a relieved breath. "Thank you. I'll see you and Dean soon."

I hang up. "Ready to meet the servant of the Devil?"

CHAPTER FORTY-ONE

GET A TEXT AS WE'RE GETTING IN THE CAR TO HEAD BACK TO JASON'S
property.

"The second meeting with Benson Mandeville is set up," I tell Dean
and Xavier. "That means they should be setting up the drop next week."

Dean gives an almost imperceptible nod. He knows the significance, but he's not going to comment. Until it's over, there's nothing
he's willing to say.

A call when we're nearly there confirms the team Eric sent has
arrived in town. I give them directions to the property and tell them to
wait with the officer securing the area until they receive further instructions. I want the chance to confront Jason with the evidence we pieced
together first, but I'm glad to have them available as backup in case
something gets out of hand.

I purposely wait until we have already arrived and are walking
through the wooded area to the yellow tape surrounding the delineated
crime scene to contact Jason. He tells me he's on his way and hangs up.

Julian Ruiz is on duty providing security and surveillance for the scene along with an officer I'm not familiar with. He smiles when he sees us, giving Dean a hug.

"Good to see you, buddy," he says.

"You, too," Dean says. "Thanks again for getting in touch when you saw this place."

The new officer looks around, a somewhat bewildered look on his face as they greet each other.

"I had no idea it was going to turn into anything like this," Julian says. "But I'm glad Agent Griffin was here."

"I really appreciate you guys continuing on with us for the investigation," I say. "I feel better knowing this place is secure until we're able to search the entire thing. My team is going to be arriving shortly. I've instructed them to wait with you until I tell them otherwise. Jason Hoyt is also on his way here. When he gets here, let him through."

"But I thought…"

"Please just let him through," I insist. "Tell him that we are down in the building and make sure that he goes directly through the hatch. If you can, watch his movements and pay attention if he seems to be looking in any particular direction or taking notice of anything."

Julian nods. "Absolutely."

We thank him before heading toward the hatch. I pause before we get there.

"Xavier, you don't have to go down there. This is a lot, and I don't know how you would feel about what you would see," I say.

"I want to go," he says.

Dean turns to him. "Are you sure? I know we've talked about these places and you've seen pictures, but it's different being down there."

"I want to go," Xavier repeats.

He doesn't need to add any insistence to his voice or give us any justifications. He's made his decision and there's no arguing with him. Except in very extreme circumstances, we don't even try anymore.

"Alright," Dean says. "If you change your mind and it gets to be too much for you, let me know and I'll get you out."

"I know you will."

I'm never going to fully understand what Xavier deals with. I'm never really going to be able to put myself in his position and go through what he does every day. But I know he experiences something the rest of us don't. I often can't tell if a situation is going to be something he can handle or if it will unsettle him. There are things he loves that I would think would disturb just about anyone, and things that are perfectly normal that agitate him. I've come to terms with the reality that I'm never going to really be able to know everything about him or catch up to his thoughts and the amorphous way he moves through life. I'm alright with it. I'll just keep trying.

I open the hatch and head down first. Dean steps back so Xavier can go ahead of him, then brings up the end, making sure to keep a watchful eye on our surroundings. I walk directly to the door across the vestibule and open it. The smell isn't as overwhelming as it was the first time I came inside. Almost like all our coming and going aired it out a bit.

"It's going to be dark in there until we get to the controls," I tell them. "Go ahead and turn your flashlights on."

As we left the hotel, I'd warned both of them of how incredibly dark it would be inside the lair and advised they bring flashlights along with them. Since they didn't have any on them, we made a quick detour to pick up some from a hardware store. I have to know they are both in control of their environment, even if it's only to the extent of being able to illuminate the space around them and see where they are going.

We go through the door into the hallway that surrounds the arena.

"This is why it felt so wrong when I came down here the first time," I tell them. "Those doors shouldn't have been unsecured. It felt so vulnerable. There was almost a trap quality to it. I kept my hand ready to grab my gun the whole time we were down here."

"What is this?" Xavier asks, moving his flashlight back and forth along the corridor.

"It's a hallway. It encircles the arena and gives access to some of the older rooms. There are some observation windows along it and gates leading into the area," I explain. He nods and we continue.

"There has to be a set of controls around here somewhere," states Dean. "There had to be a way for Jason or the Emperor to control the lights when they came inside rather than having to wait to get up to the observation box."

"You know who I am."

The voice startles me slightly and we turn to the sound behind us. The gate in the stone wall slowly opens and Jason walks out. He's clapping slowly, menacingly, and the echoes ring out into the empty space as he walks toward us. His sudden appearance, especially that way, makes me angry.

"Yes, I know who you are," I growl. "And I suppose all the blood on your hands from helping Marini find all those victims entitles you to the drama of that entrance."

Before I can continue, he nods toward Dean. "I was talking to him."

Dean takes a step toward him. "She told me who you are."

"But you already know."

There's a tense pause and then Jason turns, walking back into the arena. The lights burst on as we follow him. He's walking across the dirt without any urgency or rush. I watch Dean watch him, seeing the curiosity in his eyes as he tries to figure out what Jason means. The man casually unbuttons his shirt as he approaches the display of weapons on the wall. He reaches for a large broad-bladed sword and takes it from the wall.

My gun is in my hand in an instant and I point it at him, taking long strides across the dirt as I command him to put the weapon down. Instead, he turns his torso toward Dean, revealing a long, jagged scar across his ribs and down onto his waist.

"Put it down!" I shout at him again.

I'm ready to call out for the police officers above ground, but Dean shouts from behind me to stop. I stake my ground but don't lower my gun from its poised position directed right at Jason. Dean appears in the corner of my vision, walking past me and closer to Jason.

"You," he says. "You were with me in the arena."

CHAPTER FORTY-TWO

THE WORDS MAKE THE BLOOD RUSH HOT AND FAST THROUGH MY veins. It roars in my ears and makes the edges of my vision hazy. I take another step closer.

"Move, Dean," I order. "You. Get on your knees. Hands behind your head."

"Emma," Xavier says behind me. "Stop."

His voice is calm but strong. He sees something. I don't care. This man is responsible for so much bloodshed and he's standing far too close to my cousin with a deadly sword in his hands.

"Hoyt, on your knees. Now!"

Dean takes another step closer to Jason and his head swings back and forth slightly, like he can't believe what he's seeing.

"I didn't remember. This whole time, ever since that day, there's been a blank space where there should be the memories of what happened. I could only remember little bits, enough to know I was forced to fight in an arena, but not how I got there or who exactly was there with me. But ... it was you. You were there."

Dean lets out a low burst of incredulous laughter and closes the space between them. The sword falls from Jason's hand as the two men grasp each other in their arms. Xavier's hand touches my back, making me jump and breaking the tension that formed over me like a glaze of ice.

"He didn't bring Dean to the arena. He was already there," Xavier whispers. And that changes everything.

As I lower my gun with some reluctance, Dean and Jason step apart. Dean looks him over.

"I didn't recognize you at first. You cut your hair and you don't have a beard. And your eyes ..."

Jason nods. "It's easier not to see their real color sometimes. I was held in that cell for so long. Dragged out to fight when it amused him. I didn't think I would survive. But you freed me. I got another chance because of you. Thank you. I never had the chance to say that. Thank you."

"I'm alive right now because you fought alongside me. You helped me get out. I still don't remember everything, but I remember that sword in your hand. I remember someone taking a smaller one and slashing you. Was it another fighter? Were there three of us?" Dean asks.

"It was Marini's new assistant," Jason explains. "I was meant to die that fight. He'd kept me captive for more than a year, but he'd started referring to my status as *noxii*. A criminal condemned to death in the arena. He wanted us to destroy each other. He believed you would fight rather than try to handle the situation in any other way."

"Dean, what the hell is going on here?" I ask, feeling the urge to remind them that we're standing here in this place, surrounded by death, and Jason is at the top of my list of suspects for helping facilitate it all.

Dean turns around and beckons me forward. Jason reaches down and picks up his shirt, slipping back into it as I take a cautious step forward.

"The day I was brought to the arena, I was dragged inside and released through a gate into a place just like this, only a little smaller. You've seen it. You remember the gates. There was already another fighter in the ring and he came at me immediately. I can't remember how it happened, but the next thing I knew, he was unconscious on the ground.

"I heard Jason in one of the cells at the edge of the arena and I went to help him. I was able to figure out how to get the door open and got him out. He was weak. I didn't know if he was even going to be able to defend himself if that man got up."

"But it wasn't him that we had to worry about," chimes in Jason. "The arbitrator was already out in the arena by the time we turned around."

"Arbitrator? The person who helped Marini get Dean there?" I ask. Jason nods and a jolt of something like hope goes through me. "Who was it?"

His head shaking back and forth fizzles out that hope as quickly as it came.

"He was fully covered. Hood, mask, everything. For ritual. And for his protection. He was a Charon. That position is one of honor, but it can be a very delicate balance. It's not just about bringing new people to the palaces," he tells me.

"Palaces, Emma," Xavier whispers behind me. "Not lairs. It's a palace."

Jason nods at Xavier and finally explains everything. "The Charons are deep into his inner circle. They have to be able to charm people, to get close to them. They deliver victims to the Emperor on his whim and play a key role in determining which of them survive and for how long. Sometimes the Emperor even allowed the Charon to make that choice."

"Ferryman of the dead," I whisper. "The name I found in Serena's notes."

Jason nods. "They are responsible for all aspects of these indulgences. From bringing the fighters and slaves, to procuring the weapons, to taking care of the blood. Disposing of the bodies. Making sure the tracks are covered. But also providing the gladiators with food and first aid between fights, making sure they were up to fighting shape for their next bout."

"So there were multiple ferrymen?" I ask.

"Yes. But they are always masked. You can never truly know who it was who betrayed you. Your friend that came into your life and suddenly dragged you to fight to the death in chains. The work acquaintance who drugged you and condemned you to a life of horror. The person you trusted. All of them were put there to lure his victims in. But in a way, the Charons are slaves, too. Just of a different kind."

He's speaking in the present tense, like he's still unsure that it's not all going to start happening around him again.

"Was there more than one while you were being held?" I ask.

"Yes," he answers without hesitation. "The one who came after me was a woman. She was around for a long time. But there were men, too."

"How did so many people come through this place and all the other... palaces, and no one has ever come forward to talk about what they witnessed?" I ask.

"If you were the kind to enjoy the entertainment of this kind of place, do you think you would risk the Emperor's wrath by ratting him out to the authorities?" Jason points out. "People tried, of course. And he buried them. But after a while, there wasn't any more resistance. The Emperor would only invite those he deemed truly worthy. He had a series of tests."

He practically spits this last word as if to shudder at the memory.

"Small indulgences at first, to test the water and determine if potential spectators could really handle his true hedonistic world. And over time, those chosen got closer to sitting in one of the observation rooms watching men fight to their death, then sitting in one of the themed rooms until a woman was sent to them.

"By the time any of them would have seen anything that could be considered horrific, they were already invested. They were entwined in it and weren't going to be able to extricate themselves. Even if they did want to talk to the police about it, which very few of them would in the first place, the Emperor had already gathered enough dirt on them to ensure their silence."

"You know all this because you were one of them," I say.

He nods without hesitation. "Yes."

I lift my gun again and Dean rests his hand on top of it, lowering it down.

"Emma, stop. Listen to him. I'm here. I'm alive. He fought alongside me and got slashed through to make sure both of us got out of there. There's a reason he did that."

"You left after getting out of the arena," I say to Jason. "You stole property and money from Salvador Marini and have been living a lush life funded by that stolen capital. Isn't that right?"

"Yes," he admits. "But not for me. I was forced to witness things I will never forget and thrown into the gladiator arena, kept in one of those cells for more than a year because my uncle wanted to punish me. For my relationship with Miley Stanford."

CHAPTER FORTY-THREE

"**Y**OUR UNCLE?" I ASK. I'M NOT READY TO FULLY BELIEVE HIM. Details can trickle down and anyone can spin a pretty story to make a situation look good from their perspective. It doesn't mean anything they are saying is true. Jason is going to need to prove himself. "Salvador Marini only has one sister and she doesn't have a son."

"I know," Jason replies without hesitation. "He's not really my uncle. Not by blood, anyway. But that's how I've always known him. When he was young he had a foster family that had other kids there from other families. One of those was my father. He and Sal bonded more than the other children did. He did everything he could to help Sal, and when Sal finally left the house, my father was there to help him assimilate to the world around him. They got even closer during that time. They always considered themselves brothers even after aging out of the system at eighteen. And so when I grew up, I always knew him as my dad's brother."

"Why didn't he help his biological sister?" I demand. "She was going through hell there. He knew what she was dealing with because he'd been there. He grew up in it, too, and he obviously knew how bad it was because he got out of there as fast as he could. If he was so quick to latch onto his foster brother, why didn't he do anything to take care of Gwendolyn?"

"I don't know," Jason admits. "We never talked about her. Look, I know it was horrible of him to leave her behind and not help her. I can't imagine what she went through. I don't want to imagine it. But I had an opportunity with him. I didn't know what it was going to turn out to be. He was going to make sure I never went through that kind of desperation. And when you're young and being told that this man is your uncle and wants to take care of you, you are grateful. You look up to him. I was much older by the time I found out who he really was. And by then, he had me. I was deeply involved and he knew every way he could hurt me and destroy my world if I turned against him."

"What about Miley? How do I know she meant anything to you? You could have heard her name mentioned in relation to the case and thought it would change something."

"When searching her house, did you find a pale pink miniature car-abiner?" Jason asks.

I'm surprised by the directness of the question and the precise detail. "Yes."

"I gave that to her when we'd been together for a few months. I considered it a pre-engagement gift. It was a joke between us. And she told me about her love of rock climbing and I didn't believe her. So, she decided to bring me. It was something I had never done. Neither of us was very good at it that first time, but we had so much fun together."

"Oh my god. You are the same person. It isn't two people. An assis-tant and someone that he jokingly called his nephew. It's the same per-son," I say.

My mind is reeling with the sudden crashing of the two images, the two people I was trying to identify. Thinking of the possibility of a foster sibling having a child felt like such a desperate leap, but now it's playing out in front of me. And I'm having to reconcile the contrasting images of these two stories that have suddenly merged.

"If you were in a relationship with her and supposedly loved her, why were you blackmailing her?" Dean asks. He explains what we found in the property listing and in Miley's financial records.

"You are good," he says, looking at me with admiration. "I didn't think anyone would ever make those connections. But I wasn't blackmailing her. I would never do anything to hurt her. Not intentionally. We wanted to be together. We wanted to leave and have a fresh start. But my uncle was never going to let that happen. We were going to have to do it on our own, to run and hope he couldn't track us down. So we started saving money. She didn't want to just be taken care of. She wanted to be a part of it, to contribute to the life we were going to have together. So, we came up with the idea of her making supposed rent payments to something that looked like a rental company."

"CC DIVE," I say. "Central Enterprises, 404."

Jason nods. "Yes, you interpreted the name of the company correctly. It did represent those Roman numerals and the letters C and E. But they didn't have anything to do with Central Enterprises."

"It's a date," Xavier chimes in. "404 CE."

Jason nods. "The year the Gladiator fights ended."

"Where is she now? Where's Miley? Do you think that skeleton that was found is hers?"

A devastated, broken expression crosses his face and he seems to stumble back a partial step as if just hearing the question is enough to almost knock him down.

"I don't know. I don't think so," he admits. "I've been looking for her. That's why I came back here. I need to find her. That's why I agreed to work with you, Agent Griffin. You are the very best and that's what I'm going to need if I'm ever going to be able to find her and see my uncle be held accountable, even in his death. I will tell you everything. Just help me find her and I will tell you everything you want to know."

I don't know if I trust him, but I don't know what to believe anymore.

"Why don't we talk somewhere else about all this?" I ask.

Jason nods. "That works for me."

Slowly—and with Jason taking the front of the line—we climb out. After him is Dean, then Xavier, then it's my turn to take up the rear and keep a close watch on our surroundings. My hand is still on my hip, ready to draw if Jason tries anything, but he seems genuine.

We emerge to see the group of agents Eric sent to help with the investigation and I walk over to them to talk for a few seconds. I thank them for coming and let them know they don't need to be there anymore today. But that they will need to be back first thing in the morning for us to start the full investigation of the area.

Julian looks confused when Jason walks past him. "How did he get inside?"

"It's alright," I tell him. "Don't worry about it. I've got him."

As we walk away, Jason leans slightly closer so he can speak without his words being overheard.

"There's a secondary entrance. It's much harder to find, but it was used for the Emperor to make rapid escapes when he needed to slip out unnoticed by his guests. I was going to show it to you tonight."

I nod. "We'll see it in the morning. Right now, I need more information."

Jason comes back with us to the hotel so we can compare my notes to what he's telling me. The conversations we have are illuminating and seemingly genuine. He describes the first time he saw Miley at Marini's house when she was there with Angelo and the immediate way they connected. That the next time they saw each other was at the farmer's market, and from that instant, they were inseparable. But it was obvious from the very beginning that his uncle would never allow their relationship.

"He was critical and cruel of anyone associated with who he referred to as 'the help,'" Jason tells me. "The very fact that this girl had come to his house with one of his staff members rather than as an invited guest put a black mark on her and made her undesirable—but not for him, of course. She was beneath him. She wasn't someone worthy of a relationship. Certainly not of love or of being brought into the kind of world he lived in."

"Didn't you live in that world, too?" I ask.

"I lived in a version of it," he admits. "It was never really mine. That was why she and I were taking so much time to prepare. I needed the time to build up resources, to figure out how to successfully transfer assets to myself so that I'd not only be able to give her the life she deserved, but so I could stop him.

"My uncle would always say that she wasn't worth any of that. She was tainted. But he still wanted her. He wanted her all to himself. I don't know if he had any indication about us the first time he told me to bring her to him. I obviously knew what that meant. Someone like her wouldn't be used up and destroyed quickly. She would languish there, in his favorite palace. He'd consider her his most prized possession. She would be his alone to toy with as he pleased. But perhaps he'd offer the privilege of watching the entertainment to some of the disgusting men he brought there.

"I couldn't let that happen to her. I knew we needed to hurry up and get ready to leave faster while I tried to put off her delivery as long as possible. I told him I couldn't get her alone to talk to her or capture her. That I couldn't find her. I gave him every excuse I could think of. But it wasn't enough. Whether he knew then or he figured it out along the way, he knew what was happening between us. He wasn't going to stand for it. We tried to run, but we couldn't escape him."

It's suddenly like Jason can't breathe. He's starting to tremble and the look in his eyes is pure terror, like he's reliving all of it and can't get out.

Xavier moves closer to him.

"All around me, people spend their lives like they are on a pane of glass above everything they are experiencing. They can experience it, but as an observer," he says gently. "But that glass rarely exists for me. I slide all the way down into it so I can hear and smell and see and feel and even taste everything. Far too much. There were moments standing in that arena that overwhelmed me because the dirt wasn't lined up right, the sound of the wind going past the open hatch was loud, I could smell rust, and there was too much feeling in my toes.

"It's like drowning. But instead of water, it's the intensity of experience. When that's happening, all you can do is throw up a hand. Break through the surface and someone will be there to pull you out. Especially with Dean. You said he already saved you once. He'll do it again if you ask him to."

Dean reaches out his hand and Jason looks at it, for a second seeming to be in that cell again, desperate to be freed. He takes his hand in both of his and squeezes it for a second.

"Thank you."

"We will help you," I tell him.

"Even knowing what I did?" he cringes, looking down like he's going to be sick. "I hate myself for the things I did. I was trying to better my life. Then I was just trying to survive."

"There's so much more to you than that part. For now, we're willing to look past some of them to get what we need to put the final nail in this case. But you have to tell the absolute truth. Starting with Salvador Marini. Did you kill him?"

Jason shakes his head. "No. But I made sure he was dead."

CHAPTER FORTY-FOUR

HAVE MY NOTEPAD READY TO TAKE DOWN THE FULL STORY ONCE and for all.

Jason clears his throat and begins. "Sal could be reckless in what he considered his entertainment, the way he indulged himself, but never when it came to the possibility of getting caught. The people he allowed to know about the Emperor were few and kept very close to him. Some out of loyalty. Some out of fear. He kept very tight control of everyone in his circle. And as the years went on, he needed others to help him without needing to know anything about him or the details of what happened. He discovered the Cleaners. He heard about them from your uncle, Emma."

I nod. "That makes sense from what I've been able to piece together from what I've been given. Jonah—Marini probably knew him as Lotan—wasn't exactly impressed by the Emperor. He considered him a hack, someone living a fantasy of idle pleasure instead of really philosophically committing. Jonah always says he was righteous and justified in every horrific crime he ever committed. He has a warped worldview that he tries to bring out as justice. But it wasn't like that for Marini. He only killed for pleasure. For petty personal reasons."

"Sal always chose victims because of their looks or where he'd seen them before," Jason concurs. "He tried to bring in Lotan once, but he was just brushed off, and that infuriated my uncle. He went on and on about the disrespect. Soon enough it turned into a full-blown obsession. He wanted to be powerful and notorious like him. He started gathering every bit of information he could find about Lotan, which is how he found out about the Cleaners. And that solved his problem of needing someone to do the dirty work for him."

"They would come back and dispose of whatever needed to be disposed of," I say.

He nods. "That became another of my responsibilities. When something needed to be taken care of, I reached out to what they referred to as 'the agency' and let them know what needed to be done. Then they came and cleaned up.

"When I found out that he was being charged with Serena's murder, I couldn't cope with the idea of him going to trial. With all his money and connections, he could get out of it so easily. He knew that. He could get acquitted. And if that didn't happen, he could appeal, find technicalities, or simply bribe his way out. He'd be free and that was something I couldn't handle. So I called the agency. I told them I needed him cleaned up."

The impact of his words settles heavily into the air around us.

"Did you know Serena?" I finally break the silence.

"Are you asking if I know she took over Miley's life? That she lived in her house and pretended to be her? The bitter, revolting irony of my own uncle dating her? Yes. I knew of her. He never knew Miley's name. He didn't care enough to know. And he never saw her house or anything else about her. He had no idea what was going on. But Serena did. And Lotan did. And after the fact, I did, too. By the time Serena could have been any help, she was dead."

"What happened to Miley?" I ask.

"We were brought to his favorite arena first. He put me through my first fight and I didn't know if I was going to survive it, but he made sure I did. There was much more on his mind for me than just one fight. Then he forced me to watch him use her for the first time. Right there, on the ground, in the pool of my blood. I did everything I could to get to her and stop it, but I was chained to the floor. There was no way to get to her.

"For the next two weeks, we were forced to watch each other be brutalized. There were times when the Charon asked why I didn't just give up. I could not fight back as hard, or I could purposely move in a way that would allow my opponent to kill me. But I couldn't do that. If I died, Miley would be alone. I couldn't get to her, but I was at least there, alive. I loved her. I couldn't leave her.

"But Marini made sure I did. He had me transferred to the other arena. I never saw or heard about Miley again. She's gone. I know she is. But I can't find her."

His voice breaks and tears start to roll down his cheeks. "I just want to be able to take her away from there like I promised I would."

My stomach rolls at the description of what he went through. It's compelling testimony and something I definitely want heard.

"Would you be willing to talk about this again?" I ask. "I doubt there will be any kind of trial since Marini is dead and we can't bring up charges against a dead man, so unless we're able to identify someone else who helped him, there won't be anyone else to hold accountable."

"But me," he says.

I wasn't going to say that yet. I didn't want to broach that reality and possibly stop him from cooperating. But he looks unshaken by the declaration.

"There are things we can do," I start, but he shakes his head.

"I know what I did. I'm not trying to shirk responsibility or pretend I'm only a victim. The only thing that matters to me is finding Miley. After that, you can do anything you want with me. I'm willing to lie down and die beside her the way I should have. I just want her found," he says. "And I can do better than just talk about what happened. There's evidence."

"Evidence?" I ask.

"Marini liked documentation. He wanted to be able to go back and relive what he'd done with his favorite captives."

My heart starts to pound in my chest. "And he has some of Miley?"

"And of me. And of many of the others. Pictures and video. Sometimes other souvenirs."

That makes bile wash up my throat. "Where would he keep those?"

"He used to have them in a locked case in his wing. Right next to the bed. But when I opened it, everything was gone. He must have believed someone was on his trail."

"He might have destroyed it all," Dean offers.

Jason shakes his head. "No. Those things were far too important to him to destroy them. Besides, he would enjoy the idea of the secret.

He'd like knowing he had these sensational pieces of evidence some-where and no one knew about them. It's out there somewhere. It's just a matter of figuring out where he could have hidden them."

I go to the duffel bag of pictures and bring them over to him.

"I got these from his sister," I tell him. "She removed all the pictures she could find from his house while she's trying to figure out what to do with his estate. I'm sure there was a time when he would have wanted you to inherit it all, but there was no will."

"I don't want it. I want nothing to do with that place."

"Do you think he could have hidden the stash of evidence there?" Dean asks.

"I doubt it. He constantly lectured me about keeping your worlds separate. He apparently didn't follow his own rules, though. He designed it with some features that would allow him to indulge his twisted fanta-sies right at home rather than going anywhere else," Jason says.

I nod. "We found them. The rooms that don't open from the inside. The doors in the hallway that have nothing behind them. Twisted is probably the nicest word you could use to describe it."

"He almost got caught once. One of the girls was stronger and more outspoken than he thought she would be. Before her, he laced their drinks with drugs that made them anxious and caused hallucinations."

"The same thing he did to Serena," I say.

"They made it so that he could do what he wanted with them, then drop them off somewhere and they might feel like something hap-pened, but never really know. Definitely not enough to be able to trace it back to him. But this girl was stronger. The drugs didn't affect her enough. That was the first time he used the Cleaners. And the last time he brought anyone to his house."

"I used one of these pictures to figure out that the trees were trans-planted." I show him the picture of Marini by the tent next to the park-ing lot and the trees beyond. "You said he likes souvenirs. He likes to feel smarter than people, like he's getting one over on them. Having a picture like that around would do that. Hiding the truth in plain sight. Can you go through these and see if any of them mean anything to you?"

Jason's face hardens and I try to sound reassuring.

"I know you don't want to see his face. I know that's probably the last thing you ever want to see again. But I need you to do this."

He nods and I hand him the bag, then the pictures I'd taken out.

It doesn't take long.

Xavier picks up one of the pictures I'd taken out of the rest, the one with Marini giving the thumbs-down beside a boulder. He hands it to Jason.

"What is that?" I ask.

"We need to find this rock," Jason says.

"The thumbs-down," Xavier notes. "It was the symbol used to indicate a Gladiator's fate would be death."

CHAPTER FORTY-FIVE

'M NOW CONSIDERING JASON HOYT AS BEING IN INFORMAL CUS-
tody as part of the investigation into the crimes of the Emperor as well
as his death. He agrees to get a room in the same hotel as the rest of
us and turn over the keys to the room and his phone. Dean and Xavier
bring him back to his house to collect the clothes and other belongings
he'll need to stay for several days while I stay back at the hotel to continue piecing things together.

The plan is to start the search tomorrow morning. We'll be looking
for the boulder where we believe he hid his stash of evidence, as well as
the other nine bodies to go with the Roman numerals carved into the
wall. Including Miley. I have to debrief the team without giving away
who Jason is. Not yet. There will be a time when he will have to be held
accountable and he isn't shrinking away from it. But for now, the priority is recovering victims and making the case against Marini unshakable.

Sam calls while the guys are gone and I feel like I'm going to burst
with everything I want to tell him. It's hard being away from him and

not being able to spend our evenings curled up together on the couch, eating, watching TV, just living. I want him here with me to be a part of this, and I want to be in Michigan with him to be a part of that, but we are both where we should be. We're doing what needs to be done. We will always be waiting on the other side.

I tell him everything, then sit in silence while he processes it all.

"Do you believe him?" Sam asks.

"I do. I was so sure of what I thought happened, and I was close. But everything he said fits. If we can actually find the pictures and videos, that will clinch everything," I say. "Now you. Tell me what's happening."

"I found the magazine Marie was writing the piece about Alfa-Corps for," he tells me. "I got in touch with them and they confirmed she had approached them with the idea of an investigative article exposing the company's shell corporations and other covers, the damage they've done to so many people, and the pathetic way they've handled it. She wanted to bring these things to light and hold them accountable for everything they've done."

"Wow. Sounds like she was really insistent on it."

"Yeah. And they were actually really looking forward to a hard-hitting piece like that. It's something they had considered investigating before, but no one had ever really been able to pin them down and get hard evidence. But Marie had been telling them things she found out and people she had spoken to. Apparently, she had really made some fantastic progress and had even turned in a couple of preliminary drafts of the article. There was information missing from those drafts, of course, but they were really impressed. They said it was good enough that she would probably have been immediately offered another when this one was finished. They were really disappointed when she withdrew."

That strikes me. "Withdrew? What do you mean she withdrew?"

"Apparently, they got a note from her stating she had reconsidered the work and was no longer comfortable writing the piece," Sam explains. "She believes she'd presented false information and that she had been misled by the people she spoke with, and she couldn't in good conscience continue the article for fear of defamation lawsuits."

"No, that doesn't make sense," I reply. "She'd put far too much time and effort into that research, and was taking the entire project so seriously. She wouldn't just suddenly change her mind about everything she'd found out."

"That's exactly what I told them. Especially after they told me the date they got the cancellation. It was two days *after* she disappeared," Sam says. "The magazine told me they were expecting something from her that day because she'd sent an email saying she would have more details for them and would send notes."

"She was out researching answers the day she disappeared," I say. "She must have found something."

"I think she had an appointment with someone from the company. She was planning an interview. I just need to find out who she was supposed to be meeting."

The next morning we're back in the forest above the Coliseum just after sunrise. I've scheduled the briefing with the team for a couple hours later, wanting to give us some time to search without them. I know when the team arrives, the extra people who don't know what's going on will put Jason on edge. I want to give him the chance to think clearly and try to remember anything that might help.

But two hours pass of us carefully inspecting every inch of land, and we don't find anything. The team shows up and I go over the instructions with them carefully. I want every aspect of the search to be documented. Anything that seems out of place or that might have been added, I want to be marked so it can be further searched later.

They head out in groups of two and I go over to the table set up with coffee and pastries Jason ordered. I'm sipping a cup of coffee and thinking about whether I should give iced coffee another chance considering it's already miserably hot despite it still being early when my phone rings in my pocket.

Thinking it might be Dean telling me they'd found something, I yank it out quickly. But the number isn't Dean's. It's from Breyer Correctional Facility.

"Agent Griffin," I say almost breathlessly.

I didn't expect the visit to happen so early this morning, or for it to go so quickly. It immediately puts me on edge.

"It's Wright. The plan has changed."

I walk away from the table, putting more space between me and the agents still in the area.

"What do you mean the plan has changed? Did Benson give it up?" I ask.

"No. He did exactly what you told him. But the guy who came today said Jonah wants to meet with me this afternoon. He doesn't want a representative or to wait. He says if Benson needs something, it needs to get done now," Wright says.

"Shit. What time?" I ask.

"Two," he says.

"I'll get the first flight I can. Don't go in without me. If you don't see me, you do *not* go into that building. Do you understand me?" I demand.

"Yes."

"I'll see you in a few hours."

The rest of the morning is a frantic whirlwind of telling Dean and Xavier what's going on, restructuring the instructions for the team, and rushing to find a flight that will get me to the empty house near Breyer on time.

I barely make it, driving at breakneck speed to the spot we chose to park our cars and meet before going to the house. I don't want to risk Jonah seeing me. The fact that I'm using a rented car helps. I don't put it past him to survey the entire area to ensure he really is meeting with Deandre Wright.

It's why he changed the plan. He's trying to maintain control. He wants to make sure this is done on his terms. He chose to make an alliance with these people when they helped him escape from prison. He could have gone a different way, but he made the decision to maintain a relationship with them, to make sure they were all linked to one another. He wants to be able to use them as he pleases. He likely wasn't prepared for them to use him.

This is his way of flexing. He's making sure no one mistakes who is the one in power and who is the one in charge. And he almost succeeded in fucking everything up.

Wright looks both relieved and more anxious when he sees me park and come toward him across the back lot of the small restaurant several blocks away from the house. The owner of the restaurant was none too pleased to receive my call this morning essentially commandeering the restaurant for the two hours before the time of the meeting and through the rest of the day, but seemed appeased when I told him the FBI and police department would ensure it was full the entire time and the kitchen would stay busy.

I need the home base, a place to set up surveillance equipment for the extra officers and agents I need to have on hand. Ensuring it's empty except for the owner and kitchen staff reduces the danger in the possibility that Jonah does figure out we're there.

We're cutting the time very short as I go over my instructions with Officer Wright. He looks uneasy, and I can't blame him. He's planning to face and trick one of the world's most dangerous terrorists, who has a sea of blood on his hands and has managed to avoid capture for more than a year and a half.

But I'll be right behind him and my backup behind me. Eric arrives just as I'm starting on foot out of the parking lot. He gives me a quick hug.

"We have to stop meeting like this," he says.

"Glad you got here."

"Wouldn't miss it." He looks around. "Dean isn't here?"

I shake my head. "I didn't think he needed to be a part of this. Not if we want it to end smoothly."

Eric nods. "Let's do this."

CHAPTER FORTY-SIX

W E GET IN POSITION AROUND THE HOUSE AND WAIT. FROM MY vantage point, I can see the front of the house and watch as Wright drives up and parks in clear view of anyone around. The rest of the team and I walked the few blocks to the house to get in position so that there wouldn't be several cars parked around. It was a risk. Jonah could have been roaming the area and caught sight of us. But risks have to be taken. Especially for something like this.

Wright gets out of the car. He's in plain clothes rather than his uniform, by Jonah's request. He doesn't want anyone in the neighborhood to look out a window and get suspicious seeing an officer going into the empty house. If it's a uniformed officer, they are far more likely to think something is wrong. A person in regular clothes could just be someone representing the house or considering purchasing it.

I can't see it from here, but I know he has the specified symbol drawn on his hand. He didn't know if it was still needed since Jonah had changed the plan of sending a different representative and needing to prove their identity, but I told him it is never a bad choice to follow Jonah's instructions. He knows everything he delineated. It's always safer to expect that he will check every one of them.

Wright glances around, then heads through the gate and into the house. This is the most terrifying part of the plan. He's going in alone with no visibility. The team back at the restaurant can hear and see what's going on using the tiny, highly advanced surveillance equipment they've placed on him, but that won't protect him. It could possibly just provide footage of his ambush and death.

We can only hope that this time, Jonah will be true to his word. Wright won't be inside alone for long. As soon as Jonah is seen entering the building, we will close in. My heart pounds in my chest. I've been waiting for this for a long time. Now it almost doesn't feel real.

I radio the team at the restaurant.

"Do you have video and audio?" I ask.

"Yes. Both are working fine," the agent monitoring the equipment tells me.

"Do you see anything?"

"Nothing so far. The house is empty. Officer Wright is staying in the front room."

"Good."

Time stretches and slows. It feels like we must have been waiting for hours, that Jonah has decided not to come, when I see another car come up behind Wright's. I quiet the team around me and brace myself. My gun is in my hand and I'm ready for whatever is about to happen.

It takes several seconds for the door to open and Jonah to get out. I don't think I'll ever get over the strangeness of seeing him and the split second in the beginning when my mind thinks I'm looking at my father.

He walks through the gate and hesitates for a second. He looks around and my skin prickles. I wonder if he senses he's being watched. It doesn't matter. I'm not going to back down. The roads leading into the neighborhood are already being blocked. Officers are taking up spots at the end of the block to keep a visual on every house and pathway. He has nowhere to run.

Finally, Jonah makes his way into the house and I surge forward. I run around the side of the house to the front door and wait just outside. Others circle around to the back. The plan is to give Wright a few moments to collect recordings of Jonah admitting what he did. But that is low on my priority list. If anything seems even slightly off, I'm going in.

I listen carefully for any shout or other sound from Wright. It stays quiet until my radio crackles and the surveillance agent tells me they've got what they needed.

That's all I need to hear. One solid kick opens the front and back doors at the same time. I run inside and find Wright facedown on the floor and Jonah's back to me. For a brief second, I'm worried something might have happened to the officer, but I realize he's just doing as he was instructed and getting out of the way as fast as possible.

My gun trained on Jonah's back, I look at Eric.

"Get Deandre out of here."

Eric moves forward, his own gun held steady, and grabs hold of the back of Deandre's shirt. He tugs him to his feet and guides him past the team filling the front of the room and out the front door. He'll hand him off to someone outside and ensure he gets back to the restaurant to be debriefed.

"You didn't use our code, Emma," Jonah says. He doesn't even bother to turn around and face me.

"Shut up," I snap.

"There's no need to be rude. Can't I at least enjoy our reunion for a moment?" he asks.

He starts to turn around, his hand going to his back, and I see the officers behind him ready themselves to shoot. I hold my hand up to stop them.

"Back off," I tell them. "He won't hurt me."

"Are you so sure about that, Emma?" Jonah asks, facing me now. The scar along his face seems brighter. His eyes are darker.

His hand still hasn't moved from his back, but I don't even shift my weight.

"Yes."

"I have before," he says.

"No. Other people have hurt me in your name. You never intended it."

"So, why not now?" he asks. "I have nothing to lose."

"Because you didn't make a choice. You made a mistake. You told me I would never bring you back to prison until you made the decision to let me. But do you know what your mistake was?" I ask.

"Underestimating you?" he asks with a hint of a smirk.

"Thinking you ever had a choice at all," I say.

His hand drops to his side and a knife falls from it, reminding me of my first confrontation with him in the house in Florida, the day I got my father back.

"On your knees," I growl. He lowers himself to the floor and I gesture for the officer behind him to put him in cuffs. "Jonah Griffin, you have the right to remain silent…"

A smile starts to curl on his lips as I Mirandize him. When I'm finished, I walk around behind him and grab his cuffs, yanking him to his feet.

"It was nice working with you, Emma," he cracks. "It's disappointing you weren't able to do what I needed you to do. But you know I'll forgive you."

I walk around again so I can look him directly in the eyes.

"I know what happened to Miley Stanford. You never, ever will."

His face drops and I nod my head back toward the door. Two officers take hold of his arms and guide him out of the house. The rest of the team starts to leave, but I stay where I'm standing. When everyone else is gone, Eric puts his hand on my back.

"Emma? You okay?"

"I just need a second," I say.

"We'll be outside."

And then I'm alone. I breathe in air owed to the last year and a half. It's done. It's finally done.

CHAPTER FORTY-SEVEN

DON'T WANT TO HEAR THE CONGRATULATIONS COMING AT ME FROM every angle when I walk back into the restaurant. I don't want the applause.

This isn't a celebration. It's not a party.

I want my husband.

I want my mother.

I thank Wright for his service and go to say goodbye to Eric.

"You're not going to stay for his arraignment?" he asks.

"No. I don't need to be a part of this anymore. I'll watch him walk into the prison when that day comes. For now, I need to get back to my investigation."

He pulls me into a hug. "I love you, Emma. I'm proud of you."

"I love you, too." I step back. "And Eric?"

"Hmm?"

"Get my office ready for me."

He nods, just a touch of a smile lifting the corners of his mouth.

I take a box of food and a styrofoam to-go drink cup handed out to me by one of the staff, not even knowing what it is. When I walk outside, I feel the heat on my face and hear birds chirping somewhere. The world is completely different and exactly the same. Just as it should be.

There's a message waiting on my phone when I get back to my car. It's from Dean and only has three words.

"We found it."

I'm exhausted and don't want to travel anymore. I would have thought I would be energized when this was over, but instead, I feel like my body has finally relaxed and my brain is letting me feel and think what it's been protecting itself from since my wedding reception, when the call from Jonah informed me of his escape and sent my life spiraling off course after I had just put it back together.

It's that odd time in a summer day when the sun is still hovering in the sky even as the hour keeps ticking later until it almost seems like it will never set. But I know there will only be a second between vibrant daylight and darkness.

I told Eric I need to get back to my investigation, and I do, but not tonight. Tonight I need some time to myself.

The hotel room is cold. The basket of snacks is sitting on the desk. Everything is so quiet until I hear a voice in my mind. It takes a few seconds for me to realize it's my own. My thoughts are mine again.

I take some time to eat and relax before getting in touch with Dean.

"Is it over?" he asks when he answers.

"It's over."

He lets out a breath. "I never want to waste another second on him."

"Neither do I. So, start now. Tell me what you found."

"If you want we can do a video call and I can show it to you," he offers. "But if you're not up for it..."

"I'm up for it," I tell him. "Give me a minute to get my computer set up."

The truth is, I don't know if I am up for it. But I have to be. I can't let Jonah take any more time from me ever again.

A few minutes later I'm fighting nausea as he shows me bits of the pictures and videos they found hidden, just as we expected, inside a fake boulder hundreds of yards from the entrance to the underground lair.

Saying it's horrific is a massive understatement, but it's too overwhelming to even come up with another way to describe it.

I've only seen a few pictures of Miley during her life, but I couldn't help but feel close to her. I didn't realize how much I'd built up my hope around the idea that she had run away and was happy somewhere until I watch the brutality of the last moments of her life. Even knowing Jason is the man Angelo spoke about, the one we hoped was making Miley happy wherever she was, and hearing him say he believed she was dead, didn't take that thought away from the back of my mind.

Now I was forced to accept it. I'd been searching for someone I couldn't save.

"We still need to find her," Dean says. "The team has identified at least three more places that could be graves or other places where he hid things. They're waiting for you to get back here to begin the excavation."

"I'll be there tomorrow."

I close out the video call and call Sam. I know he's burning with curiosity about the details, but he has the grace not to ask. All he needs to know is that it's over. I'm safe. And everything will be okay.

"I love you," I say.

"I love you."

I fell asleep last night to the sound of Sam's voice telling me he'd found another witness, a woman whose brother had tried to stand up to Alfa-Corps after his wife developed cancer and died. According to her, he came back from the meeting changed. He was withdrawn and didn't talk about them anymore. A year later, he disappeared. They were still searching for him and she was able to give Sam information about how to contact the same people in the company.

I'm still thinking about it, wondering if I should call him back and have him tell me again, while traveling back to the scene. I decide to wait until tonight. It's going to be a long day and I need to focus.

As soon as I arrive, I'm swept into the depths of the investigation. Now that the stash of evidence has been found to finally implicate the Emperor for all his brutality, all attention has turned to looking for Miley and the rest of the victims. Jason brings us through the underground palace, showing us every hidden crevice and room, every place he knew of where we might find anything. But he'd searched these places before. He hadn't found anything. Showing us was only out of hope that fresh eyes not clouded by the single thought of searching for Miley might notice something.

Bright pink and blue flags dot the area where inconsistencies or potential carvings caught the attention of those searching. I told them to identify everything and not to make assumptions. I want to see anything that they think might be important, and they didn't disappoint me.

The sheer volume of what needs to be excavated is daunting, but I'm not afraid. We're getting closer. There's one victim that has been reclaimed, waiting in the medical examiner's office to be identified and returned to her family. No matter how long it takes, it's better than it was. She has a chance now. She doesn't belong to Marini and she never will.

At the end of the day, I go back to the hotel hot, sweaty, and streaked with dirt. I step into the water and close my eyes, waiting for the image of three more skeletons pulled up from the ground to fade from my eyelids before washing my hair.

Another thing I love about hotels is that the hot water goes on for hours without running out. I can stand under it and let it create a buffer between me and the rest of the world for as long as I want.

I don't know how long I stay in there tonight. I end up sinking to the bottom of the tub and closing the drain so it will fill as the shower rains down on me. It lets me slip into a state of meditation, my mind filled only with steam and the hazy sound of the water.

By the time I finally drag myself out of the shower and walk back into the room, I feel like my muscles are on their way toward melting. I climb into bed and am asleep as soon as the light is off.

The room around me is still dark when something wakes me up. I'm groggy climbing up out of the deep sleep and it takes me a few seconds to realize it's the sound of my phone ringing. I can't get to it before it stops ringing, but it starts again immediately. I finally find it still in my pocket from earlier and see Sam's number on the screen.

"Hey, babe," I groan. "I'm sorry, I was asleep. I ..."

"Emma?"

It isn't Sam's voice. It's Rose's.

My heart sinks and jolts up into my throat at the same time.

"Rose? Is everything alright?" I ask.

"Emma, you need to get here."

CHAPTER FORTY-EIGHT

I STORM THROUGH THE HOSPITAL DOORS AND RUN DOWN THE HALL, ignoring nurses calling after me until I find Rose. She wraps her arms around me and squeezes me tight.

"I'm so sorry, honey."

"Where is he?" I ask.

"The last room. The doctors are in there now."

"What have they said?"

"Two of the bullets couldn't be taken out in surgery. They might go back in some other time, but for right now they are too dangerous to move. They removed three and as many fragments as they could. He lost a lot of blood, but they stabilized him. He's still critical."

She's struggling to keep her voice controlled, but I feel like I'm about to snap. She wouldn't tell me anything while I was traveling here, only that Sam had been hurt and I needed to get to the hospital. I walk around her and jog down the hall to the room.

A nurse steps in front of me as I walk in.

"I'm sorry, no visitors," she says.

"I'm not a visitor. I'm his wife," I snap, pushing past.

A steel vice closes around my heart when I see my husband lying in the bed, attached to tubes and wires, bloodied bandages covering part of his head. A doctor turns away from the bed and the nurse gestures at me.

"I'm sorry. I tried to stop her."

"I'm Sam's wife. Agent Emma Griffin." I show him my shield. "I want to know what happened."

My throat squeezes tight, aching as I fight tears. They aren't going to keep anything about him away from me.

"Agent Griffin, I'm Dr. Pryor. Right now, we have Sam stable. He lost a tremendous amount of blood and there is still a high risk of infection and other complications. The detective will be able to tell you more. Are you going to be staying with his aunt?"

"I'm going to be staying right here," I say.

"Ma'am, I highly recommend…"

"I am staying *here*," I repeat forcefully. I go to the other side of the bed and sit down, taking Sam's hand. "Tell the detective to find me when he gets here."

He looks like he's going to say something else, but a harsh look from me stops him. He walks out of the room and my head drops to the bed beside Sam as the tears start flowing.

I sit beside that bed for the next three days.

I hold Sam's hand and talk to him, sharing memories with him, laughing where I know he would. Sometimes I watch the machine that's tracking his heartbeat, listening to the rhythm that comes with the peaks. I stroke his hair and trace the edges of his face.

The doctors and nurses come in regularly to check on him, giving me those little pacifying smiles and encouraging nods, but not really saying much.

On the fourth day, they're ready to wean him from his medication and see how he'll fare coming out of the medically-induced coma that has been allowing his body to heal. Time is slow and painful as I wait for any change. Finally, the doctor comes in and tells me to take a break while they check him again. I reluctantly go to the cafeteria for coffee and head back as quickly as I can.

From the second I enter the room, I notice the change.

Sam's eyes are open.

The coffee falls from my hand as I run to the side of his bed and grab his hand, leaning down to kiss him over and over. The breathing tube is out of his throat, but his face is dented and reddened from the tape. I touch the places softly, choking back tears even through my smile.

"Hi," I whisper.

"Hey," he croaks, his voice rough and strained. "I thought I was the one who was supposed to be sitting next to your hospital bed when you wake up."

I laugh again. "I'm sorry to switch it up this time."

"I guess it was my turn." He chuckles but immediately winces from the pain. He looks around. "What the hell happened?"

"You were shot," I tell him. "The detective handling the case said if you hadn't told the department you were having that meeting, you wouldn't have made it. Do you remember anything?"

He takes a deep breath and scrunches up his face.

"Take your time," I tell him.

"I'm okay. I... set up a meeting with Harrison Groening," he says slowly. "From Alfa-Corps. I pieced together some of Marie's notes and I think he's the one she had contacted and told about the piece she was doing."

I nod. "He was. Marie reached out to the company to let them know about her article and ask if they wanted to cooperate. She was trying to get them on the record. The company refused and tried to threaten her out of writing it. They had their lawyers contact her, but they didn't intimidate her."

"Freedom of the press," Sam manages to say. He tries to shake his head, but it comes out as more of a wobble. "I don't remember anything else."

Fortunately for him, I've been able to piece together the answers in these last few days. "Groening reached out to Marie and offered an interview. That was what the magazine was talking about. He convinced her that he was going to go rogue and fill her in on everything so that it could go public. He told her that he believed in what she was doing and wanted to help her. But what he was actually doing was trying to convince her not to do it. He wanted to pay her off. But it didn't work. So he threatened her. He told her if she didn't back off, he would ensure all the information about her past drug use and brushes with the law would come out.

"She tried to walk away from him and he grabbed her, wanting to try again to stop her. She fought back and fell and hit her head. She was still alive, but barely. He called the Cleaners in to handle it and they staged the overdose."

"How do you know all this?" he asks.

"The detective got his confession. Groening didn't mention the Cleaners by name, just that he had some people handle it for him, but you know what that means. You set up a meeting with him and when you got there, he shot you. He didn't expect you to have backup nearby. He was planning on staging it as retaliation from a drug dealer you confronted to avenge your cousin. But they have him. Because of you."

"Have you been here the whole time?" he asks.

"Of course, I have," I answer.

"I know. I just wanted to hear you say it."

"I haven't left your side for three days."

He gives me a hint of a smile.

"You kind of smell like you haven't left," he wheezes.

That makes me laugh. Actually laugh. Full on, doubled over, body shaking, tears coming out laughter. Sam joins in, but his laughter quickly turns to pained coughing and I calm myself down enough to make sure he's alright.

"You're going to have to be here for a while longer," I say, brushing the tears from my eyes. "But then you're coming home. I'm bringing you home."

Sam cups one cheek with his hand, rubbing my skin with his thumb.

"Don't cry," he whispers. "I'm here."

"I know. But I'm glad to hear you say it."

EPILOGUE

Three weeks later

"HOW IS SAM DOING?" DEAN ASKS, HUGGING ME.

"Getting there," I tell him. "It's going to be a long recovery, but he's much better than they were expecting. He wants to go back to the office, but I convinced him to take one more week. He's going to be on pure desk duty for a good while."

"How's he feeling about that?"

"He's glad he's alive. I think he's willing to deal with paperwork for a bit." He nods and I look behind me at the open church door. "Are you ready for this?"

He takes my hand and we climb the brick steps to the top where Xavier is waiting with Jason. The pews inside the church are empty. Later I'll be here again, sitting through Miley's formal funeral alongside Angelo. But for now, it's just us. I want to give Jason the chance to say goodbye without being watched. Tomorrow, I bring him to the District Attorney. He's not afraid.

The four of us walk up the aisle together and I feel Jason's hand tighten around mine. His eyes are locked straight in front of him. He won't look away from the casket sitting among a lavish display of flowers in front of the altar.

Miley's remains were found a week ago. She was the eighth body to be exhumed, and the only one actually found inside the palace. For someone he hated so much, Marini had been adamant to keep her close.

The investigation isn't over. There's still far more for us to do. The third picture, the one of Marini sitting at the top of the hill, is still in my bag. It means something. I know it does. And one day, I'll know. But today isn't about him. As of today, we've claimed back six more victims. There are still four more to identify, but we're getting closer. Today, we celebrate Miley. Today, Jason says goodbye.

He walks up to the casket and rests himself over it. After a few seconds, he lifts his head and kisses the lid. We sit in the pew for a long time, talking about who she was and who she could have been. It's good to see the light in Jason's eyes, even behind the pain.

When it's time for us to leave, he walks back up to the casket and reaches into his pocket. He pulls out a small velvet box and from it takes a diamond ring. He nestles it into the curve of the pink carabiner already sitting on the top, wrapped in ribbons and sitting among white rose petals. They'll be put into the casket with her before she's buried.

"I love you," he whispers softly against the smooth wood of the lid, then straightens and looks at me.

His shoulders are more relaxed now. He's not carrying a burden that was dragging him down for so long.

"Thank you for this," he says. "I'm ready for tomorrow."

"Are you sure?" I ask.

"Yes," he nods, resting his hand on the side of the casket like he's trying to reach for hers. "I have a long time of redeeming myself ahead of me so I can see her again. It could take years. But every one of them will be worth it."

Two weeks later…

Sam went back to work a few days ago. The town of Sherwood was so proud of their courageous sheriff that they threw a parade and we rode down the street in a convertible like it was high school Homecoming all over again. He's still dealing with pain and I know he's going to be dealing with the consequences of the attack for the rest of his life. But it's something he's willing to face. He gave Marie the truth.

The police department has launched an internal investigation into the way her disappearance was handled, and so far three officers have been fired and brought up on charges related to the corruption. They believe Gerard 'Rocky' Collins was a casualty of a much deeper web of bribery and retaliation involving the police dealing with drug dealers in the area. It will be difficult to prove, but I'm glad they've started.

I'm sitting on the front porch drinking peach iced tea and watching a thunderstorm rolling in on the horizon. I can't wait for the rain. It's been miserably hot for days, so humid it's like I could take a bite out of the air around me. When the clouds finally open up, the deluge will break through the heaviness and bring some relief.

It'll wipe us clean. And we could all use a little bit of that.

My phone buzzes on the table in front of me and I glance down at it. I'm expecting a call from Bellamy, but it isn't her. It's Dean.

"Hey," I say.

"Emma, where am I?"

My initial reaction is that it should be a funny question, but the sound of his voice isn't funny.

"Dean, what's going on?"

"Where am I? Where was I supposed to be today?" he insists, an edge of panic coloring his voice.

"I don't know. Where's Xavier?" I ask, taking my feet down from where they were folded on the table.

"I don't know. Emma, what day is it? I don't know how long it's been since I remember."

"Dean, look around. What do you see?" I ask.

It's been a long time since he had a blackout like this, and I've never heard him with this level of fear in his voice when he talks about one. I haven't heard from him in a couple of days, and he didn't tell me what he had on his schedule for this week.

"Emma, I think there's something really wrong," he says.

"Why?"

"I'm outside in the woods. There's a woman here with me."

"A woman? Who is it?"

"I don't know who she is. But I think ... I think she's dead."

AUTHOR'S NOTE

Dear Reader,

Thank you for reading *The Girl and the Twisted End*. I hope this book answered most, if not all of the questions you might've had for this season of Emma Griffin mysteries. **I guess this is the perfect time to announce that Dean is getting his very own series!** I've been working on Dean's series for a while now and can't wait for you to read it.

If you can please continue to leave your reviews for these books, I would appreciate that enormously. Your reviews allow me to get the validation I need to keep going as an indie author. Just a moment of your time is all that is needed.

My promise to you is to always do my best to bring you thrilling adventures. I can't wait for you to read the Ava & Dean books next!

Yours,
A.J. Rivers

P.S. If for some reason you didn't like this book or found typos or other errors, please let me know personally. I do my best to read and respond to every email at mailto:aj@riversthrillers.com

P.P.S. There will be more Emma Griffin adventures in the future!

ALSO BY
A.J. RIVERS

Emma Griffin FBI Mysteries by AJ Rivers

Season One
Book One—The Girl in Cabin 13*
Book Two—The Girl Who Vanished*
Book Three—The Girl in the Manor*
Book Four—The Girl Next Door*
Book Five—The Girl and the Deadly Express*
Book Six—The Girl and the Hunt*
Book Seven—The Girl and the Deadly End*

Season Two
Book Eight—The Girl in Dangerous Waters*
Book Nine—The Girl and Secret Society*
Book Ten—The Girl and the Field of Bones*
Book Eleven—The Girl and the Black Christmas*
Book Twelve—The Girl and the Cursed Lake*
Book Thirteen—The Girl and The Unlucky 13*
Book Fourteen—The Girl and the Dragon's Island*

Season Three
Book Fifteen—The Girl in the Woods
Book Sixteen —The Girl and the Midnight Murder
Book Seventeen— The Girl and the Silent Night
Book Eighteen — The Girl and the Last Sleepover
Book Nineteen — The Girl and the 7 Deadly Sins
Book Twenty — The Girl in Apartment 9
Book Twenty-One — The Girl and the Twisted End

Other Standalone Novels
Gone Woman
* Also available in audio

Made in the USA
Las Vegas, NV
30 July 2022

52444561R00152